Griff Hosker qualified as an English and Drama teacher in 1972 and worked in the North East of England for the next thirty-five years. During that time he wrote plays, pantos and musicals for his students. He then set up his own consultancy firm and worked as an adviser in schools and colleges. The financial crash of 2010 ended that avenue of work, and he found that he had time on his hands. Griff started researching the Roman invasion of Britain and began to create a novel. The result was *The Sword of Cartimandua*, his first book.

Lord Edward's Archer is Griff's first collaboration with another publisher, having up until now published through his own company, Sword Books.

PRAISE FOR LORD EDWARD'S ARCHER:

'From the first page to the last, *Lord Edward's Archer* grabbed me and did not let go. Hosker's depiction of life and struggles in that slice of early English history is real, brutal and utterly captivating.' – Eric Schumacher, award-winning historical fiction author of *Hakon's Saga*

'Medieval adventure with the pace and power of a war arrow in flight. Griff Hosker has ~~able~~ ~~willing~~ ~~ee why!'~~ – Matthew Harffy, b

Also By Griff Hosker

Series

The Sword of Cartimandua

The Anarchy

Norman Genesis

Border Knight

Struggle For a Crown

Combined Operations

Aelfraed

Wolf Brethren

Dragonheart

New World

British Ace

Novel

Carnage at Cannes

LORD EDWARD'S ARCHER

GRIFF HOSKER

ENDEAVOURQUILL

AN ENDEAVOUR QUILL PAPERBACK

First published by Endeavour Quill in 2019

Endeavour Quill is an imprint of Endeavour Media Ltd
Endeavour Media, 85-87 Borough High Street,
London, SE1 1NH

ISBN 978-1-911445-66-1

Typeset using Atomik ePublisher from Easypress Technologies

Printed and bound in Great Britain by
Clays Ltd, Elcograf S.p.A.

www.endeavourmedia.co.uk

Table of Contents

PROLOGUE

The Welsh border during the reign of Henry III

"Gruffyd, watch the horses!"

I nodded. I was the youngest archer in the company. I had seen more than seventeen summers, or so I had been told, but I was still a new archer. I was the one designated for every task deemed to be unworthy of the older archers. I was also the youngest warrior, and so the sergeants at arms also put upon me. My father warned me that this would happen. He said it was inevitable and would make both a man and an archer of me. My father had been an archer. He had served King Henry, the son of King John, and he had prepared me for such things. He had told me to watch and to learn. He had told me to keep my head down. I listened to my father. He was not only my father; he had been a captain of archers and men had deferred to him.

We served in a border castle. We guarded Chester against the Welsh. We had left Denbigh eight days since and crossed into the area controlled by the Welsh. Baron Henry of Clwyd was Norman and wanted both cattle and captives. He was running short of money. He was not with us and remained in the castle; his lordship rarely came to raid or to war. He had good men to do that for him. The baron enjoyed hunting and wenching. I had been told that he had fought. That had been many years since. Now he sent us to do his fighting for him.

There were twenty-five of us: ten archers and fifteen sergeants at arms. We were led by Hugh of Rhuddlan. He was a grizzled greybeard who had fought as a sword for hire until he tired of lords dying and failing to pay him. He was Welsh, but he fought for pay, not honour. He would fight any foe so long as he was paid. He had chosen Sir Henry. Sir Henry was not warlike, and it suited him to pay Hugh to do his fighting for him. Hugh ruled us with an iron fist. He was the only one with a hauberk. The other men at arms had helmets and they had shields and swords, but Hugh of Rhuddlan was the one who looked like a warrior. Half of us were Welsh and the other half English; these were the borderlands. Disputed and debated land. We raided the Welsh and they raided us. My mother had been Welsh and my father half Welsh. It was said he was the bastard son of a Norman archer who came north with Henry FitzEmpress. Who knew the truth of such matters? My grandmother had died and kept the secret of his birth from him.

I took the reins of the four horses we had brought and watched as the archers and men at arms made their way up the slope towards the hall. The Welsh lord who lived there, Iago ap Mordaf, was little better than a brigand. He stole from his neighbours as much as he stole from the English. He had many sons and brothers. They were more like a clan than anything; with thirty men and boys, he had warriors he could call upon. They lived in a rambling old hall with a single wooden tower. That was why Hugh of Rhuddlan had chosen this approach. He and the men were scrambling up the side of the stream. It was rocky and difficult to climb, but it had the advantage that the hall hid us from the tower, which watched the valley.

I tied the reins to the branches of the willows which hung over the stream. I chose the thicker ones - I would be beaten if any of the horses broke free. That done, I strung my bow.

This was my first raid. It was why I was guarding the horses and not protecting the sergeants like the other archers. Gerald One Arrow, my father, had drilled into me that an archer had to be ready at all times.

While I was waiting, I chose my best arrow. My father had taught me how to fletch, and I had made all of my arrows. I had stained one of the goose feathers in each arrow red with cochineal. I used that to identify my own arrows and to help me aim. Some of the other archers did not fletch. They bought them from a fletcher. I was happier knowing that each arrow I used would be true. I chose the first one I had made, and I nocked it.

Although young, I was large for my age. Most of my comrades were squat and broad. I was tall and powerful. Perhaps that was the mix of Norman and Welsh. However, I was able to move silently any time I chose.

One of the horses raised her head and pricked her ears. That might have meant nothing. Horses can be sensitive creatures, but I was curious and I cocked an ear and listened. There was a noise. It was above me. I did not think it was our men. I sniffed the air. My father was a good huntsman - he had taught me to use my nose. I smelled sweat, and I smelled mutton fat. There were Welshmen, and they were above me. I used the rocks to step silently up the bank. Further up lay ferns and bracken. I would be able to use those for cover. My brown leather jerkin was old and dull, it would blend in. My face, also, was tanned and not white. I was rarely indoors.

As I neared the top, I dropped to my knees. As much as I wanted to be able to send an arrow at any Welshmen I spied, I needed to know their numbers and their position. I had seen the footprints in the mud by the side of the stream when we had ascended. I had been suspicious, but as no one else had said anything I had remained silent. I now saw that had been a mistake. The Welshmen had been waiting for us. They were going to turn the ambush around.

I lifted my head above the bracken and edged forward. It was not easy, holding a nocked arrow and a bow. Forty paces from me, I saw the line of twenty Welshmen, crouched and ready to strike. Some had helmets and some had shields. All held a weapon. I was relieved to see that none of them held bows. I could not see our men. I guessed they were edging towards the hall. Should I shout to warn them? Would I be punished by Hugh of Rhuddlan if I did so? My decision was made for me as I saw one of the Welshmen, with a helmet, a shield and a war axe, stand and raise his arm. They were going to attack.

I stood and brought my bow up in one swift motion. I drew back the string. I had trained for ten years, and it was as natural an action as scratching my ear. I aimed at the leader. As my arrow flew, straight and true, I heard him begin to shout. I was drawing and nocking another arrow as he fell dead. Fortune favoured me, or perhaps it was God, for the men looked, not at me, but at their dead leader. I sent another arrow at the man next to him. Then they saw me.

From behind them I heard a shout and the clash of metal. I drew another arrow and, as four of them ran at me, I sent it towards the nearest man. It hit him in the chest. This was a test. How fast could I nock and release? There were three of them now. My next arrow hit one in the throat. Two remained, but they were just ten paces from me. The next Welshman to die was so close to me that I could smell his breath. My arrow went through his screaming mouth and out of the back of his head. It was his body that saved me, for the last of the men could not get at me directly. I flung aside the bow and pushed the dying man at the Welshman with the sword and shield. As he fell, I took my dagger from my left boot and grabbed the sword which had fallen from the last man I had slain. I knew how to use a war bow. A sword was a different matter.

The Welshman grinned. "Boy, I am going to hamstring you first and then have my fun with you! You have killed my brother and you will pay. Your man–sacks will adorn my wall!"

There was a temptation to shout something back at him, but I was terrified. He was my size. He had a leather helmet and a long sword. His round shield had a boss. I would have no chance against him. My father had taught me to look for weaknesses. That applied to animals when hunting, or men when killing. This man was overconfident. He came towards me and I backed through the bracken. He laughed and swung his sword at my head. My descending the slope meant he was above me. I jerked my head back. The sword seemed to hum as it whipped past my face. I knew that if I looked down I was dead. I had to move slowly and feel each footstep before I took it.

Behind him I could hear the battle raging. I had my own battle here on this slippery slope which lead to the stream and the horses. Fate took a hand and my left leg slipped on a rock. The Welshman saw his chance and he raised his sword. Even as I hit the ground I saw the blade coming for me. I am no swordsman, but I am strong. To me the sword was just an iron bar. I held mine above me and the Welshman's sword rang into it. He looked surprised, for he had not beaten me down. I lifted my dagger and rammed it into his foot. He screamed and made the mistake of pulling his injured foot back; my dagger was embedded in the earth from the strength of my blow . He tore my dagger through his foot. Blood spurted. As he fell backwards, I jumped to my feet and brought the iron bar that was my sword across his head. The skull split and I saw brains within.

I put my dagger back in my boot and rammed the sword into my belt. I ran up the slope. At the top, I picked up my bow and I ran past the dead men I had killed. When I reached the flat ground, I saw that the battle was finely balanced. I drew an arrow. Even as I aimed at one of the two Welshmen fighting Hugh of Rhuddlan, I wondered why our archers were not doing as I was. My arrow hit one of the Welshman in the back. I saw the other glance to the side, and, in that moment, Hugh of Rhuddlan slashed him across the middle with his own sword.

I nocked another arrow and saw that seven of my comrades, archers all, lay dead or dying. The other three were having to use their short swords. I aimed at the men the three archers were fighting. As my arrow took the first one, I saw Ralph raise his arm in acknowledgement as he grabbed the bow which lay on the ground. He ran to me. I took another arrow and aimed at the massive Welshman who looked as though he was about to smash his war hammer into Harry Warbow's head. My arrow went through his neck. It did not kill him immediately. He seemed frozen. Harry took his sword and hacked it down on the Welshman's skull. He picked up his bow, and he too ran to me. Even as I took another arrow to help David ap Llewellyn, the Welshman he was fighting skewered him.

Now that Ralph and Harry joined me we had three bows. I sent another arrow into the man who had slain David. I heard Hugh of Rhuddlan shout, "Shield wall!"

Suddenly Harry fell with an arrow in his leg. They had archers. I reached for an arrow as Ralph sent one towards the archer who was in the tower of the hall. I nocked the arrow and aimed at a head I could see peering out from the tower. Even while my arrow was in the air, I saw the head rise and a second archer raise his weapon. My arrow hit him in the chest and he plummeted to the ground.

Ralph said, "I think that is the last of the archers. We have to help Hugh of Rhuddlan. He is outnumbered. How many arrows remain?"

I looked in my quiver. "Eight."

"Then use them wisely."

Hugh of Rhuddlan had just seven men with him, and there were still thirteen Welshmen left alive. I saw one of the sergeants fall to a billhook. The Welshman hooked the sergeant's shield and pulled it towards him. Then he rammed the pointed end into the sergeant's throat. My arrow struck him in the shoulder. Ralph sent his next arrow into the thigh of the next Welshman, whose shield prevented a kill. As the Welshman faltered, I saw a gap between his helmet and his shoulder. My arrow went into the tiny space. It was now six against eleven. Suddenly, Ralph went down as though poleaxed. He appeared to have no wound, and then I saw the boy whirling his sling. I had an arrow nocked, and as I saw the sling release, I dropped to my knee and sent an arrow into the boy. A second boy ran towards me with his sling ready. I nocked and sent another arrow. I plucked him from the air. The two boys had seen fewer than ten summers.

In the time it had taken me to kill the boys, we had lost another man at arms. I grabbed one of Ralph's arrows and sent it into the back of a Welshman. I was now beginning to tire. I had to grit my teeth. I took another of Ralph's arrows and ended the life of the Welshman with the axe, who was about to finish off John of Chester. The sergeant at arms lay on the ground. I had to get closer. I nocked an arrow as I ran. I made sure that I had stopped when I released. My arrow hit another Welshman in the side. I was fewer than twenty paces from him; I could not have missed. Some of these men had mail but that did not stop my arrows. I slew another two before Hugh of Rhuddlan killed Iago ap Mordaf. The five sergeants slaughtered the rest of the Welshmen. They did not give quarter. We had lost too many of our band for that.

With one of my last arrows nocked, and watching for danger, I walked towards Hugh of Rhuddlan.

"I thought I told you to watch those horses!"

I turned to look at him. "Sorry, Sergeant!"

He was grinning. "I will let you off just this once, but don't make a habit of it, archer!"

Ralph sat up. I thought he was dead, but he had a thick skull. He grinned at me when he saw the sword in my hand. "An archer with a sword! Who would have thought! I hope you killed that little bastard who hit me with the stone."

"I did!"

"Good! For that, I shall buy you an ale."

We headed back to the castle, purses filled with the captured coins, the cattle, swine, grain and horses from the farm and with the war gear we had taken from the dead Welsh clan. We did not bother with slaves. Hugh was angry at having lost men, and the women and children had fled. The baron would be unhappy. The church now frowned upon the taking of slaves, but I knew that the women and the children who were left would struggle to survive the winter. Life was hard here in the borderlands.

CHAPTER 1

That one battle made me what I became. I was now not only an archer but also a warrior. It had been a costly raid our lord had sent us on, but it had shown me and the men with whom I fought that I could kill. It showed me that I could hold my own with archers such as Harry and Ralph. I was no longer the untried novice. I had used a sword to kill a man. I felt like a veteran. Even Hugh of Rhuddlan began to show me a little respect. I would still receive a cuff and a blow when I displeased him, but I had saved his life, and, for that at least, he was grateful.

Life was not easy in the castle. We had sentry duty and archery practice. The only day we were not working was Sunday; at least one Sunday in four was allowed for ourselves. On that one Sunday in four we went to church and then had the afternoon off. On each of these Sundays I ran, after church, the twelve miles to my father's smallholding. It was not a farm. He had a cottage garden which grew leeks and greens. He fished and he hunted. He gathered. I called him foolish, for he would often hunt, fish and gather in the land of the Welsh. We were just over the border. He had laughed at me and told me that he was too good a scout to be caught.

He lived alone. My mother had me and then left when I was eight summers old. She ran off with a man purporting to be a doctor selling

9

cures. My father was away, and in those days my grandmother lived with us. When my grandmother died, I lived alone when my father was on campaign. That was one reason he had left the service of the Earl of Chester. He wanted to raise me as an archer.

I headed to his home. It was not far from the castle. I took the woodland way. The woods were his lordship's personal hunting ground. My father's home was in the land just beyond his lordship's. I passed Ada's cottage. Ada lived with her two sisters. All three of them were widows. Some said that they were witches. They were not. They were just three women who had outlived their husbands. With children fled the nest, they now had a comfortable life, raising goats and making cheese. They had offered to help my father, but he was an obstinate man. He liked his isolated existence. However, each time I passed, I always bought some goat's cheese and milk. Ada's cheese was the best in the valley. She used some flavours and ingredients which were a secret. I knew that my father liked the taste.

"How is he these days, Gammer Ada?"

"The same as ever, young Gruffyd. I know why your mother left him. Some men cannot abide the company of women. Your father is one such. I think he spent too long at the wars." She handed me the milk in the jug and the cheese wrapped in dock leaves. I gave her the silver pennies. "But I confess that I like him. He is independent. Still, you will not end like him. You could have any girl in the valley!"

I blushed, "I have time enough for that, Gammer."

She smiled an enigmatic smile. "You will not end your life with a girl from this valley. There is greatness in your future."

Father was not in the hut when I arrived. He had chickens and fowls in a pen. There was a female goat he used for milk and butter. Inside the hut was a simple bed. There was a log he used as a table and two small logs for chairs. The hut was conical, and there was no chimney such as the great halls had. There was a fire, which he kept burning in the centre all year around. The smoke kept the wildlife from the thatch. It was a simple existence, but my father enjoyed it, or, at the very least, he did not complain.

I had bought a flagon of ale from the alewife in the town, and I placed it on the table, along with the cheese and the milk. I would have two empty jugs to take back with me. I knew that he struggled to get bread so I had bought him a four-pound loaf. Even when it went stale he would still eat it. Stale bread in the broth he made each day was nourishing. It had been how I had lived while he was away. With little coin and the nearest bakers twelve miles away, bread became a luxury. There were wild greens and trapped animals which made healthy stews. To hunt game on a lord's estate could result in death. A lenient lord could take a limb or a nose; perhaps an ear. I knew that my father risked such punishments, but he could outfox the gamekeepers used by Sir Henry. I too had been forced to poach on many occasions. I think it honed my skills as a hunter and a scout. I had learned to move silently and avoid those who hunted me.

I took the leather pail and marched down to the stream to fetch water. As I arrived I heard my father. He was approaching through the woods. Most men would have had no idea that he was there, but I heard the most minute of sounds. Even though I expected it to be my father, my hand went to my newly acquired sword.

He grunted when he spied me. He had with him his old dog, Wolf. There had been a time when Wolf had been a fierce wolfhound. Now he was like my father, old and watching life drift by. "I smelled you half a mile away. How many times have I told you to make your clothes smell of animals?"

I laughed. "The other archers in my lord's hall would object, I think. Good to see you Father."

"Then they are tosspots! A good archer cares not what his bow brothers smell like, so long as they are accurate. Tell them Gerald ap Llewellyn told them so."

I saw that he had a pair of rabbits over his shoulder. "They are not from his lordship's land, are they?"

"He only eats them in winter! Two rabbits will hardly bother him."

I shook my head as we headed to his hut. "I know not why you sent me to him. He is about as much use as a three-legged horse!"

"I told you. The Earl of Chester is not a good master. He cares not for archers. But at least you are close to home if you serve the master of Denbigh." He put his arm around me. "Remember, my son, that an archer is born and not made. You have archer's blood and I have made you work hard to become an even better archer. I am good, but you shall be great."

I laughed as we entered the hut. "Whoever heard of a great archer? Knights; yes, even men at arms, but archers? We do not move the thrones of this world."

"Then you shall be the first. Our ancestor came north with Henry FitzEmpress and each generation has been stronger. Come. I have talked enough and I have an appetite. Skin the coneys. I will put the water on to boil. If we have ale first, then I will have them so tender that I can suck the meat from the bones!"

"Your teeth are bothering you again!"

"I am old. It is to be expected. Surely you do not mind tender rabbit?"

I shook my head. "You need a woman to watch over you."

"I tried a woman once and she left me."

"That was my mother!"

"Aye!"

My father was gruff and could be taciturn, but we got on well together.

He would never praise me. A nod was the most fulsome acknowledgement. However, he had taught me well.

He saw the sword at my side. "That is new."

"I took it from the Welshman who tried to skewer me with it."

I handed it to him. He felt its balance. "Not a bad sword. It is shorter than most, but it will do." He felt the edge and then flexed it against his thigh. "It is made of good steel. It looks like it had a jewel on the pommel at one time. I bet the thieving Welshman you took it from sold it. When you have time, polish a river stone and place it there. It will improve the balance. You need a scabbard. If you do not then it will rust and become dull. You do not want to be ever sharpening and cleaning it. Come, while the rabbit cooks we will make one."

I was intrigued. I had never seen a scabbard made before. I wondered how my father knew to do so. He seemed to read my thoughts.

"When we were on campaign, I watched Old Edward, the earl's bodyguard, when he showed the earl's squire how to make one."

Behind the hut were lengths of willow. They were cut and were being seasoned. He found one log, slightly longer than the sword. He took a metal spike and, using the back of his wood axe, split the log in two. He split one half in two, and then the next, until he had two thin lengths of rough wood. He talked as he worked. "People asked me why I chose this spot for a hut. The Earl of Chester offered me larger plots than this one. It was the woods and the stream. I can hunt in this wood, for I have the earl's permission. I have water and I have willow. Willow is a very accommodating timber."

He took his adze and began to smooth the two lengths. If he had not been an archer, then he could have been a carpenter. He knew how to work wood.

"While I do this, take the cured skins from the hut. They will make the lining. I have some deer hide to bind it."

By the time I had found the seasoned skins, he had finished the wood. He placed the sword between them to make sure it fitted. He took his pot of glue and placed it by the fire. He used the hooves of any dead animals he found to make the glue. Taking his sharp knife, he cut the rabbit skins so that they were smaller than the sword. As soon as the glue bubbled, he coated the wood with it and then placed the skins on the wood. Putting them fur to fur, he laid them on the ground and put two logs onto the top. Over time, the rabbit's fur would flatten. At first, the sword would be hard to draw.

As he passed the pot with the rabbit cooking, he stirred it and then took a length of deer hide. "I was going to discard this. It is an awkward width, but I think it will just do for you." The deer hide had been scraped and tanned. It was flexible and it was tough. He handed it to me. "Here, make holes a thumbs' width apart. I will get us bowls. The rabbit is almost ready. We can finish the scabbard when we have eaten."

My hard, calloused hands and my powerful shoulders make short work of the holes. I knew what would be needed next, and I took my knife and slit a length of hide from the edge. It would bind the scabbard together.

"Come, get your food."

My father was a good cook. Wild garlic and rosemary infused the stew, along with wild greens. He cut a hunk of bread for each of us and we ate. We did not eat all of the stew. We each ate a saddle of the rabbits. It would last my father three or four days. By adding more water and greens each day he would have a thin soup left on the fifth day. He would use it to soak the stale bread. When next I returned I would bring him more. It meant he had bread once a month, at least. We washed the stew down with half of the ale. The rest would be eked out over the next two days.

"Now then. Let us finish the task." He put the sword between the two fur-lined boards and then began to bind them together with the length of hide I had cut. We were both strong and the bindings were tight. He fashioned a loop for my belt, and he positioned the sword on my left hip.

"Draw the sword." It did not come out easily. "Good, it is a tight fit. Over time, it will become easier. You are an archer. You should not need to draw a sword. If you do, then it means you have run out of arrows."

I slid the sword back into the scabbard. It was plain and unadorned, but it would do. I took the piece of deer hide which remained. "I will use this to make a sheath for my dagger."

He nodded, "Aye, I never liked the idea of jamming it in your boot. It asks for trouble."

I stayed until dusk and then departed. "I shall see you again in four weeks." I handed him three silver pennies. "Buy yourself more bread." He was going to refuse. He was a proud man, and he liked not the idea of charity, even from his son. "I took the coins from the dead Welshmen I slew. I have more. Buy bread."

He nodded. "In that case, I will." He held out his arm and I clasped it. "One more thing, my son. Call it advice if you will. I wasted much of my life. I served others. I should have served myself. If you find an honourable man then serve him. I thought Sir Henry honourable. I know that I was wrong. You swore an oath to him, and until he is dead, you cannot break it, but watch out for yourself."

"I will." Wolf came and nuzzled my hand. I ruffled his fur and left.

I loped off through the woods. The sword, in its scabbard, rested easily against my leg. On my way there it had banged. My father was right. He always was. I wondered about the stone. I had seen the hole and wondered what should have been in it. I would find a stone from the Clwyd.

*

I had found and begun to polish the black and white stone when we were ordered north. As usual, his lordship was not with us. We were joining the men of the Earl of Chester. Hugh of Rhuddlan gathered us together. There were just four archers and ten sergeants.

"Well, my lucky lads, you get to ride this time! We don't need to march! You will need your blankets; we will be sleeping under the stars for the next week or so!"

Ralph asked, "Where to this time?"

Garth, one of the men at arms, said, "You can bet that his lordship will not be shifting off his arse anywhere."

Hugh of Rhuddlan brought his mighty hand to smack Garth on the back of the head. "Watch your mouth! Scots have raided south of Carlisle. The earl wishes to scour the land between Chester and Carlisle of the vermin who infest us. That is why we need horses. Now get your war gear and get mounted."

They were not horses we rode. These were ponies. Hugh of Rhuddlan had a palfrey. He towered over us. The ponies were hardy and they would be able to keep up with the rest of the mounted men. They were as wide as a sumpter but your feet almost scraped the ground. One advantage of raiding the Welsh was that they always had plenty of ponies.

We headed north for Chester. Our path took us through Delamere forest. This was where outlaws lurked. Periodically, the earl would send his men to hunt down those who lived outside the law. There were many such men. If you offended the lord of the manor, or one of his priests, then you had to find somewhere to live. The forest offered a home. We rode warily through it. Sometimes there would be enough outlaws to take on a small band such as ours. When we emerged, I breathed a sigh of relief.

The Earl of Chester was also the Prince of Wales, Edward Longshanks. I ventured, "Sergeant, will the Earl of Chester be leading us?"

"No, for he is in France. Sir Ranulf de Kevelioc will be in command."

I had heard of him. My father had served under him. When my father had been one of the earl's archers, the Earl of Chester had been John of Scotland. He had been dead for some years.

While we waited for the other knights to join us, I finished polishing my stone and fitted it in the pommel of the sword. My father was right, it had a better balance. Just as importantly, it looked right. I felt like a warrior with it at my side.

It was a motley band which left the city of Chester to head north on the old Roman road. Sir Ranulf led ten knights. There were thirty sergeants and just fifteen archers. We were tucked at the rear with the servants and baggage.

Ralph turned to me. "Now I see why they needed us. We make up over a quarter of the archers. If there are Scots, then you need archers."

One of the other archers, riding a sumpter, spat, "Don't get ideas above your station! We are the earl's own archers! You lot will just be here to clean up horseshit." The earl's archers wore a distinctive livery. They rode palfreys.

Ralph was not a man to suffer insults. "When we stop, friend, then you and I will have words and perhaps a blow or two. There may just be four of us but this young warrior next to me slew twelve Welshmen in one battle. When was the last time you popinjays did anything other than strut the walls of Chester?"

They had leggings with stripes and a colourful tunic. We looked like poor relations by comparison.

"He does not look old enough to have killed any. Has he begun to shave yet?"

17

That made them all laugh. I smiled at Ralph. These days, I was more confident. I was not afraid of this loudmouth archer. "He reminds me of that last Welshman I gutted with my dagger. He squealed just before he died." I turned to look at the archer. "I would watch a man fight before I insulted him, friend."

The captain of archers, riding at the front of our column, shouted, "John of Warrington, shut your mouth. If you annoy me, it will be you who cleans up the horseshit!"

That made the four of us laugh.

We rode hard that first day. I enjoyed every moment of it, for Ralph and Harry told me of battles in which they had fought. They told me how an archer could use a pavise and outwit a crossbowman. They gave me tips on how to make a bow and a bowstring. For my part, I gave them my father's tips on how to fletch. We stopped after a long day's ride and we camped by the River Ribble. Hugh of Rhuddlan organised our tents. "Gruffyd, son of Gerald, and Harry Long Stride, you two will be guarding Sir Ranulf's tent."

Harry moaned, "Why us? What is wrong with his own archers?"

"Just do what you are told. His own archers are leaving before dawn. They have horses and are going to scout out the Forest of Bowland. Ralph and Alan of Denbigh, you get to watch the horses. Don't let his lordship down!"

It was on the tip of my tongue to say that Baron Henry let himself down all the time, but it would have been wasted and put me in Hugh of Rhuddlan's bad books.

The sentry duty meant that one of us would have to be awake at all times. We led our horses to the horse lines. Ralph and Alan had an easier duty. They could just tie a piece of cord to the end of the horse lines and would be woken if the horses moved. One of us would have to stand outside the tent and make sure that no one entered while the knights slept. We would alternate.

We ate with the other archers. I kept a wary eye on John of Warrington. I was bigger than he was but he had the look of a treacherous man. When Ralph went to make water, I saw John of Warrington follow him. I was about to rise when Harry said, "Just sit. Ralph can handle himself."

They both seemed to be away for a long time. Darkness descended. Captain Jack looked up as Ralph appeared. His knuckles were bloody and his lip was bleeding. He sat down and winked at me. John of Warrington appeared a short while later. His face looked a mess and he was slightly doubled over, as though he was in pain. Captain Jack said, "Have you got the shits or something?"

He mumbled, "Something like that, Captain."

Ralph drank some of the ale Harry offered him. "He is all mouth! I wouldn't want to rely on him if the Scots get close. He will find it hard to ride tomorrow!" Harry gave him a sideways look. "I kicked him between the legs. You didn't think he really had the shits, did you?"

Hugh shouted, "Right you two, duty time!"

We picked up our bows and our blankets and headed to the tent. The knights were seated around their own fire. Their servants and squires were tending to them. Sir Ranulf pointed to their tent. "One can sleep behind. The other stand by the door." The door was just a flap. Harry and I had tossed a coin. I would have the first shift and the middle watch. He took my blanket. We would be more comfortable than the others; we would use one blanket as a bed and cover ourselves with the other. My bow was not strung and I laid it down in its cover, where it would not be stepped upon. I moved back into the shadows. I could still hear the knights as they spoke.

"When do we get a real war, that's what I want to know?"

"And where is Lord Edward these days?"

Sir Ranulf hissed, "Stop moaning. Lord Edward is in France, as you know, and we are preparing for war. It will come. Regard this as practice, Raymond."

"Chasing Scots? There is no honour in killing them. They do not even bring knights south anymore. They are more like bandits!"

Another saw me and said, "And what of Henry of Denbigh? He sends a handful of men and does not come himself!"

The one called Raymond, laughed, "Better without him. He is fit for hunting and that is all. He is so fat that he needs a warhorse to hunt!" I smiled at that. It was true that our lord was excessively fat. He liked his food, there was no denying it.

Sir Ranulf raised his voice as though to silence them. "Do not speak ill of a brother knight. Without Baron Henry, we would have Welshmen to deal with as well as Scots. When was the last time the Welsh raided your lands, Sir Roger?"

"You are right, but I am not sure that the baron dirties his own hands. I have heard that his captain, Hugh of Rhuddlan, is the real warrior."

"Then be grateful that we have him! Now it is time we retired. Our archers will find the Scots on the morrow and then we can deal with them and return to Chester."

"I hope your information was correct, Sir Ranulf. If they have headed north into the old Viking lands, then we shall need more than this handful of men to flush them out."

"Fear not, the abbot of the White Friars monastery was the one who reported their presence. They will be in the forest. The Scots think that it will hide them. Captain Jack will find them."

My watches were uneventful. In those days, I was young enough to go without sleep and the lack of it did not bother me. When I awoke, the rest of the archers had gone. The Baron of Denbigh's archers were the only ones left to protect the knights, squires and sergeants. We headed upstream to cross the Ribble by the old bridge. The forest of Bowland lay to the north. It was the hunting ground of the Earl of Chester. As such, it was free from bandits and brigands. The forest lay just below the high ground. It was what made it such a fertile hunting ground. All types of beasts lay within its eaves. Ahead, I saw birds flocking. I knew birds. These were crows and magpies. They were feasting on flesh. I wondered if I should say anything. Surely someone else would know what the flocking birds meant? I watched the banners of the knights at the head of the column as they entered the forest. Suddenly, Hugh of Rhuddlan spurred his horse and galloped to the head of the column. When he reached his lordship, we all stopped.

Ralph chuckled, "Our captain will be in trouble. I don't think his lordship will take kindly to being stopped by a sergeant at arms, even one as experienced as Captain Hugh!"

To our surprise, Hugh of Rhuddlan stood in his saddle, turned and waved at us. "Archers!"

We galloped forward. Ralph was our leader and replied, "Yes, my lord."

Sir Ranulf pointed ahead. "Hugh of Rhuddlan is not happy about those birds in the distance. Investigate them."

We dismounted. We were archers and not horsemen. We took our bows from their canvas sleeves and draped the sleeves over our saddles. We strung our bows and slipped our wrist-guards on. Nocking an arrow each, we prepared to move. Ralph led us at a lope, and we did not enter the forest on the trail but ran through the trees. We were not armoured men. We could move easily. We were light-footed and did not trip over roots nor step into rabbit holes. We formed a diamond. Ralph led, Henry and Alan followed and I brought up the rear. Compared with these three, I was the novice still.

When we had covered four hundred paces and were hidden by the trees and undergrowth, Ralph held up his hand. We stopped. We were far enough from the horsemen to be able to hear the forest. There was silence. That in itself was a warning. There should have been noise. Animals should have been skittering through the dead material on the ground, and there was nothing. Ralph waved to the west and we began to move towards the trail. Alan and Henry moved further apart. I scanned the ground. It had rained recently, and I saw footprints in the mud. Someone with bare feet had been over the ground. We wore boots. Often the Scots went barefoot.

As we neared the trail Ralph stopped us again. This time we heard a noise. It was the sound of squabbling birds. From the sounds, they were magpies. It was the fluttering wings of a pair of the birds that alerted me. They were pecking at a dead archer. I saw his leggings with the black and white stripes. They were now besmeared with blood. They were his lordship's archers. Ralph saw them at the same time. He gave a low whistle and waved for Alan and Henry to keep watch and then gestured me forward.

There were seven dead archers. Of their horses, there was no sign. I saw that John of Warrington would insult us no more. From the blood at his groin, I guessed what had happened to him after he had died. It begged the question, where were the others, and where were the horses? I headed towards the trail and saw signs of a struggle. The bracken and the grass had been flattened and was bloody. I saw hoofprints that led north and west. I pointed to them.

Ralph nodded. "The Scots are gone. Go back and fetch the column."

I nodded, and putting my arrow back in my quiver, slipped my bow over my back. It made running easier.

"My lord, there has been an ambush. We have found seven dead archers. The captain, the others and the horses are not there."

He nodded and turned to the men at arms and knights. "Follow me."

Hugh of Rhuddlan said, "Fetch the ponies."

I mounted my horse, and taking the reins of the others, rode after the column. This was a disaster. We had had pitifully few archers to begin with. Now that the Scots knew we were coming we would find the task even harder. I guessed they had taken the four archers either as hostages or to extract information.

When we reached the scene of the ambush I saw that Ralph was examining the ground. He was a good tracker. "They have headed deeper into the forest, lord."

Sir Ranulf looked at Hugh of Rhuddlan. "What think you, Captain, a trap?"

He nodded. "They would draw us deeper into the forest. Your horses make much noise, lord, as does your mail."

"We have been sent to rid the forest of these raiders. I cannot let them wander at will."

"No, lord, but the path we were on comes out close to Craven, and there it splits into two. The Scots could go to Lancaster or head north towards Carlisle. I would wager it to be Carlisle. If we head up the road, then we can wait at the crossroads and turn the ambush onto them." He pointed to us archers. "These four can track and trail the Scots."

"They are our only archers!"

Hugh shrugged. "Then if we lose them, we have lost but four men. Better that than *we* end up like John of Warrington here!"

The baron nodded. He pointed to Ralph. "Can you find them?"

Ralph nodded.

"Then find them, and meet us at the crossroads with news of their whereabouts."

As the men at arms and knights moved off, we slung our bows over our backs and prepared to move off. Harry grumbled, "So it is fine for us to die, eh? I have a good mind to join the outlaws in Delamere!"

Ralph hissed, "I know that you are fooling, Harry, but words like that could cost you your eyes. We will not end up like John of Warrington. We are used to the forest. Gruffyd, you have the youngest ears and eyes. Even a blind man can follow this trail. You lead. If you sense danger then drop to a knee. No heroics!"

"No, Ralph!"

I jammed my hat into my belt. I needed to see, hear and feel as I ran through the forest. Ralph was correct. The trail was easy to follow. They had taken horses. Horse tracks are the easiest to follow. I ran but I did not run recklessly. I did not want to be out of breath, and I did not want to stumble into an ambush. After half a mile I stopped. I smelled something ahead. I left my sword in my scabbard and drew my knife. I crept towards the bole of a large elm and crouched. I saw a foot. As soon as I saw the black and white legging, I knew it was another archer from Chester. I stepped around the tree and saw the body of Alan Red Fletch. He had a wound in his leg and his throat had been cut. He must have been slowing them down.

Ralph appeared behind me. I pointed. He nodded and gestured for me to carry on. Captain Jack now had just two archers with him. Would they survive? Had they been taken, and if so why? After another half a mile I became aware that the Scots were now following a wider trail than before. They must have known where it was. This had been part of Scotland for some years. It was only in the time of King Henry that it had reverted to England. The trail was a hunter's trail. I moved a little faster. I saw ahead of me a stinking pile of horse manure. It was steaming. The horse that had dropped it had to be less than half a mile ahead of me. I was getting close and I slowed, waving Ralph forward. I pointed to the horse muck and he nodded. He waved Harry and Alan forward.

He slipped his bow from his back and nocked an arrow. We did the same. He pointed to me and Harry and then to his right. Then he tapped Alan's chest and led him to the left. We moved through the forest now and avoided the trail. It was obvious where the trail was going. I began to hear voices. It was the Scots. A horse neighed and I heard a slap as someone struck the beast to silence it. Harry and I crept. The sound of the neigh and the voices gave us an indication of where they were. Harry nodded towards the trail. We were now thirty paces from it. We moved diagonally so that we were closing alongside the trail but still moving in the forest. I caught the flash of black and white. It was an archer.

Once I saw the archer's leg I stopped and moved my eyes slowly upwards. I caught sight of bare flesh. Often Scots warriors did not bother with anything above the waist. It was, to them, a sign of their courage. Once I had seen this glimpse of flesh I soon saw others. It seemed the Scots had stopped to rest. Without looking at the sun I could not work out the exact time, but I guessed it was shortly after noon. They must have thought that they had lost us. I realised that there were many footprints surrounding the horse's dung. They had waited. They would have been listening for pursuit. Men on horses make a noise; perhaps they had also been listening out when they had slain Alan Red Fletch.

I looked at Harry. What could four of us do against an unknown number of Scots? He must have read my thoughts. He pointed further down the trail. Up ahead Sir Ranulf was waiting with forty men. Our job was just to keep watch. We continued to creep and I heard the voices of the Scots. Their words were unclear, for they were speaking quietly. The horses stamped their feet. I heard them tearing grass from beneath the trees. I caught the sound of a man making water against a tree. We moved another few paces and then Harry froze. Suddenly we saw men. We had reached the head of the Scottish column. I could see a mailed warrior and he was astride a horse. Harry squatted and I copied him. We waited. Archers are patient creatures. Most of us are hunters and know how to stalk. We were now stalking humans. It was no different.

They did not stop long. I heard the warrior in the hauberk snap, "Move, we have fifteen more miles yet to travel." I heard grumbling. "Scouts out!" I saw three half-naked men lope off to the north.

They were not going to Lancaster. They were heading for the valley which led up past Coningeston. They could not possibly reach Coningeston. I knew they must be heading to a camp which was north of the Lancaster road. We moved as they moved. Acutely aware that sudden movements would make it easier for them to see us, we used the trees for cover. Only one of us moved at a time. Each time I moved I watched the column of men and animals. I spied Captain Jack. He had been beaten. He had a bloodied head. I marked him and the two men who guarded him. I did not see the other two, but I suspected they would keep their three prisoners separate. No one had told me what we were going to do if it came to a fight, but saving the three archers would be a priority for the four of us. The knights and men at arms could deal with the others.

Not knowing these woods, nor the distance we had to travel was unnerving. We had been told to follow, to track and trail. We had done that. What next? As the trees began to thin, I had my answer. There was a cry from the far side of the Scots. One of the mailed men was thrown from his horse. He shouted as he fell and his horse bolted towards the thinner trees. Suddenly every back was turned to us as the Scots faced this threat. I raised my bow, ready to end the life of any Scot who came within range, but Harry restrained me and nodded for me to follow him. He was my senior and I did as he instructed.

Ralph and Alan were using their arrows well. Men fell and the Scots had to lift their shields to protect themselves. I heard the warrior shout, "After them! There cannot be many!" The numbers before us thinned as the Scots scattered. I saw that the prisoners were bound, but they had now brought the three of them them together. Tim and Walther looked as bloody as Captain Jack. Three men guarded them. I now knew what Harry intended.

We moved silently. I saw Harry slip his bow over his back and take out his short sword. When we were just ten feet from the column of Scots, he pointed for me to guard his back. Harry was a killer and he was the toughest man I knew. He crept close to the Scot on the right and, in one motion, pulled back his head and slit his throat. I sent an arrow into the back of the one on the left, and even as the middle one turned to stab at Harry, I had drawn a second arrow, nocked it and sent it through the side of his head. Harry cut the bonds of the three archers. I had an arrow ready. There was too much noise for the three deaths to be noticed.

Captain Jack and his two archers grabbed weapons from the dead Scots and moved back towards me. They were seen.

"The prisoners! This is a trick!"

Harry had his bow out, and the two of us ended the lives of the first two heroes who ran at us. Captain Jack led his two men deeper into the forest. They were not moving quickly, for they were wounded. I was pulling and nocking arrows as fast I could, but the Scots were now using the trees and their superior numbers. Had it just been Harry and me, we could have melted away, but the three wounded men would slow us down. Ultimately, they might just get us killed.

Harry and I had been moving closer together as we moved back. Once we used our last arrows we would have to fight together with our swords.

I sensed a movement to my left and I spun and loosed, almost without thinking. One of the Scots had sneaked around and was just ten feet from me. My arrow ripped into his chest, only the feathers protruded. Even so, he continued to run at me. I took an arrow from my quiver. I had no time to nock it, and so I rammed it through his eye and into his skull. The arrow broke but he died. I was down to three arrows.

Then I heard a cry, "England!" It was Sir Ranulf, the knights and the men at arms approaching. We were still in danger. The men who pursued us had lost friends. Just as we would have done, so did they seek vengeance.

"Back to us!" I heard Captain Jack's voice. I sent another arrow towards the advancing men. My arrow hit one in the shoulder. He broke it off and continued to charge. These men were hard. I flicked a glance over my shoulder and saw that Captain Jack and his two men were between two oaks. They had their captured weapons ready and were making a stand. I used my penultimate arrow to end the life of the wounded Scot and ran back.

"Get behind us."

"I have but one arrow left!"

"Then use it well!"

I stood behind them and saw the ten Scots who advanced towards us. Most were not mailed. They wore no helmets and most were bare-chested with wildly tattooed bodies. In their left hands they held small bucklers, whilst in their right, they held weapons ranging from axes to swords, clubs to small hammers. These were not warriors, but they were killers. One had a mail vest and I used my last arrow on him. At a range of ten paces my arrow would not be stopped by mail. He looked down as the arrow struck him in the chest. The strike must have hit something vital for he fell backwards, as though poleaxed.

I dropped my bow and drew my sword and my hunting knife. It

was sharp enough to shave with. I stood next to Tim. He gave a wan smile. "Nice arrows, archer!"

"Thank you." The fact that I was complimented by his lordship's archer made me swell with pride.

"I hope you are as good with that sword or it could all be in vain."

Harry had also used his last arrows and he stood next to Walther. There were seven of them and five of us. The fact that we had three injured men, and that my lack of beard made me look like a boy, must have given them encouragement, for they raced at us, swinging their weapons wildly. Had I not fought with a sword before I might have been intimidated. Because I was on the outside, two men came at me. One was ahead of the other. I had been taught to take the closest target first. The other would only be a heartbeat behind his companion. The first Scot had an axe held in two hands, while the one behind had a buckler and a short sword.

I must have appeared like a frightened rabbit to the Scot with the axe, for as he swung and I didn't move, he shouted, "Are ye filling yer breeks, Englishman?"

In answer, I dropped to one knee, and as the axe cracked into the bole of a tree, rather than my head, I drove my hunting knife up between his legs and into his guts. I had gutted wild boar. This was easier. With the axe embedded, his hands went to his stomach. I stood and used my powerful shoulders to drive his body into the swordsman behind him. The dying man fell backwards and I slashed my sword sideways. It was more in hope than expectation, but the swordsman's buckler was ineffective. His dying companion lay against it. My sword struck the swordsman's thigh and, as I pulled it backwards, I saw that it was slick with blood.

I was learning that, in a battle, you concentrated upon your own fight and didn't worry about others. I heard screams and shouts from behind me but I ignored them. The man I had wounded could still fight. I had seen wild pigs, stuck with boar spears. They had still eviscerated an unwary hunter. The Scot seemed enraged that I had hurt his leg. Blood was pouring from the wound. It was not mortal, but it needed attention. He tried to strike me in the face with his buckler. His left leg did not give him the support he needed, and the blow was easily blocked by my knife. He swung his sword at me, thinking that my sword could not reach him. He was right, but he didn't realise how strong I was. I hooked my left leg around his right, and as he swung, I pushed. With a weakened left leg, he tumbled to the ground. As I lay prostrate, I hacked my sword across his neck. It was a powerful blow and the head rolled away.

"Gruffyd!"

I turned in time to see Tim's butchered body and both Harry and Captain Jack fighting two men each. I ran, screaming. It distracted one man who was fighting Captain Jack. He turned, but he turned too late. I swung my sword hard across his middle. Scraping off his ribs, it hacked deep into his body. He was dead, even as I withdrew my sword. I stabbed the other Scot in the arm, and that allowed Captain Jack to ram his sword deep into his body. Harry was struck, just as I turned to go to his aid. I saw my friend fall. He had been hit by a small war hammer. I stabbed with both knife and sword at the two men who had fought him. Both found flesh and made the men turn. Captain Jack's sword hacked across the face of one man. That left one other . I had stabbed his left arm. He was bleeding but he was not willing to die.

Swinging his sword from on high, he attempted to bring it down and split my head in two. Instinctively, I brought up my own sword. I was an archer. I had muscles as thick as young oaks. Our swords jarred together. My father had told me that it was a good sword, and the clash of steel proved it. The Scot's sword bent. He looked up in surprise as

I drove my dagger up between his ribs. As it scraped off bone I twisted. His eyes glazed over and blood oozed from his mouth.

I looked around for more enemies. The battle at the path still raged, but we were now an island of the dead. Walther was lying, like Harry, unconscious. They had both been struck in the head by the small war hammer. I knelt to see to Harry and Captain Jack did the same for Walther. As he did so I heard him say, "Jack of Warrington could not have been more wrong about you, Gruffyd son of Gerald. I would offer you the chance to fight for his lordship."

I was too busy looking at the wound of my friend to take in the offer. I often wondered what would have happened if I had accepted. I just dismissed it. "Thank you, Captain, but I will serve Sir Henry a little while longer."

Harry groaned. Captain Jack said, "Your friend must have a harder head than poor Walther here. My archer, like Tim and the others, is dead."

I took Harry's water skin and forced some between his lips. He coughed and said, with his eyes still closed, "Are you trying to poison me? You give a wounded man wine, or, at the very least, beer."

Captain Jack said, "He will survive. Now look lively and arm yourself. We are not out of danger yet."

As it turned out we were. Ralph and Alan came racing through the woods with swords drawn. Alan had a bandage around his head and a bloody face. They had fought hard too. Ralph grinned when he saw us both alive. "I thought to find two butchered bodies here. I am right pleased you live. And you too, Captain Jack. Come, the Scots are dead. Let us see what offerings these miserable vermin hold."

Captain Jack said, "Whatever is here goes to these two archers. But for them, I would be dead. They could not save my two archers, but this young Ajax slew four and wounded one. They deserve it."

CHAPTER 2

We did not do badly from the bodies. They had coins. They had raided some churches and some farms. They had known where the farmers hid their gold, and we shared it between us. We collected their weapons and took back the two dead archers. The wildlife would feast well on the Scots carrion. Sir Ranulf had not emerged unscathed. There was one dead knight, Sir Giles, and eight dead men at arms. The Scots had fought hard. The animals they had captured were not to be found, and Sir Ranulf assumed that there were more Scots ahead of us. He ignored us, but was fulsome in his praise of Captain Jack.

Hugh of Rhuddlan came up to the four of us. "You four did well. Ralph, tell me what happened while the high and mighty decide what we do next."

"We tracked them, and I knew that you would be close, Captain. I gambled. I thought that if we loosed arrows and killed a few men, then they would shout and cry when they died, and you would hear. What I did not expect was that Harry and Gruffyd would have the sense to rescue the archers. I know two died, but I had thought that all three were dead men walking."

32

Hugh looked at the two of us. "I can see that you two have a future."

I know not why I said it, but I did. "Captain Jack asked me to join his archers."

Alan was aghast. "And you refused?" He began to feel my head, "I thought it was me who had a blow to the skull. If you serve Sir Ranulf, then you live in Chester Castle. You do not have to seek out wild Welshmen who wish to feed your bollocks to the dogs, and you are paid!" He shook his head. "Just when I thought you had something about you, then you do this!"

Hugh of Rhuddlan put his arm around me. "Do not listen to him. I admire your loyalty and it will be rewarded. When I tell Sir Henry what you have done for his lordship there will be coin for you."

Sir Ranulf shouted, "Hugh of Rhuddlan, yours are the only archers now. North of here lies a castle; Hornby. The knight is Richard fitz Meldred. Take your horses and see if the way to it is clear. We will follow."

Hugh said, "You heard."

We mounted our ponies and headed north. "Not so much as a kiss my arse there! I tell you, Ralph of Appleby, I like not this duty. You would have thought we did nought." Harry was not happy.

"We are the only archers now."

Alan said, "Aye, but even if all of Captain Jack's men had survived, we would still have drawn this duty. It is not as though Sir Henry values us. We are paid less than any other archers in the county."

Ralph was silent. He was torn. Even I could see that, and I was new. He was loyal to his lord, but he saw the injustice. When he spoke, it was measured. "Look, I am not saying you are wrong, but I am not agreeing either. I will speak with Hugh of Rhuddlan when we return."

Harry was like a dog with a bone. "I have heard that English and Welsh archers are prized in France. They are paid well."

Ralph turned in his saddle, "You would serve the French?"

Harry shrugged. "Longshanks is in France now. He has relatives there. French, Norman, English – it is all the same to the likes of us. What has the crown ever done for me?"

"You would leave his lordship's service?"

Harry laughed. "You are a fine archer, Ralph, and a good captain, but you are a fool. Of course I would. There is no reason for me to continue to serve a lord who does not value me." He turned to me. "When this is over, Gruffyd, come with me. You are handy in a fight. I owe my life to you and I would take you with me."

"You are stepping onto a dangerous road, Harry!"

"If Gruffyd and I turned our ponies and headed east, there is none to stop us, Ralph. I am not saying that is what we will do, but do not push our friendship. I almost died today, and for what? What thanks did I get? None!"

We rode north in an acrimonious silence. I had not said a word. I would not leave with Harry, but much of what he had said made sense. I began to wonder as we neared Hornby and its castle. We told the castellan of the arrival of the conroi and I was sent back to tell the others that it was safe. I was still the youngest and I still drew those duties. We slept in the stable. It was warm and it was dry. The food was porridge. My father ate better.

The next day we were the scouts who sought the enemy. The difference was that Captain Jack rode with us and so all disloyal talk was silenced. He did praise us and tried to persuade all of us to join his lordship. I knew that Ralph and Alan were tempted, but Harry had spoken to me in the stable. He was ready to run.

"When this is over and we return home, let us leave the rest near to Chester and let us head east. We can be at York and take ship for France. We are both good at hiding. They will not find us."

I had been tempted but I remembered my father. I could not leave without saying goodbye to him. "Let us wait until we are back at the castle. It will be just as easy to leave from there, and besides, his lordship may reward us."

"And I may grow a pair of tits and become a wet nurse! You are too trusting, Gruffyd. It will be the undoing of you."

It seemed we had killed the clever ones. We found the Scots just north of Uluereston. They had raided the town and were grazing their captured animals by the river. With sentries watching clouds, and not for enemies, they were surprised by us when we attacked from the north.

Even though we had only a handful of archers, we were able to slay those who threatened our knights and men at arms as they rode to slaughter the raiders. They could have all been captured, for we had better horses, but Sir Ranulf wished to make an example of them. Sir Ranulf had all of the Scots who surrendered maimed. Most lost their left hand. It was a harsh lesson for them. They would learn not to raid England. It took six days for us to return most of the animals and slaves. Some of the animals' owners were now dead. They became the property of Sir Ranulf. He had payment for his dead archers.

Harry was not happy as we headed south. We had gained coin and some weapons, but others had done better. I knew that he brooded upon the injustice of Sir Ranulf. The spoils from the last attack were given to his men at arms and knights. We had none. It seemed to confirm his opinion of our betters. We stayed at the estate of Sir Richard Molyneaux. It was in the village of Euxton and was just a day's ride from Chester.

We were relegated to the stable once more. Harry came to me and asked, "I would take the coins we took and ride east. Come with me Gruffyd. We will serve together and make our fortunes fighting for the French. What say you?"

I shook my head. "I will not, Harry. I would like to, but I need to speak with my father first."

"I have no time to wait. When I flee I will ride hard."

I shook my head. He held out his hand. "Then this is goodbye Gruffyd. Watch out for yourself, and trust no man!"

He took a palfrey and a sumpter. There were no guards, for all were in the hall, drinking. He took a bag of coins and he walked the horses away. He simply disappeared into the undergrowth. I watched him go and felt regret. For all his gruffness, I had liked Harry. I desperately wished to go with him but I was afraid. Harry was now an outlaw.

The next morning, when the theft was discovered, the three of us were interrogated thoroughly. Sir Ranulf could not believe that we knew nothing about the flight of our comrade. I kept a deadpan face. I had sworn no oath to Sir Ranulf. I owed him nothing. Had he treated Harry better then he would not have run. Captain Jack scrutinised my face. Sir Ranulf sent four men at arms south to try to apprehend him. Harry was heading east. He would evade them.

As we rode south, Captain Jack rode next to me. "I know that you know more than you are saying, and I understand both your loyalty to your friend and the reason for his flight. Reconsider my offer and you will be treated better."

"I will speak with my father first, Captain, and I thank you for the kind offer."

"That is a fair comment. He will advise you to join me. Of that, I have no doubt."

We reached Chester and spent a night there. Sir Ranulf came, with Captain Jack, to see us in the warrior hall where we were enjoying a feast. "You three archers have shown that you are worthy to serve under me. I know that Captain Jack asked you before, and now I will make it a formal offer. Will you serve under me?"

Ralph said, "I am the captain of Sir Henry's archers, lord. I cannot."

Alan said, "I will gladly take the offer, lord." Then he looked at me and nodded.

I shook my head. "I will not give my answer yet, lord. I will first speak with my father. It was he who advised me to serve Sir Henry. I cannot, in all conscience, make such a decision without speaking with him."

Sir Ranulf shrugged. "Let me know within this sennight." He turned and left, obviously displeased with my words.

Captain Jack smiled. "You are a man of principles. I doubt not that your father will advise you to join us, for I know his reputation. Gerald ap Llewellyn was known to be a mighty archer and a man of honour."

Hugh of Rhuddlan was less than happy that one of his best archers had been poached. He rode with Ralph and me. With dead men at arms we now had palfreys to ride rather than ponies. We led our ponies with our baggage. "I know that you think Captain Jack and Sir Ranulf offer more for you than Sir Henry, but let me speak with the baron. I am certain he will see fit to reward you two for your service."

Ralph shook his head, "He has lost two archers and there are four fewer men at arms. He has nothing to show for his fealty to the Earl of Chester. I will wager that we will receive shorter shrift than before."

"Then why did you not choose to go with Captain Jack?"

"I told you. I swore an oath." He looked at Hugh. "What say you, Captain? Can we not reward Gruffyd by allowing him to visit with his father?"

Hugh reined in his horse. We were riding at the rear. "You would return? You would not do as Harry did and run?"

"I swear that, no matter what my father says, I will return to his lordship. I would not be a man otherwise."

"Then go, and return on the morrow. I will answer to the baron for your absence. I owe you that at least, for you did noble service, and *I* appreciate it even if Sir Ranulf did not."

I left them at the baron's forest. I had no bread nor ale to take to him, but I would call at Ada's and buy some cheese and milk. It had been well over a month since last I had seen him. We had been on campaign for almost eighteen days. Much could have happened in that time. Ada and her sister Gurtha were outside cleaning out the goat pen as I rode up. I should have known something was amiss from their faces. Ada normally had a warm welcome for me. Instead she began wringing her hands. I wondered if something had happened to Seara, the third sister.

I dismounted. "What is amiss?"

The two of them threw their arms around me and began to weep. I put my arms around them in return. Seara must have died. They lived alone and my father and I were the only ones they saw. Ada stepped back. "His lordship would not let us tend to the body! We had to leave him where he is."

A shiver ran down my spine. "He?"

"Your father is dead. His body swings from a tree outside the remains of his hut."

I forced myself to be strong and to make these two upset and over-wrought women tell me exactly what had happened. When I knew all, then I could act. "Tell me all and tell me slowly. I need to know."

Ada nodded. "Aye, for you are a man now. Your father was always proud of you. He said you were the best thing to come from the time he spent with your mother."

I said, patiently, "What happened?"

"Eight days since, Sir Henry and his friends were hunting. They were using dogs and they had been drinking. They caught no animals. They stopped near to your father's hut. Old Wolf stood and growled, or so the beaters told us, and Sir Henry's dogs tore it to pieces. Your father went berserk. He took his axe and slew six of them before his lordship had him taken. He had him blinded and then hanged for damaging his property. He forbade any to touch the body. He wanted it kept as a reminder that his property is sacrosanct. He had your father's hut destroyed."

I nodded. I was numb, but I reached into my purse and took out a silver sixpence. "Here, take this for your kindness to my father." In my head I was already planning what I would do. I would join Harry, but first, there was something else I had to do. It was something so terrible, even thinking it made me shiver.

Ada took it and said, "What will you do?"

"I will bury my father and Wolf."

"And that is all?"

"Farewell ladies. I fear I will see you no more. I thank you for all your kindnesses. Think well of me, no matter what you hear." I mounted and rode away, ignoring their protestations. I knew what I would do. I could see now that I was meant to come back. It was not to seek my father's advice, it was to do him one final service.

I saw that the birds had feasted on my father's flesh. Flies buzzed around his body. Of Wolf, there was little left. His bones had been picked over. I noticed that his lord's hounds had been taken. I tied up my horse and climbed the tree. I cut the rope. My father was old and had not been heavy. I lowered his body to the ground. I saw that although the hut had been destroyed, nothing had been taken, save the axe he had used to kill the hounds. It had been thrown around as though by wild animals. I found a mattock and his wooden shovel. I went to the vegetable plot. My father had been happy tending it. He would now spend eternity there. I dug a grave. I made it deep. I found the cloak he had worn when he had served the Earl of Chester, and I wrapped his body in it. I laid Wolf's remains at his feet. I placed stones along the two bodies, and then I piled back the soft earth. I neatened the sides and then fashioned a cross.

It was coming onto dark and I lit a fire. I needed neither food nor warmth but I needed the fire. When it was hot, I used pieces of metal and my knife to carve in the cross, *Gerald the Archer*. The hot knife would burn the wood and make the letters stand out. That done, I planted the cross at the head of the grave, and then I spoke to my dead father.

"Forgive me father, for I was not here to protect you. Had I been here, then you might still be alive. I swear that your death will be avenged. I cannot serve a man like Sir Henry. I fear I must become an outlaw. Do not be ashamed of me in the hereafter. There is honour involved. When I leave here, I will no longer be Gruffyd, son of Gerald. I will be Gerald the Archer. I will take the name Gerald War Bow and begin my life anew. Perhaps that is what you meant when last you spoke with me."

I sat before the fire and stared into the flames. There were so many things I wished I had asked him before he had died. It was too late now. When I had done what had to be done, then I would head east. Perhaps it was not too late to find Harry. He might not wish an outlaw with him. Then I remembered that he, too, was an outlaw.

I did not sleep well. I was not haunted by the dead. My mind was filled with plans. I knew what I had to do but I did not wish to die.

After some time of tossing and turning I rose and watched dawn break. I searched the discarded detritus of my father's world. He had little in his life, but there were items of value. I found his bow. It was a good one and would be my spare. I found his bowstrings. I found the spare food he had buried underground to keep it from scavengers. There was a salted leg of venison. It was not a large one, but it would do. One of his most valued possessions was the bag of salt. I took that. I also dug up the arrows he had stored. I had but eight remaining. He had fifty. They were good arrows. Half of them were hunting arrows with a barbed tip, but the other half were knight killers. They had needlepoint bodkins at the end. He had dyed the feathers green. It was an affectation so that he would know who or what he had killed. I used red. I took his water skin. A spare was always handy. That was all that remained. It was not much to show for a life.

After packing the pony with my arrows I mounted the palfrey and rode towards the castle. I left the pony tied to an elder tree in the forest, two miles from the castle. When I left I would be in a hurry.

This time, as I approached the castle, I took careful note of all that I saw. It was Alf and John who were the sentries. This was their duty now, to watch the gate. They were both old and slow. They would not be an obstacle.

"You are up early, young Gruffyd." They were smiling. They did not know what had happened to my father. I wondered if others knew.

"I promised Hugh I would return, and I am a man of my word. If I say I will do something then I will."

Once inside the inner bailey, I tied my horse next to the water trough to allow him to drink. I strung my bow and held two green fletched arrows next to it.

There were horses with beaters holding them, ready for the knights

41

to ride forth and go hunting. There were no dogs. I smiled grimly. His lordship was going hunting. I saw Hugh of Rhuddlan speaking with Ralph. I walked over to them. Ralph frowned when he saw the stringed bow. He was an archer and knew that an archer did not do that. He said nothing. My face must have shown what was in my heart, for Hugh of Rhuddlan said, "What ails you, Gruffyd? Did you have words with your father?"

They did not know. "That would have been difficult, Captain. My father was blinded and hanged by Sir Henry. I buried him last night."

Hugh said, "I am sorry for your loss, but I am certain Sir Henry had good reason. Had your father been poaching?"

Hugh was clutching at straws. I forced a smile. "I will ask him that."

"Be careful, Gruffyd. Do not upset his lordship."

I nodded. Luckily, I did not have to say more, for Sir Henry, his squire and two other knights emerged. He saw me and shouted, "You, archer! Hugh of Rhuddlan overstepped himself when he allowed you to spend a night away from the castle. You will forego your monthly day off."

I nodded. "Tell me, my lord, why did you hang my father?"

He took ten steps towards me so that he was but five paces from me. "You insolent wretch! I answer not to you. I will have you whipped for that. Hugh of Rhuddlan, bind him!"

In an instant I had an arrow nocked, and I aimed it at Hugh. "One step towards me, Captain, and you will die!"

He shook his head sadly as he backed away. He had seen me at work and knew my skill. "I had high hopes for you."

"Back off, Captain, and you too, Ralph. Lower your swords to the ground, or by God I will end your lives here and now. You know I can do so."

They complied.

Sir Henry drew his sword. "Am I surrounded by cowards? I will end your wretched life myself." I loosed one arrow and it went through his leg and into the ground. He squealed like a stuck pig. He could not move without tearing the arrow out. "You will die for this!"

I had another arrow ready. I saw his squire and the two knights reaching for their swords. "If you wish to die, then draw your swords. On your knees and you shall live. I have twenty arrows, and I am the fastest archer in this castle." The squire hesitated, and my arrow smacked into his left arm. I had another nocked before the scream had died. I began to back towards my horse. I think that Sir Henry thought he was going to live. He was not.

"Sir Henry, you are a coward. You let others fight for you. You are ungrateful and do not deserve the men who follow you. I swore an oath to fight for you so long as you live. I am no oath breaker. My oath ends now!"

I do not think any expected what I did. My arrow struck the knight between the eyes. He died instantly. I was already leaping onto the back of my horse as Hugh of Rhuddlan shouted, "Close the gates!"

It was too late. Alf and John were old and slow. As I galloped over the wooden bridge they hurled themselves into the dry ditch to save being trampled. As I rode towards the wood and my hidden pony, I wondered just how long I would survive. I had cast the bones. I was now an outlaw.

CHAPTER 3

I knew I would be pursued. There were horses ready, but those horses belonged to the two knights. Hugh and Ralph would never dare ride his lordship's horse. They would have to saddle their mounts and then follow me. Hugh and Ralph might have caught me. The knights would not. I had time. I did not thrash my horse. I knew that the two knights would. They would be affronted by the audacity of an archer slaying one of their own. I was a peasant and they were nobility. The road which led to the forest was straight for a mile or so. I turned in the saddle and saw them hurtling after me. Neither was wearing mail. They were equipped for hunting. They had boar spears and swords. I recognised both of them. One was Sir William Fitz Mortimer, and the other, his younger brother, Sir Richard Fitz Mortimer. Both were wastrels who just spent their days hunting, drinking and carousing with Sir Henry. I had taken away their livelihood. They would seek vengeance.

Once the road turned, I stopped and dismounted. I tied the horse to a tree and drew two arrows. I could hear their horses and I drew my bow. As Sir William rounded the bend I sent an arrow deliberately into his leg. It went through and into the horse. The horse fell and knocked over Sir Richard. I saw his head strike the ground hard as he crashed to it. He did not move. I replaced the arrow and mounted my horse. I tore through some nearby branches and made my horse turn before diving into the forest. As soon as I found the path I joined it and rode more carefully. Ralph was a good tracker. I wanted him to follow me into the forest. I knew this forest well. There was an area of stone not far from the path. When I reached it I rode my horse along it, and then took him back through the forest. I avoided breaking branches. They would find my trail, but by then I would be long gone. Of course, if they knew me well, they would ignore the trail through the forest and they would be waiting on the road where I had left the pony. Then I would be hanged!

I reached my pony and saw no one. Leading the animal, I galloped down the road. I needed to put as much distance between myself and my pursuers as possible. I planned on heading for Delamere forest. It was known as a refuge for outlaws and even Sir Ranulf was wary of entering. That was a good thirty-five miles away. I could not reach it in one journey. If I tried, I risked losing one of my animals. In a perfect world I needed all three animals. That way, I could have changed horses and outrun pursuit. Had I been on foot I would have been as good as dead. I planned on reaching the Dee by nightfall and hiding in the woods that lay along the river. I would swim the horses across just before dawn. From the River Dee it was just ten miles to the distant forest.

However, I had two problems. One was Chester and Sir Ranulf. The other was Congleton and the powerful baron, Sir Roger de Lacy. I had to cross the river between the boundaries of their estates.

I left the road just before it crossed the River Alyn and I swam my horse and pony. It was a narrow river, but it showed me that they could swim. I then made my way through an unknown wooded area. I was many miles from my home. I relied on the skills my father had given me. I used the sun and the moss to guide me as near to north and west as I could get. Each time I smelled woodsmoke I took a detour. I wanted to avoid people. It was not that they might harm me, but they would be able to identify me. I wanted to disappear. I knew that I had committed a crime. It would be called murder. I called it justice. I called it an eye for an eye, but I was just an archer. I had no powerful lord to support me. I would have to leave England, but first I had to find sanctuary.

It was getting on for dusk. I wanted to find the river before darkness fell. It was my horse and pony who found it. Their ears pricked up and they hurried to get to the water. I dismounted and walked them, for I knew that the Dee had ships which used it. I was still trying to remain hidden. The bank was overgrown. There was no path, and that suited me for it meant that I would not be disturbed. I let my animals drink and I filled my water skin. I led them away from the river and found a bower where willows overhung the river and wild hawthorn and elder trees screened us. I risked no fire. I hobbled the animals where they were grazing. I sliced some hunks off the venison and grabbed handfuls of the sour elderberries. I spied a bramble bush and found some ripe blackberries. It was hardly a feast, but it would keep me going. By the time I had eaten and drunk it was pitch black. Darkness was my friend. I had not slept the night before and I was exhausted. I was asleep almost instantly.

Archers know when to wake up. I know not why. Perhaps because we are in the woods so much that we are like the animals, and nature courses through our veins. Whatever the reason I woke before dawn. It was not long off sunrise and I saddled the horse and pony and led them to the river. When I had looked the previous night, it had appeared to be about thirty paces across. The Alyn had been barely eight paces. This was a faster river, and wider. I held onto the pony's reins and led the horse to the river. We walked in. I allowed them to drink while I slipped my hand under the saddle of the horse. I clicked my tongue and they both walked into deeper water. We made it easily to about a third of the way across. Then they began swimming. As I had expected we were taken downstream. I was a strong youth and I held the pony's reins tightly. The horse was a strong swimmer and the pony a game one. When their hooves touched the river bed we were just eight paces from the shore. I took my hand from beneath the saddle and grabbed the reins. I was across the Dee.

After tightening the horse's girths, I mounted him and began to ride, as the sun rose in the sky, north-west towards the forest. I saw it as it spread out ahead of me. It was ten miles away, and yet it seemed to stretch from horizon to horizon. Once again I was entering unknown territory. There was no assurance that the bandits and outlaws would accept me as one of their own. Every man would be my enemy. It was a daunting prospect.

I halted half a mile or so from the forest. I saw a road enter the trees. That would not be the route I would take. I turned my horse to the north and rode across a recently harvested field. If there was a farmer nearby and he saw me, then so be it. I was close to my destination. If he reported it then it would not change my circumstance. I would lie low in the forest for a couple of days and then I would head east.

As I neared the forest, I saw that its eaves had fewer trees than deeper within. I spied a stream coming from the woodland. It was heading towards the Dee and I decided to follow the other way towards the forest. It did not look deep and would be a safe, if noisy, way to enter the hideout of the brigands. Within a few hundred paces the light disappeared and the forest became a gloomy and threatening place. The trees all strove for height and I saw that the ground was free of obstacles. I clambered from the stream. I stopped frequently, and I listened. There were no animal noises. That meant I was being watched and probably tracked. It was always easier to track someone than discover where your trackers were.

I saw a lighter part of the forest and I headed for it. When I reached it I dismounted and, standing between the pony and the horse, shouted, "I seek sanctuary with the bandits of Delamere Forest. I am an archer, and I have skills. I would talk with your leader." It felt foolish to be shouting thus, but I knew that there were men around. I could feel their presence. I allowed the horse and pony to graze, for there was a little grass, and I drank from my water skin. It seemed an age, and then I sensed movement. I hung the skin from the saddle and looked into the forest. I saw a pair of eyes peering between two branches. I scanned the trees and saw at least four others.

I stepped from between the animals and laughed. "Are you so afraid of one archer that you have to hide in the trees? I have yet to reach for my bow."

A man as tall as I was stepped out. He had a bow in his hand. He wore a leather jerkin studded with iron. He must have once been a warrior. He smiled at me. "We were just wondering if you had a death wish to enter the forest of Delamere. Few men do so and live. What makes you think that you will be welcome here? The forest is a harsh place to live."

I now saw that there were five men. It was hardly a huge band. I had been led to believe that the forest teemed with bandits.

"Perhaps I had no choice. In truth, I am passing through. My friend went to fight in France and I am following him."

"And you chose this route because you have committed a crime."

I hesitated. If I told them, they might turn me in.

"Come, friend, I like you. You have courage, do not turn that to something else. You wish us to trust you, then trust us."

"I killed my lord, for he blinded and hanged my father."

"And who was your father?"

"Gerald ap Llewellyn."

"The archer? I thought him dead years ago."

"You knew him?"

"I knew of him. I served the Earl of Derby, we campaigned against the Welsh together. I heard he was a fine archer. You slew your lord?"

"Baron Henry of Clwyd."

"I know not the name. It seems that you have all the qualifications you need to join us, save one."

"And that is?"

"The price of membership. The horse."

I shook my head. "I need the horse to get to the east. That is too high a price."

"You have courage, for we could kill you and take them both."

"You could, but in doing so, at least two of you would die and your band would be even smaller."

He laughed. "Better and better. The pony then."

I put my hand out. "My pony it is!"

"I am Roger of Talacre."

There was the slightest hesitation, and then I said, "And I am Gerald War Bow."

"Which is not your name, of course, but it is good that you honour your father by taking his name. Come, let us go to our camp." He took the pony's reins. "If you killed a knight then they will not rest until they have you. I know that the Clwyd is forty or so miles away but they will seek you out."

"By that time I will be gone, and you can tell them where I have gone. Once I am on the other side of the mountains they will never find me."

"You are confident for one so young. I look forward to talking to you. Do you have food?"

"Salted venison."

"Good."

This was not what I had expected. I had expected larger numbers who hunted where they chose and ate well. I was glad I was not staying long. They led me to a dell. It was well chosen. The trees hid it until the last moment and then it was revealed. There was a pond or small lake, and I saw that they had a sort of vegetable plot. There were eight lean-to huts. I looked at Roger of Talacre questioningly. He shrugged. "Men come and men go. This life is not for all men."

"I can see that."

"Those three to the left are empty. Choose one. Wilfred of Eaton farts when he sleeps. I would choose one at the end, away from him."

I nodded and led my horse towards the last dwelling. I unpacked the horse and then returned to unpack the pony. Roger of Talacre helped me unload my arrows. "You are a true archer. These are well-fletched arrows."

"These were my father's. Mine had red flights, but you are right. I know arrows. I am not boasting; I am a good archer."

Roger nodded and leaned in to me. "I know. Your arms and your chest speak as much. The others are bandits. You and I are the archers. It is why you live."

I looked at him in surprise. "You would have slain me?"

"For a horse and a pony? In an instant and without even thinking, but I saw that you kept your bows in canvas sheaths. I saw your arms and knew that you were an archer. I told the others to refrain from slaying you."

"You know that at the first flight I would have drawn my bow and three, at least, would have died."

He laughed, albeit quietly. "That, too, influenced my judgement." He put his arm around my shoulders. It was not an easy task. "Come, I have a feeling that you have been sent here for a purpose. I fear that you bring doom and destruction upon us. I will live with that. Your salted venison will be the best food we have had in a while. Where is it?"

I took it from my saddlebag.

"This will feed us tonight, and, with greens and some of the beans we grow, will give us soup for two more days."

This was not the paradise I had expected. It seemed I was their saviour and not the other way around. As I took the venison to the pot of water I noticed seven mounds. One had freshly turned earth. "What are they?"

"Our dead. The last was Will Green Legs. He was the leader of the men of Delamere. We were hunted by knights from Chester, some two moons since. We lost four men, captured or killed. Will had a wound we thought had healed, but it had not. He wasted away from inside and died eight days ago. Two others left to find somewhere easier to live."

"It is not what I expected." I hacked the meat from the bone.

"No one chooses the life of an outlaw. All of us here suffered because of some lord or other. This is our punishment. This is our prison."

I dropped the bone into the water. "Then I shall leave sooner rather than later."

"I thought you might."

"What is your story?"

The other four had been gathering greens and they began dividing them out onto four rough wooden platters. I did the same with the venison. What might have lasted me a few days would now be gone in one night. We sat by the fire on a hewn log.

"Not as noble as yours, I am afraid. As I said, I served the Earl of Derby as a man at arms. I quarrelled with the sergeant at arms. It was over a woman. She was his and I thought she preferred me. It came to blows and should have ended there, but he pulled a knife, as did I. I was stronger and he died. I fled for my life. That was seven moons ago. I reached here after forty days and nights of hiding and stealing. I should have headed to Sherwood. There they are more organised, but this was closer."

"Why do you not hunt?"

He pointed to my bows. "We are not archers. Oh, we can draw a hunting bow, but we are poor fletchers. When we do hunt we have to keep an ear out for the men of his lordship. Two months ago we hunted a fine stag. It would have lasted a long time. We brought it down, and before we could even begin to gut it, riders disturbed us, and we disappeared into the forest."

"Then before I leave I will hunt with you. I will need food for my journey and a forest this size must teem with game."

I heard the others' stories as we ate what was, for them, a feast. I examined them as we talked. They were all emaciated. James, son of John, had been whipped for failing to attend church. He had waited until dark and slit the throat of the man who had whipped him. Will Three Fingers had been a farmer. When he had lost two fingers and was unable to work his fields, the lord of the manor had taken his land and given it to another. Iago of Pwellhi had killed a man in Gwynedd. That was all he would say. The last, Peter of Euxton, was also the youngest. His family had died of the plague. He had survived, but the other villagers had burned his home and driven him hence. All their stories were sad, as were their mean lives. It made me all the more determined to find Harry and join him. Living outside the law was no life at all.

The next morning I strung my bow and took some of my father's hunting arrows. Roger of Talacre and the others might not be good at hunting, but they had lived in the forest long enough to know where the animals were to be found. I used them as beaters. I waited downwind and sent the five of them upwind to drive the herd of deer towards me. I readied my bow. I had two more arrows held next to my bow, and as I heard the thunder of hooves, I drew back. I could smell them as they approached. There were eight in the herd. I ignored the stag. A good hunter did not take the leader. He would sire more young animals. Instead I aimed at the older doe, which ran close to him. My arrow struck her chest and I switched to one at the rear of the herd. It appeared to be tiring. My arrow struck its head and, at twenty paces, was driven deep into her skull to kill her instantly.

Roger had had the men prepare sharpened stakes. They ran up and rammed one through the deer which lay close to me. I retrieved my arrow. I would not reuse it, but it would be good enough for the others once I had gone. I turned and ran after the herd. The first deer I had struck had struggled on for forty paces. I knelt and put her out of her pain. I took out my arrow. Will and Iago brought the stake and, after they had the deer secured, picked it up.

"Quickly, back to the camp!" Roger led, and I brought up the rear. We were a good mile and a half from our camp. Roger had told me that just killing an animal was not the end of it. They had to evade the gamekeepers who rode the trails. I had asked him why they did not ambush the gamekeepers. He had told me, quietly, that the men he led were better at slitting throats than combat. The two of us were the only ones who had fought. I began to see myself in a different light in those few days I spent in Delamere.

We were lucky. We reached our camp unseen and then began to make the most of the hunt. We gutted the deer first and put the heart, liver, kidneys and brains to cook. They would not keep. If we discarded them then they would attract vermin. We skinned them. I was the better skinner and my hide was less butchered than the one skinned by Iago. Roger of Talacre proved to be a good butcher and he jointed the animals. They only had a little salt and I was forced to use some of mine. We cooked one animal and salted the other.

That night we gorged on offal and the soup made from my venison bone. The other bones were hacked open and we ate the marrow before putting them in water for more soup.

"Tell me, Roger, how did you happen to find me?"

"Normally we head to the road each day to see if there are any on the road we might rob. Peter of Euxton has good eyes, and he can scamper up a tree like a squirrel. He spied you from afar when you crossed the fields."

I had been wondering how they had found me, and now that I knew I was relieved, but it was a warning too. I had been careless and allowed others to see me. Riding across a field had marked me as a suspicious character. I wondered if the farmer had seen me. If he had and told his lord, then we were all in danger.

"I think I will leave on the morrow, Roger. This is not as safe a haven as I had thought. I will take my share of the meat and one of the hides."

"That is fair, but cannot we persuade you to stay?"

"Roger of Talacre, you do not wish to stay, do you?" He shook his head and I lowered my voice. "You do it because you feel responsible for these four fellows."

He looked startled. "Do you read my mind?"

I smiled. "No. I have been here but a couple of days, and *I* feel a little responsible. If I stayed longer then it would be hard for me to leave." I was thinking of the men I had left on the Clwyd. Had I not been forced to leave then, I would have found it hard to desert them.

"Well, then I thank you. We have food now, that may last until the leaves begin to fall. And we now have two good arrows." Although one had struck bone, it could be sharpened and beaten to make it deadly once more. The shaft and the feathers were undamaged and that was what made them good.

"I will leave you ten more hunting arrows. I can make more, but the ones I leave with you are the best of arrows. Do not be wasteful of them."

I stayed one more day. The hide would not be tanned. I still had work to do, but it was in a good condition to transport. I had taken enough of the venison to see me to the east coast. If I was to stay hidden, then the journey might take four or even five days. I now just had my horse. I had given my word to leave the pony with Roger of Talacre. I would have to ride easier and slower. I left at dawn.

"Farewell, Gerald War Bow. I wish that I was coming with you, but we are in a better condition now than we were. We can hunt and we have food. May God ride at your side."

"And I thank you Roger of Talacre. If the fates allow, then I hope that one day we will fight side by side."

I walked Harry, for so I had named the horse, to the north-east. I would conserve him as best I could. I was sad at leaving Roger. I liked him. Sometimes you made a bond with another warrior and there was no reason to it. Thus it was with Roger. He was a man at arms and I an archer, yet I felt as though I could fight happily alongside him.

The forest was large. Roger had told me that there were others who eked out a living in the woods. He did not fear for me as I had great skills. He had recognised that. I had not thought of them much before. I had never met with my father's approval. He always criticised me. Now I saw the reason for that. Since I had tracked the Scots, I had realised that I was good at what I did.

At noon, I reached the edge of the woods and I rested. I planned on staying to the south of the Maeresea. I was heading for the Woodhead pass. I had not decided from which port I would leave England. York still had ships which headed east and it would be a shorter land journey. It was, however, a busier port than most. I had decided to seek a smaller one, like the one at the mouth of the Humber which was used by the monks to send their wool abroad. Even Grimsby was quieter than York. After I had eaten and given my horse water I headed along the path by the river. I risked riding him. The ground was flat, but there would be harder paths ahead. He now had to carry my blankets, arrows, water and food, not to mention my two bows.

I reached Thelwæl in the middle of the afternoon. It had a wooden wall around the village but I spied no standard. I risked a stop. I had seen no armed men, and if the four outlaws I had met were anything to judge ordinary men by, then I had nothing to fear from those I met. There was a water trough in the centre of the village. I dismounted and asked a pair of men who were talking, "Is it acceptable for me to water my horse?"

They looked at each other. "Aye, it is. Are you a soldier?"

There was no point in trying to deny it. I had a sword and there were quivers of arrows. "I am. I am heading for Lincoln. I thought to seek employment with the sheriff there."

The other said, "Did you come through Delamere?"

This time it was a test. I had to have come through Delamere to reach this village. "I did, but I saw no outlaws. I must have been lucky eh?"

"There are fewer of them these days. Sir Robert of Lymm has been scouring the forest for them. He came here yesterday for the dogs and our hunters. I am surprised you did not meet him and his men."

"No, I saw no one. You are the first I have seen. Tell me, do you have a baker here? I have not eaten bread for some days. I have coin."

"No bakers, but if you go to the end cottage then Gammer Lucy might sell you a loaf. She uses the town oven. She is a widow and can always use coin."

"Thank you, sirs. You have made a weary and hungry traveller happy."

I walked Harry to the rude hut. I could smell the bread. I shouted, "Gammer Lucy?"

A toothless old woman came out. She looked like an older version of Ada. "I am Gammer Lucy. Do I know you?"

"No, Gammer, but I am a traveller who has coin to buy bread."

She nodded. "Is it just bread? I make a fine cheese from goat's milk if you are not averse to that beast. I know some who think it is the devil's own animal. For myself, I find that a foolish thought."

"I like goat's cheese and milk."

"Then six silver pennies will buy you a loaf, some cheese and a drink of milk to go with it."

"That seems expensive."

She gave me a sly look. "I am a widow and you look like a well-paid archer. That is a fine palfrey and your clothes are well made. You can afford it."

I laughed. "Aye, I suppose I can."

She went inside and brought me out a wooden beaker which she filled. "You can have more. I have no larger beakers." The milk was good and I had two beakers. She brought me the cheese. It was hard and wrapped in a dock leaf. The bread was a two-pound loaf. She laughed as I sniffed it. "And I wager that you have nibbled the end before you are out of sight of my home!"

"And there you are wrong. I have had short rations before, and I will wait until I eat. I just want the smell of the fresh bread to keep me going some more miles."

I put the cheese and the bread in the net I had hung from the saddle that my father had made from old lengths of rope. It worked.

I rode another six miles before I stopped. I had come far enough and I found a good camp site close to the river. I had a tree for shelter above me. I had water and grass for my horse and there was enough driftwood on the bank to give me a fire. I did not need to hide. I got the fire going and made myself a bed under the tree. I took off my sword and placed it close to hand. After hobbling Harry I washed my face and hands. I intended to enjoy my food. I cut the loaf in two. I would have the second half in the morning. I divided the cheese in two also and then took out some of the venison. I had just begun to eat when I heard a noise.

It was Harry who alerted me. His ears pricked and he snorted. I reached out and drew my sword from its scabbard. I stood and hid behind the tree. I heard the sound of hooves. Someone was coming down the river trail. They might have been an innocent traveller but I was not willing to take any chances. A mounted shadow appeared.

A voice shouted, "War Bow! Are you there?"

It was Roger of Talacre. Was this a trap? I neither moved nor responded. I looked beyond the shadow. Nothing else was moving. He was alone. I stepped out as he came into the light.

"What brings you here?"

"I am wounded!"

He fell from the pony. The pony looked all in too. I took the beast to the river to allow it to drink and to bring some water back in my metal cooking pot. Roger had fallen close to the fire. I moved his cloak and saw that he had a bloody side. I undid the leather metal-studded jerkin. The leather had prevented the blade from penetrating too deeply but the skin had been scored and he had bled for some time. I used the river water to clean it and then went to my saddlebag. I had a medical kit. Every archer did. It was simple enough. I had a leather skin of vinegar and a pot of honey. Neither would ever go off and both could be used for a huge range of tasks. I returned to him and laid them down. I went to the north side of the tree and scraped off some moss with my knife.

He was coming to when I returned. "Don't speak. Let me bind the wound, then we will get some food inside you, and then you can talk."

He nodded and closed his eyes. I used the vinegar to clean the wound. He winced but said nothing. He was a man at arms, and I guessed he had endured such as this before. Then I smeared honey into the wound to seal it. It also seemed to help the healing. Finally I packed the moss along the wound. I went to my saddlebag and took out my oldest shirt. It was already torn and I ripped it up to make a bandage. I needed something to hold the honey and moss in place.

When that was done I sat him up and gave him some of the bread with cheese upon it. "Eat while I see to your poor beast." I went to the pony and took off the saddle. I rubbed it down with its saddle cloth and then led it to the grass, where Harry still grazed. I had spied a crab apple tree a few paces from the river and I went and picked five or six of them. I laid them on the ground for the pony.

When I returned to Roger he looked happier. "What happened?"

"Knights came hunting for us. I was riding the pony, or I too would have been slain like the other four. I heard the screams and the shouts. From a hidden vantage point I saw them butchering the four of them. There was nothing I could do. I fled. They had men all over. I managed to kill one of them, but his horse galloped off, and I could not catch it. The horse alerted others. Two of the men chased me. I killed one but the second stabbed me. I just managed to knock him from his horse and escape. I headed for the river. I rode hard. I think I lost them. I followed your trail and the old lady in Thelwæl told me that you had passed through."

"Then we will need to leave before dawn."

"But why?"

"If she told you, then she will tell Sir Robert of Lymm, for it was he and his men who hunted you. His castle is not far away. He will follow in the morning. We will have to cross the river."

CHAPTER 4

Roger did not sleep well. The wound was hurting. I woke before dawn and saddled the horse and pony. I roused Roger and we shared the last of the bread and the cheese. Neither would survive the dousing they were about to receive. Roger looked at me. "I will slow you down."

"Aye, you will, but I will not leave you here to be butchered like your friends. Now the pony is a practised swimmer. Hang onto the saddle and kick with your feet. Do not worry if we are swept a little downstream. Just so long as we cross. Come. Let us go."

I led Harry by his reins and patted his flank. "Come, this is the third time you have done this. We will show Roger of Talacre how it is to be done." I turned. "Follow me and be brave."

I found it easier than the first two times I had done this. I had no pony to distract me. I held onto the saddle and kicked. We were across in a few heartbeats. As Harry scrambled up the bank I turned and watched Roger. The sun had not fully risen yet. The grey light was sufficient for me to see close by. The pony was not as strong and he was being taken downstream. I walked down the bank and, jumping into the shallows, pulled the man at arms from the pony and to the shore. Freed from the weight, the pony scrambled lithely onto the bank.

"Quickly, mount your pony and let us ride. We need to be well hidden before the Lord of Lymm seeks us."

As we headed away from the river my original plan was in tatters. The Warre family had a castle at Mamucium. That lay at the junction of the Irk and the Irwell rivers. We would have to travel further north. I knew there was a high pass over the hills at Saddleworth. We would head there. I knew that the weather would soon be turning. We had no furs with us. I was confident I could survive the high ground but I was uncertain about Roger of Talacre. When I had tended his wound I had seen his ribs. He was not well fed.

We rode hard, skirting every village and settlement we saw. I could not risk buying bread any longer. I questioned Roger as we rode. "The men who hunted you, what was their livery?"

"White surcoats with green stripes. Why?"

"We look for those. We might be able to bluff our way past others, but the ones in those tunics will be seeking us."

We rode for twenty miles without stopping, the ground steadily rising. I knew that we would have to rest our animals. We skirted a village, and I was about to stop when I saw a castle rising to the south of us. I took us up a sheep track. It dropped down into a sheltered dell. It would have to do. It was noon when we stopped. Roger fell asleep after we had eaten a frugal meal of venison and drunk some water. I left him, and taking my bow, quiver and three water skins, headed to find fresh water. I descended the slope. The water would be lower down. I used the terrain to guide me, and when I heard the bubbling water, I knew that I had found it.

The water had white bubbles. I looked upstream. There were no dead animals. It was good to drink. I filled all three skins. I worked out that there was a more direct route back to Roger. I strung my bow and took out a hunting arrow in case I spied a rabbit. Fresh meat was always welcome.

I heard horses. I knew the noises Harry and the pony made. These were different, and there were three of them. I switched the hunting arrow for a bodkin. I crept and used the ground to shelter me. I heard voices.

"Outlaw where is your companion? Where is the man with the horse? The old lady told us he was an archer." I heard something, but it was incoherent. Then I heard a slap and a cry. "I will happily take your bollocks from you to make you speak. You are a dead man. But I can make your end quick."

I risked looking over the top and I saw three men with their backs to me. They wore the white and green tunics Roger had told me of. I dropped my head down and took out two more bodkin arrows. I jammed them in the earth and then I stood and drew. The men were just thirty paces from me. I could not miss. The question was how many would I hit before they could get to me? I sent the first one into the back of the man who had just struck Roger. He seemed to me to be the leader. He fell face down on Roger. Seeing the arrow the other two turned to face me. That gave me the chance to nock another arrow and send it into the chest of the second man. Roger pushed the dead man from him and tried to rise.

Even as I took my third arrow the last man grabbed Roger and held him before him. His sword was at Roger's throat. Only half of his face was visible. "Drop your bow or he dies!"

I nodded and lowered my bow. I saw his hand relax a little and I pulled the bow up and released in one motion. The arrow plunged into his eye and he fell dead. I raced across the ground with another arrow nocked, though I knew it would not be needed; all three were dead. Even as I ran I knew that, although we now had three horses and would be able to travel faster, the three dead men at arms would point Sir Robert in our direction.

Roger looked up. His wound was bleeding. "I owe you my life again!"

"Thank me later. See if they have coin and if their swords are better than yours. I will gather the horses." I walked slowly towards the skittish horses. Blood always made horses anxious, though I had a way with them and gathered the three of them. Harry was a better horse, but they were all much more useful than the pony. I was already working out that we would be able to cover another thirty miles before nightfall. If one animal became lamed we would still have spares. We had to outrun our pursuers.

Roger had taken one of the swords. "This is a good one. They had coin."

"Keep it. We need to move. Choose the best horse and mount it. I will tie the others and lead them."

"I can lead one!"

"You are as weak as a newborn calf. You will do your share when you are fitter. Now mount." I was younger, but Roger of Talacre had been an outlaw for six months. He had lost his warrior skills. If we were to go to France then he needed to regain them. I mounted one of the captured horses and tied Harry and then the pony to it. I led the other horse. I would change after fifteen miles or so. The land undulated and then the road dropped into a valley. We had done the hard part. We had negotiated the high pass of Saddleworth.

As we descended I was able to spy out the settlements. I left the road before we came to each of them. Roger was in pain. He needed his wound tending but we dared not stop. Sir Robert had obviously sent men on both sides of the Maeresea. When the three did not return he would seek them out. As we headed east I knew that soon I would have decisions to make. When we approached Loidis I would have to decide if we were to go to York or head due east to Hull. Both involved risk. Which was the lesser?

Nightfall made our decision. I dared not ride further in the dark so we stopped in a hollow, half a mile from the road. There was a spring, but we were so exhausted that any place which was not exposed would have done. I did not risk lighting a fire and tended Roger's wound by moonlight. He had burst the dressing and I had to use my honey again to repair the damage. One horse had become lame and I let her go. We ate because we had to and we drank from the spring. I knew that I should have kept watch, but I was just too tired. I slept and relied on Harry's ears.

When I awoke, in the dark, it was to the sound of a tolling bell. There was a monastery close by. I had been saved from making a major mistake. I might have ridden on and been discovered. I would not kill priests, but they would have happily reported seeing two men with three horses and a pony. Roger slept on. I was awake and so I saw to the horses. I gave them water and I made sure that they grazed. I roused Roger when I saw silver in the east.

After more venison we headed east and passed the monastery. That determined our route. The road to York passed by the huge monastery so I took us along the stream which skirted it. Our course was set. We would go to Hull and seek help from the monks who traded wool there. The forty miles we rode took us all day. Roger was still not fully fit, although he was better than he had been. When we neared the monastery, I said, "Let me do the talking. Remain silent."

The monks of Meaux Abbey were clever men. They used their farms to raise sheep and export the wool to France and the Low Countries. The revenue helped them to become one of the richer orders. I had heard of them through Hugh of Rhuddlan, who had travelled through the port when he served with the Earl of Chester. Knowing that, I was able to appeal to their mercenary side.

The monk who spoke to me was a senior one. "Brother, I wish to travel to Flanders. You have ships which ply the seas. I would trade our horses and ponies. We seek passage on one of your ships. We could act as guards for the crossing."

The monk's eyes flashed as he saw the profit. "How much would you want for the animals?"

"You are an honest man. You tell me."

The price he paid was well below their value, but the animals had cost us nothing and his silence was assured. It was a buyer's market and we agreed the price. We spent three days in the abbey awaiting the ship. The monks tended to Roger's wound. I was sad to lose Harry, but he had served me well, and he would have a better life with the monks. He would be away from war.

While we waited we met a merchant. We could see he was a merchant by his dress, but he carried a short sword and he had sharp, inquisitive eyes. I would have said he was the same age as Roger of Talacre. Dickon of Doncaster was a plain-speaking man, and he walked up to us as we sat on the wood quay awaiting a ship. "You two look like likely lads. I see swords, war bows and arrows. Are you archers?"

I nodded. "I am. Roger here was a man at arms."

As I learned later, Dickon was a shrewd and perceptive man. "You are leaving England, and I am guessing in something of a hurry."

I was startled. Roger was quicker to hide his face. He smiled. "We are in no hurry, sir. We await a ship."

The merchant nodded. "It will be here tomorrow. It is my ship. Yet you sold your horses for much less than they are worth. From your clothes, Roger the man at arms, I would say that you have seen better days, and yet you owned three horses and a pony."

We had a dilemma. His words were becoming uncomfortably close to the truth, and yet if we wished to sail, we had to use his ship. My world was one of hunting and the woods. This was a world of deception we had entered, and I was ill prepared.

Dickon of Doncaster smiled. "I care not for your past. It is your future which interests me. Where are you bound?"

I was on firmer ground now. "France. We hear they pay archers and men at arms well."

"They do. You two, however, have first to pay for a berth on my ship or, if you choose to wait another six days, for another ship. I have to tell you that the money you were paid for your horses will barely cover your berths and leave you without the means to buy horses in France."

I frowned. "How do you know this?"

He laughed. "You did not think I came here early just to watch the waves break upon the shore, did you? I was here to negotiate the cost of carrying the monk's cargo to France. They are keen to help me, and they volunteered the information about you two." He lowered his voice. "They think you are fleeing some crime. Your friend's wound was made by a sword."

For a brief moment I thought to return to the monks and demand that they sell us back our horses, but I knew that would be rejected. They had made profit from us.

"So will you hear my proposition?"

I looked at Roger who shrugged. What had we to lose?

"I take that as a yes. You two need to get to Gascony. As it happens, that suits me. I have need of guards for both my ship and for my wagons when we get to France. We will land at Honfleur and travel across Aquitaine to Poitiers. I have carters to drive my wagons, but I need men to guard them. I will feed you and mount you. I will give you berths on my ship. When we reach Poitiers, then I will give you the horses. What say you to that? Gascony and the conflict you seek is but a day or two south of Poitiers."

Roger said, "Would we be paid too?"

Dickon laughed. "You will be fed, given a bed and a horse. What more payment can you expect?"

It was better than I had hoped. I nodded. "I am your man." I glanced at Roger who nodded. "As is Roger of Talacre."

"And what is your name, archer?"

"Gerald War Bow."

And so a new part of my life began. It did not begin with a lie but, like much in life, a half-truth. I discovered, as we waited for the ship, that Dickon transported a wide range of goods. When we were finished in Poitiers, he would travel down to Bordeaux, where he would meet his ship and take wine back to England. He had a family in Doncaster. There, he kept his valuables and his family well guarded. I learned that he did not surround himself with armed men, for that attracted attention. He rarely carried coin with him. There was a group of men who did business with each other. They used paper instead of coin. It meant that if they were robbed, the paper was useless and they had lost nothing. It explained why we would not be paid in coin. He had none to give us.

The ship arrived on the evening tide. The *Maid of Beverley* was larger than I had expected and had a small forecastle as well as an aftcastle. The forecastle would only have accommodated three men, but, as we discovered, it also doubled as sleeping quarters. James of Whitby was the captain. He was a big man, and he ruled his crew with his ham-like fists. He reminded me of Harry. He had his crew load the wool so quickly that I knew they had done this many times before. It was practised. It was done so quickly that we left the river lit by the setting sun behind us. The dark sea awaited us.

Dickon of Doncaster seemed to forget about us once we set sail. The first mate, James of Whitby's son, took us to the forecastle. "This is where you will sleep. There is an old piece of canvas there. If you rig it over the top it will give you protection from the sea." He smiled. "Unless we hit a storm, and then nothing will stop a soaking!"

We had been fed by the monks before we left. Dickon had influence. It looked like that would be our last meal until the next morning, and so we made ourselves as comfortable as we could. We stored our weapons, arrows and saddlebags between the ribs of the forecastle. That left us just enough space to curl up and sleep. The canvas above us shut out all light, but as we left the river and the larger waves struck us, we were glad of it. The water broke over the bows, and we heard it splatter onto the canvas.

I found the motion quite restful and I was soon asleep. I was disturbed twice by Roger of Talacre. He proved to have a weaker stomach. We woke to a grey day with a wind which was not doing what the captain wished. We had to tack back and forth. Roger and I were soon taught how to help the sailors. I found it easier than Roger. Hauling on sheets and stays was nothing for someone who had been trained as an archer. It took twelve days to reach Honfleur. By the time we got to the river we had both picked up skills and got to know the crew. They taught us some words that would stand us in good stead. They mainly involved paying for wine or women.

We were used to help unload the ship. The merchant was getting his money's worth from us. There were wagons waiting for us, and we loaded them while Dickon went to hire drivers. The crew helped us to protect his cargo. It was not just wool. There were also blanks which would be made into swords. We saw many shifty looking characters who hung around the port.

Roger pointed to two such men. "I will wager they have accomplices. Unless I miss my guess, our skills will be needed on the road. I am glad that my wound is healed."

He did look much stronger. The food on the ship, whilst it had not been particularly exciting, had been both plentiful and filling. He had regained his strength. He would need it. On the voyage he had made a second scabbard for the sword taken from the dead man at arms. He wore them across his back. He could use both hands to fight. That was unusual for it meant he did not use a shield. He had regretted not taking the helmet from the dead men at arms. Archers did not like them but I knew that a good helmet could stop a blow to the head.

Dickon returned with the six drivers who would accompany us. He also brought three horses. His was a palfrey and ours were sumpters. It made sense. They were the same horses as the ones which pulled the wagons. Our job was to stay as close to the wagons as we could. After giving instructions to James of Whitby, we set off and headed south towards Aquitaine.

"You two stay close to me and, Gerald War Bow, keep your bow strung. There were greedy eyes at the port. We may soon discover if you are as skilful as your name suggests."

I did not like to keep my bow strung but I had a spare bow and bowstrings. This was my new world and I had to embrace it. I had spent part of the voyage making my father's green arrows red. I was not disrespecting my father's memory. I needed the comfort of my familiar red fletch.

It became clear that Dickon had done this before. The length of our ride was dictated by villages and inns. Dickon liked his comfort. We slept with the wagons but he slept in a bed. However, it meant that we would be safe from robbers at night. It would be during the day when we might be set upon.

Our first stop was at Lisieux. The twenty miles we had ridden had been nerve-wracking for me. The smells of the land were not what I was used to. The words of those we met were foreign. I was glad when, as dusk approached, we reached the safety of the town. We unloaded some of the sword blanks. I saw no money changing hands but Dickon of Doncaster seemed happy with the paper he received.

It was Roger's outlaw eyes which spied the men we had seen in Honfleur. As soon as the two men realised they had been spotted they disappeared, but Roger had seen them. He came to me to tell me and we reported to Dickon. He did not seem put out. He merely nodded. "Good, my investment begins to pay off. Tomorrow the road passes through a forest. I suspect the men you saw may try something there." He smiled. "They are Normans and they know not what a good bow can do. You are fast?" I nodded. "Good."

"But I cannot loose from a horse, and if they ambush us I will need to have a solid platform."

"Good, you are a thinker. Then on the morrow, you ride next to Alain who drives the lead wagon. Will that be solid enough?"

"Aye, so long as it does not jerk too much."

"And you, Roger of Talacre, must make them fear you!"

Roger laughed. "That they will do!"

I placed the quiver of red-fletched arrows in the well of the wagon, along with my sword. I wore my cloak to disguise my frame and I hunched over. Alain spoke a few words of English. "You wish me to stop the wagon if we are attacked?"

"Aye. Will we be attacked?"

"Three times in the last year we have been attacked in these woods. The lords who live close by try to protect the road, but the men who will try to take our goods know the woods and the road well. They can move around. Last time my brother was slain. Do not show these rats any mercy."

"I will not."

I had begun to think that Alain and Dickon of Doncaster were wrong, for we were almost through the woods when the eight men burst from hiding. They had swords and spears. One of them shouted, "You are surrounded. Surrender and you live."

Even as he was speaking I was nocking an arrow, which I sent directly into his chest. My second and third took the two men next to him before they had even realised what was going on. Dickon and Roger charged some others, and I nocked another arrow and sought one of the men behind us. There were four men remaining and they had knocked the driver of the last wagon to the ground. My first arrow hit the man who sought to replace him, and my second hit the one who tried to climb up. The other drivers had dismounted and, along with Alain, raced to attack the last two. I turned and nocked an arrow. A brigand swung an axe at Dickon's horse. My arrow went through his arm and into his neck. The last man fled.

I heard a scream from the last wagon as Alain and the other drivers butchered the last man. Dickon rode up to me. "You did not exaggerate, Gerald War Bow. Those arrows were both fast and accurate. I owe you my life." He turned. "Roger, see if they have anything of value and then push their bodies into the ditch. We have wasted enough time."

Alain returned. "Serge is a little groggy but he will live. Thank you, archer. We are indebted to you."

I mounted my horse and rode at the head of the column with Dickon and Roger. Dickon nodded to Roger. "You two may share what coins and weapons they had. You too impressed me, Roger of Talacre. If you choose not to find another lord, I would employ you all the time."

I looked at Roger and shook my head, "No master. We have set our course and we will follow it where 'e'er it leads."

By the time we reached Poitiers we had both picked up a little Norman and a little French. I knew that we would need it. We had coins in our pockets. Some was from the sale of the animals in England, some from the dead brigands. As we parted with Dickon he gave us twelve silver sixpences each. "Call it a bonus. If ever you need work, then find me. I am to be found in Bordeaux or Honfleur. All know me." He pointed south and west. "There are small wars being fought there. If you seek work, then travel on the road towards Toulouse; you will find a master who needs your skills."

We spent one night at an inn. We would be sleeping rough for the foreseeable future. Our horses were not in the best state and so I bought a bag of grain. Winter was coming and the grazing would not be as nutritious as we might have liked. I also spent some of my money on a better cloak. I decided to head for Agen. We had heard, at the inn, that Gaston de Béarn was fighting against the English lords of Gascony. This struck both of us as a perfect opportunity to earn coin and still serve England. We were both Englishmen at heart. It was rumoured that Edward Longshanks, known as Lord Edward, was campaigning south of Agen. Given that he would be the next king of England, we hoped he would wish to hire two warriors such as we.

Looking back, it was such a vague idea that I am amazed we even contemplated heading south with such flimsy evidence of employment. I believe that had we not met Dickon of Doncaster, we might have ended up on the borders of Normandy and might even have fought against the English. We headed south, keenly aware that we were seen as the enemy by many Frenchmen. Officially our two countries were not at war, but it would not have taken much to spark one. Our French was improving day by day, but we would never be taken for Frenchmen. My longbow clearly marked me as an archer and therefore English.

The road to Gascony was not a quiet one. There were others such as ourselves, warriors seeking paymasters. We were the only Englishmen, although there were some Normans and Angevin. They had been part of the Empire of King John until that foolish king had lost them. We fell in with six Angevin men at arms. They were happy to have an archer with them.

"What do you know of this land to which we go?"

Gaston was a grizzled old veteran. The others deferred to him and it was he who answered. "De Montfort ruled Gascony for a while, until he was found to be taking coin. I think King Henry did not like his ideas. It did not help that the Lord Edward, Edward Longshanks was a friend of De Montfort. The prince is there now, trying to exert his authority over the men of Bearn."

One of the younger men at arms, Jean, added, "He married well, or at least his father married him off to a Spanish bride. He now has Castile backing him."

"I take it we try to fight with Prince Edward?"

Gaston leaned in to speak to Roger and me, "Timing is all. If the English prince loses a battle, then he will be more inclined to need to hire men, and he will not worry about the cost. Gascony is well endowed with coin and goods and the prince is rich."

"You would have him lose?"

He laughed. "This is not England. The battles are more like skirmishes.

You will be much sought after, for if there are enough archers on the battlefield then that can often decide the outcome. Knights do not like to risk expensive warhorses in charges. Princes and dukes are happy to pay a few coins for the likes of us, but paying pounds for lost horses is a different matter. Here, men fight for coin and not flags."

The eight of us stayed together for wecould negotiate better prices for food, and we watched out for each other. One of us would stand guard if there were Frenchmen close to our camp. It took eight days to reach Agen. It was a border town with a fine castle and it was filled with French. Roger and I remained silent and let Gaston and the others do the talking. I had asked everyone about Harry but no one knew of an English archer recently arrived. I guessed he had stayed in the north. In the end we were too desperate to await news of a battle. The Angevin had coin. Ours was limited. We heard of an English lord across the river from Aiguillon. It was sixteen miles away and guarded two rivers, the Lot and the Garonne. There was a bridge to the south of Aiguillon. We would cross into Gascony and hope that the Englishman who lived there would pay us.

Gaston thought it foolish. "There will be a skirmish or a battle. Edward is young and inexperienced. He will lose. Just be patient."

"Thank you for your advice, but we have had a long journey from England. I am losing my touch!"

It was lonely riding the river road but our journey was almost at an end. When we reached the bridge I saw that it was a rickety, wooden affair. We dared not risk riding our horses across it. I walked mine across first. If it held me then it would easily hold Roger. I was relieved when we reached the other side. I saw a huge forest stretching before us. We had been told that the castle of Sir John Woodville lay twenty miles on the other side of the forest at Saint Justin. We decided to camp at the edge of the forest and ride through in daylight. It did not do to chance an unknown forest in a strange land at night.

We risked a fire. We had bought food, and a warm fire would make our camp seem more comfortable and less lonely. When we had eaten and we had rolled in our cloaks, we talked. This was the first time since Hull that we had been able to do so. We had become firm friends. We could ride for hours without speaking and not feel uncomfortable. Now we both wanted to speak.

"This time tomorrow we may have a lord to serve."

I nodded. "I still have a worry, my friend. What if they have heard of me? It has been weeks since I slew Sir Henry. Word may have travelled here."

"How would they know it was you? You are an archer. You do not have a Welsh accent. Your name is not an uncommon one. Men will be seeking Gruffyd who was an archer on the Welsh border. They will not be looking for Gerald War Bow who served Dickon of Doncaster."

"I am certain he knew my story. He kept giving me strange looks."

"Perhaps he did, but thanks to him, others now accept you as an archer seeking his fortune and not a murderer."

"Listen, Roger, if I am recognised then disown me. Tell them you knew nothing of my story. I would not have you suffer for my foolishness."

"We are friends and I will not desert you." He stretched. "I tell you one thing. The forests of Gascony are warmer and more welcoming than Delamere. A man could easily live in the forests here."

"Aye, it is pleasant. It does not smell like an English forest. The birds are different too. I have seen birds I thought I knew, but they have different calls here. I have much to learn."

We slept well, until our horses woke us as they grazed close to our heads. After finishing off the food, we mounted and headed into the forest. We did not follow the main trail. It was wide and almost like a road. We took the hunters' trails. I felt safer doing so. Roger just followed my lead. He deferred to me on many things. Using the small hunters' trails meant we made less noise than on the hard-packed earth.

I heard the sound of metal on metal in the distance. I strung my bow and took out three bodkin arrows. I slipped my cloak over my horse's neck, nodded to Roger and dug my heels into my horse's sides. I headed towards the fight. Perhaps this was Sir John Woodville. We might have a chance to aid him and win a place in his household. I did not gallop. The sound of drumming hooves would attract attention. I saw a flash of colour ahead. I stopped my horse. I could not fight mounted, but Roger could.

Tying my horse to a tree, I began to make my way through the undergrowth to reach the fight. Roger would follow my lead. I was looking for a sign which would tell me that this was Sir John Woodville. I had been told he had a wild boar as his standard. I heard Roger draw both of his swords. I concentrated on my own approach, using the trees to move closer. I could hear steel on steel and the cries of men as they were struck. I heard the neighs and whinnies of horses. I saw a surcoat. It was yellow with two horned cows. I had been told that was the symbol of Gaston of Béarn. I had identified one side. I saw that there were others dressed as he was. This was a mounted battle, and I saw that the men of Béarn were winning. These had to be my enemies, and so I approached to within thirty paces and knelt. I sent an arrow at the nearest man. It struck him so hard that it came out of his chest. His companion looked around and my arrow struck him in the chest and threw him from his horse.

They knew there was an archer present and eight of the men at arms turned. I saw that there were at least seven others who were fighting. Just then, I heard a cheer and the sound of galloping hooves. It was Roger coming to my aid. It was brave, but it was foolish. I had not identified the men who were being attacked. I sent another arrow at the warrior in the centre. Roger would distract the two nearest him. I took my fourth arrow and the man at arms held his shield up. It saved his life, but the arrow struck so hard that he fell from his saddle. There were still three men racing towards me. I did not panic. I drew and sent an arrow through the ventail into the neck of another man at arms. The two to my left were fewer than ten paces from me. I heard the sound of Roger fighting his foes. I could not allow myself to be distracted. I would be able to release one more arrow only. I did not manage a full draw, but my arrow still hit the thigh of the nearest man at arms. I dropped my bow and, spinning around behind a tree, I drew my sword and dagger.

As I spun I saw Roger fall from his horse. One of his foes remained.

I was the hunted now. One man at arms had an arrow in the thigh, but the other was fully fit and desperate for vengeance. He had a spear and he spurred his horse and lunged at me. The temptation was to try to strike upwards at him. That would have been foolish. Instead I used my dagger to flick up his spear. I dropped to one knee and swung my sword into the back of the hindquarters of the horse. The other man at arms galloped at me. He was wounded. My arrow had pinned his leg to his horse. Both were in pain. Whilst his companion was trying to save himself as his horse crashed to the ground, the wounded man came directly at me and I saw him raise his sword. He intended to strike at my head. He jerked his horse so that his right side faced me. He pulled back on his reins to allow the full force of the blow to strike me. I held up my sword and lunged with my dagger at the same time. Our swords rang and sparks flew. My dagger went inside his mail chausses and into his groin. I twisted and pulled.

I was aware that the fallen man at arms had risen. He was unsteadied. I rammed my sword into the ground and picked up my bow. I had an arrow nocked before he had taken two steps, and by the third step, he was dead.

I turned and, picking up my sword, ran towards Roger, who lay prostrate on the ground. That was when I made my mistake. The man whom I had stabbed in the groin had hobbled from his horse and he slashed at my leg. I felt it bite into the calf. I turned and, raising my sword, brought it down so hard that it took his head from his shoulders.

The sounds of battle had faded as I knelt next to Roger. He was barely alive. I saw that he had a stomach wound. Blood oozed from his mouth.

"Well, my friend, it was a short adventure, but I thank you for it. This is a better end than I might have had in Delamere. Take my gold and swords. In return, give me a warrior's death. I would not die slowly."

I shook my head. "I will not for…" I got no further. His head lolled to the side and my friend was dead.

I heard a voice behind me. "Archer, you have done Lord Edward a great service, as has your friend. Rise and tell me the name of the man who saved my squire and me."

I turned and saw the three lions passant. It was Prince Edward. With his long legs and lazy eye, he was unmistakable. I dropped to my knee. "My lord."

His squire said, "Lord Edward. He is wounded."

The prince dismounted and said, "Lie down. I will staunch the bleeding. You and your friend drove them off, but they have done for my men. Barely six remain alive. Had you not come when you did, then I fear we would have been captured." He tore a piece of cloth from the surcoat of a dead man at arms and bound my calf.

His squire said, "I have a horse for him."

I shook my head. "I have one tied up in the woods."

"I will fetch him."

"My lord, if you give me your arm."

"Are you sure?"

"I need to see to my friend. We were brothers in arms. He asked me to take his weapons and his coin." I shrugged. "We were poor warriors seeking a master. I fear he has served his last lord."

"What is your name, archer?"

"Gerald War Bow."

"Then I offer you the chance to become my Captain of Archers."

"That is a great honour, but I am young. What will the other archers think?"

He laughed. "Very little, for I have none. But having seen what one man can do, I intend to raise a company of them, and you shall be the man to choose them. What say you?"

"I say aye."

"Good, then you will be the first of Lord Edward's archers. We will take our dead back to Sir John's castle. I have much I need to say to him."

CHAPTER 5

His squire could not believe that I eschewed the palfrey he had offered and that I chose to ride a sumpter. I patted the sumpter affectionately on the neck. "I am sorry, lord, but we have ridden a long way together. He is my last companion. I could not leave him in the woods."

Lord Edward said, "I can see that you are loyal. That is a rare trait in many men." He gave a strange look to his squire. They seemed to have an understanding which needed no words. It was the squire who organised the men, shouting orders and instructions.

His surviving men led horses carrying the bodies of Lord Edward's dead. I led Roger's horse. As Lord Edward waved his arm for the column to move, I waited to take my place at the rear of the short line of men. "No, Gerald War Bow, I would have you ride behind John and myself."

"Aye, lord."

As we moved, they began to speak, and I could not help but overhear their conversation. The squire, John, appeared to be roughly my age and little younger than his master. They spoke easily together as though friends, rather than knight and squire.

"That was a trap, John."

"Aye, lord, but was Sir John in on it? If he was, then we are putting ourselves in an even worse position. With this single archer, we still do not number ten."

Lord Edward turned in his saddle, "I fear you have joined us, archer, when we are surrounded by enemies and men we cannot trust. Had I not seen the evidence of your loyalty by the red-fletched arrows sticking from the bodies of my enemies, I might have mistrusted you too."

There was little I could say. I was just surprised that the heir to the throne should have been placed in such a parlous position. His face invited conversation. Lords did not usually speak to me. Sir Ranulf and Sir Henry had barely noticed me when I had followed their banners, and here was a future king of England speaking with a low-born archer.

"Lord, your squire and your men address you as Lord Edward, but you are Prince Edward are you not?"

"I am, but I fell out with my father a while ago. I can see now that it was a mistake. I took the title of lord to insult him. It was an error, but we are used to that form of address now. Do you get on with your father, archer?"

"I did, Lord Edward, but he is dead now." I hesitated.

Lord Edward turned in his saddle. As I discovered, he was a very perceptive man. His father, King Henry, was a pious and studious man, who was more at home with books. His son was not only a warrior but someone who could divine men's thoughts.

"Speak archer. I like honesty above all things. I meet it so rarely. Everyone seems to have plots and plans of their own."

"I was just going to say, Lord Edward, that although I got on well with my father when he was alive, I did not speak with him enough. Now that he is dead, I can never ask him that which is in my heart and mind."

"For one so young you offer sage advice. I will give you your first task when we reach the castle of Sir John Woodville."

"Of course, Lord Edward. I am yours to command."

"Ah, Gerald War Bow, but with some men, that does not mean the commands will be obeyed as they were intended, but I feel I can trust you. You will be housed in the warrior hall when we reach the castle. Keep your ears open. Men talk, and if they are in their cups, then their lips become looser. I would know if Sir John had a hand in this."

I nodded and was silent for a moment. "I fear your squire is right, Lord Edward. If he is, then when we stay in his castle are you not in danger?"

"I would be if I did not suspect a trap. We will drink little and listen much. The sooner I am in the castle at Bordeaux, the better."

I wondered if I would see Dickon of Doncaster there. Thinking of Dickon made me realise that I still had the problem of my past to haunt me. If I stayed with the prince, then the odds were that I would come into contact with someone who knew my story. That was especially true as Lord Edward was Earl of Chester. Sir Ranulf would remember me. So long as we stayed in France I could remain silent, but if we left for England I would have two choices. I could run or I could confess. If I confessed, would I be signing my own death warrant?

We reached the castle at Saint Justin in the early afternoon. It was a strongly built stone castle which used the river along one side as a moat. Sir John must have been warned of our arrival as he awaited us in the outer bailey. I was close enough to hear the conversation.

"Lord Edward, what has happened?"

I dismounted. I knew of Lord Edward's suspicions, and yet his voice did not betray his thoughts. He was a clever man. He was much taller than Sir John, and he had to stoop a little. "We were ambushed by men from Béarn. They were waiting for us just south of the Garonne."

"I knew nothing of this, you must believe me, my liege! You cannot think that I had aught to do with this."

"Did you, Sir John?"

I could not see Lord Edward's face but I saw the fear on Sir John's face. He was not a young man and he paled under the baleful glare of the future king of England. "No, lord. I passed the message on from Lord Henry."

"Montfort?"

"Aye, lord. He told me that he had heard the men of Béarn were gathering in the south and threatened the border. He said he was returning to England to be with his brother."

"Then it is Henry de Montfort who must account for his words."

"He may have been speaking the truth. The men of Béarn *are* gathering, Lord Edward. That is true. We have had reports this past month of men assembling. Tarbes was threatened, and we assembled men to send there. My son, Sir Richard, led them six days since."

Lord Edward put his arm around the old knight. "Then we will stay the night, before I head south."

His squire said, "We do not go to Bordeaux?"

"No, John. We have a snake to quash first. Sir John, we have dead to bury."

"I will fetch my priest."

Roger of Talacre was buried with honour in the small graveyard of the church at Saint Justin. He would be in heaven. The rest of our past companions, Iago and his company, would be wandering between worlds. I doubted that Sir Robert of Lymm would have had their bodies buried. They would have been left for the creatures of the night. I said a silent prayer for my friend.

After my wound was tended by the healer in the castle I joined the rest of Lord Edward's men in the warrior hall. I received accolades from the six who had survived. They regaled the men of the castle with the tale of my arrows. They exaggerated. When I tried to have the truth told, it was put down to modesty. However, the consequence was that they all spoke freely before me. It became apparent that Sir John had spoken the truth. Either that, or he had deceived his men, too.

I was not privy to the conversation between Sir John and Prince Edward, but the next day half of the garrison marched south with us. John, Lord Edward's squire, had persuaded me to ride a palfrey and use my sumpter for my arrows and belongings. It made sense. It meant we could travel faster. Sir John had given us six servants to lead the horses with the baggage. Lord Edward's squire rode off soon after he had given me my instructions. I was to ride next to Lord Edward. I felt honoured and a little intimidated. How did I speak to such a high-born noble?

I knew Prince Edward for many years. There was much about him to dislike. He could be cruel, and he could be treacherous. Others found that to their cost. He bore grudges. Yet, with me, he was always the same. He never played me false, nor did he abuse my loyalty. You cannot change a man's nature. His line had come to power in Normandy and England. Through marriage and conquest, they had built an empire. That does not come from being pious and noble. You need to be ruthless, and Lord Edward was the most ruthless man I ever met.

"We have a long way to ride this day. Tell me how you came to be here in Gascony? There are few English archers who make the journey and even fewer with connections to Wales."

I felt a chill. How did he know of my connections? I had to tread carefully and that was not in my nature. I was naturally an honest and plain-spoken man. I told a version of the truth which did not involve a lie. "My lord was killed and I sought a new one. A man I served with told me that there was coin to be made in France, and we came here seeking our fortune."

"And your friend's fortune was six feet of earth in Gascony. A high price to pay."

"War is the only trade that Roger and I knew, Lord Edward."

"I meant what I said. When we find the men led by Sir Richard, we shall see if there are any archers. I would have you form them into a company of archers. Are you an exceptional archer?"

"My lord?"

"Can others release as many arrows as quickly as you? Can they kill as efficiently?"

"Perhaps, but yesterday is not an example of what archers do best, Lord Edward. You need fast hands and reflexes to be able to kill a man who is fewer than twenty paces from you. There is little skill. Anyone could hit a target at that range."

"What do they do best?"

I could tell from his tone that he was genuinely interested. I reached behind me and took out an arrow. "This tip can penetrate mail, Lord Edward. If I had ten archers, then we could send such a shower of these, that every warrior you lead this day could be slaughtered before they could close on us. A good archer can send an arrow more than two hundred paces. How long would it take mounted horsemen to cover such a distance?" I saw him calculating. "We could send six flights over before they closed on us. The arrows that did not hit men might hit horses. It matters not how you stop a horseman, just so long as you stop him."

"And if the men were on foot?"

"Then they would all die. A man on foot in mail does not move swiftly, Lord Edward. Archers fear horsemen. If we are caught close to them we are in great danger. That is how I came to suffer my wound. It is why Roger of Talacre sacrificed himself. He knew, better than any, the danger I was in."

"Yet you used your sword and dagger well. Ralph, my sergeant at arms, watched you as you took on those two mounted men. He was impressed by your courage."

"I am strong. I may not have much skill with a sword, but I know how to win. I have learned that is what is important."

"Then I can see that God sent you to me. He wishes me to regain all that my grandfather lost. When time allows, we will see that you are properly attired and rewarded."

We talked as we rode. He seemed happy to confide in me. It had been the same with Roger of Talacre. There had been a bond between us before we had spoken, and so it was with Lord Edward. We headed for Auch. It was the capital of Gascony with, as I discovered, a fine cathedral, city walls and a castle. Lord Edward confided, as we rode, that he hoped to pick up more men there. "Tarbes is a strong city with six castles close by each other. Even if one has fallen I would hope that the remainder have held out."

Roderigo of Auch ruled the town for King Henry. He was a big, bluff soldier. He needed a warhorse just to carry his weight, but his men adored him. He drank as hard as they did and did not know the meaning of defeat. He welcomed Lord Edward. I saw John, Lord Edward's squire. Now I understood why he had ridden off early. Lord Edward was not about to allow the grass to grow beneath his feet. He would strike quickly. We might have fewer men than the enemy, but he would take them on. I admired that. I did not see Gaston and the others. They would still be waiting in Agen. Nor did I see Harry. I kept hoping that I would run into my old friend.

Now that we were in a castle, I was relegated to the warrior hall with the other men at arms and crossbowmen. I appeared to be the only archer.

Matthew, Lord Edward's sergeant at arms, explained why. Sir Richard of Saint Justin had taken all the archers he could find. As rare as hens' teeth in Gascony, they had hired twenty. "They will be with Sir Richard, but what I cannot understand is why he did not come here first. Everyone knows that Roderigo of Auch hates the men of Béarn and would happily have joined him."

One of Roderigo's men, who had had to move his bed to accommodate us, said, "I heard it was because Sir Richard wanted the glory of destroying Lord Edward's great foe. He thought he had enough men."

I had rearranged my arrows and stored some. I asked, "Did he?" He nodded. "He had archers?"

The man at arms seemed to see me for the first time. "Perhaps. I know that the long war bow you use is a powerful weapon, but Gaston de Béarn is a cunning commander. If he hides behind his walls what can archers do?"

I smiled. I had heard this argument before. "More than you might think, but they need to be led well. What kind of leader is this Sir Richard? Is he reckless or thoughtful?"

"I am not sure. He is fierce and he lays clever traps."

"Men have to stand on walls to defend them. The difference between a crossbow and a bow is that we archers can stand safely behind a pavise or large shield and send arrows inside castle walls. If he is a reckless leader, then he may sally forth to destroy the archers who hide within."

Matthew said, "You look young, and yet you know much. Have you seen much fighting?"

"Enough, and I served with archers who passed their wisdom on to me. I listen." He nodded. I turned to Roderigo's man. "Tell me, were there many archers who rode with Sir Richard?"

"Twenty, perhaps twenty-five. He picked up a couple who had come here seeking work."

"Was there one, a big archer with fists like shovels? Went by the name of Harry Long Stride?"

He shook his head. "There was an Englishman who sounds like your chap, but his name was Ralph."

I smiled. That was Harry. Just as I had changed my name to protect myself, so had he. I felt much better knowing that he was ahead of me. I would soon have my old companion at my side. I would take him on as the first of Lord Edward's archers.

The next day we began to move just after dawn. We had fifty miles to go. Had we all been mounted we could have made it in one long day, but we were men who fought on foot. I did not have the luxury of riding at the head of the column with Lord Edward this time. We now had thirty knights and I was relegated to the rear of the mounted men. I was ahead of the foot which included crossbowmen. Crossbowmen and archers do not get on. I had heard of violence between them if drink was involved. I was alone, and so I ignored their jibes and their banter. To be truthful, I was anticipating a meeting with Harry. I would tell him of my adventures, and, I had no doubt, his would be as interesting.

We had stopped once to water and feed the horses and were on our second march, just after noon, when we halted once more. It was unusual. Word rippled down the column. I had no doubt that by the time the message reached me it would have changed beyond all recognition. Surprisingly it had not. It was simple and it was black. Sir Richard and his column had been attacked, and more than half their number were either captured or killed. Sir Richard had been badly wounded and it was feared he would never fight again. We rode just another two miles after the halt, and we camped by a small town which had a solitary tower for defence.

Matthew and Lord Edward's men at arms had taken me under their wing and I camped with them. They were led by Captain William, and I liked him. He was bluff and he was honest. I was anxious to find out more about Harry and his fate. I made my way to the camp of the survivors. It was close to Lord Edward's. He and his knights were in deep conference. No one had expected Sir Richard to defeat Gaston de Béarn, but to have lost more than half his men was a disaster. When I reached the survivors I saw the scale of the disaster. Half of the men I saw had wounds.

The archers, there were six of them, were seated together. That was the way with archers. None of them was Harry, and my heart sank. They looked up at my approach. One of them, a surly looking man, who appeared to have a permanent sneer on his face beneath a recently broken nose, said, "Where have you sneaked from? Managed to miss the battle, eh? Still sucking on your mammy's titty?"

I stared at him. He was obviously overwrought, but no man suffered insults without responding. "Friend, curb your tongue, lest I remove it for my peace of mind. I came to ask of a friend I believe served with you."

The surly fellow leapt to his feet and his hand came towards me. He was making to punch me. I wrapped my right hand around it and began to squeeze. I saw his face twist in pain. I hooked my right leg behind his left and pushed. He tumbled backwards. My sword was out and pricked his neck before he knew it.

Before it could escalate further, John, Lord Edward's squire, came racing over. "What is this, Gerald War Bow? A sword drawn in our camp? Lord Edward asks you to curb your temper." He gave the slightest of winks. "This is not the behaviour he expects from his captain of archers."

I sheathed my sword. "I am sorry, lord. It will not happen again. I was just getting to know this archer. We are now acquainted." John nodded and left. I put my hand out to help the archer to his feet. "And he knows better now than to insult a man he has only just met."

He stood and pushed my hand away. He held his hand to his neck and it came away bloody. He pushed past me.

The others stood. One of them grinned and held out his hand. "I wouldn't worry about Guy of Sheffield. He could start an argument in an empty room. No one likes him. We lost many good archers the other day. It is a pity that he was not one of them. I am John of Nottingham." He pointed to each archer as he named them. "Peter Crookback. Do not worry about the hunch. He is still a powerful bowman. David the Welshman, a fair archer but tends to wander off if there are sheep about."

David the Welshman laughed and smacked John of Nottingham's calf with an arrow, "That is because the sheep are prettier than any English woman I have ever seen!"

"The last two are Stephen Green Feathers and Robin of Barnsley."

I nodded. "My father favoured green flights."

"Was his name Gerald ap Llewellyn?"

"It was, did you know him?"

"No, my father served under him when he was Captain of Archers. He adopted green flights in his honour. This is a small world and no mistake. Sit friend, and tell us your tale. Did we hear aright, that you are Lord Edward's captain of archers?"

"I am." I squatted on the ground with them.

John of Nottingham, the eldest of the men, said, "Do not take offence, Captain, but you are young for such a title."

"I take no offence, and you are right, but Lord Edward seems to think I can do this. If any of you wish to serve Lord Edward, I would happily lead you. I will not be offended if you decline."

"I for one will serve. That was a neat trick with Guy and you must be strong. Had you not tripped him you would have broken his hand."

"I am strong. I was trained by the best: my father."

The others all offered to serve. Robin of Barnsley said, "Any paymaster is welcome. I doubt that Sir Richard will fight again. There will be little pay from him."

I nodded. "Tell me, was there an archer with you by the name of Ralph? He would be a big man." I smiled, "If he was my friend, I am guessing he would have had a run-in with Guy of Sheffield."

That set them all to laughing. "That was Ralph, but that was not his real name. He said it was Harry, but he wished to be known as Ralph for he had run. He was the one who broke Guy's nose."

"He helped to train me."

John of Nottingham said, "I have bad news then. He was taken prisoner."

"Harry was taken prisoner?"

"Believe me, he fought well. He used all his arrows and fought on with his sword. He was laid low by a mace. I do not think he died. We were fleeing. The six of us, and two others, were lucky enough to capture horses. We escaped. The rest did not."

I had gone from the joy of believing that my friend was alive, to the despair of knowing that he was a prisoner.

CHAPTER 6

I was heading back to Lord Edward's men at arms' camp when John found me. "Lord Edward would like a word with you before you retire."

"Of course." I wondered if I was about to be reprimanded for my actions.

He was seated on a chest, which had contained salted meat, and was staring into the fire. "I am afraid you will not have many archers when we ride to Tarbes tomorrow. Can you do anything with the handful of men you have?"

"That depends upon the target."

"I have sent Sir Richard home. He will never be a knight again. He has lost the use of his left arm. He told me, before he left, that Gaston de Béarn has captured Bourg Neuf. It is one of the six citadels at Tarbes. It has its own wall. How the fool of a castellan lost it is beyond me."

"You say that there are five others, lord. Are any close to it?"

"Yes, Gerald, Bourg Crabé. They even share some walls."

"Then my archers can use the walls of this Bourg Crabé to rain arrows onto their walls. We can clear them as crossbows cannot. If they hide behind embrasures, then still our arrows will be able to hit them."

"But there are only seven of you."

92

"Actually Lord Edward there are only six. I am not certain how reliable Guy of Sheffield is. It matters not. We do not have to send them over quickly, just so long as it is a constant shower. It is like the drip which hits the same spot on the stone. Eventually it wears down. Men are not stone and they break quicker."

Lord Edward still looked dubious.

"And we can send fire arrows over at night. They would work as effectively during the day, but there is something terrifying about fire at night."

"I need something. I am loath to lose men storming the walls. I just need to defeat Gaston de Béarn. I am needed in England. The de Montfort brothers are causing trouble. This attack by Gaston de Béarn is to keep me here." He lifted his head. "John."

His squire came over and took out a purse. He counted out ten gold coins. Each was the equivalent of three months wages for an archer. "Lord Edward would have you bind the archers with these coins. One for each of the six and four for you."

"It is too much, Lord Edward."

Lord Edward laughed. "A modest man. Take it Gerald. If nothing else, it pays for the lives of the men at arms you saved. Tomorrow we will encircle Bourg Neuf and you and your archers can find somewhere within Bourg Crabé."

I returned to the archers. Guy of Sheffield was not there. I cocked my head to one side. John of Nottingham shrugged. "He ran."

I nodded. "Then more fool him, although I would not have wished him to be part of our company." I gave each of them a gold coin. "This is the payment to secure your services. You receive the same each month." Their faces showed their joy. I took out another of them. "This one is for whichever of you manages to set the castle alight tomorrow night."

"Castle?"

I told them what Lord Edward had planned. It pleased me that none appeared discomfited by the thought.

John of Nottingham said, "And we will call you Captain. David, fetch the captain's war gear from the other camp. It is right that the company of archers stays together. We are now a band of brothers."

They made me feel welcome. I know it was not just because I had given them a gold coin. We were few in number, and, David apart, we were all English. More than that, they now served the future king of England. When my gear arrived, we worked out exactly how six of us would do what an army could not. Reduce a castle.

When we marched towards Tarbes, the whole army went prepared for war. We had a vanguard made up of armoured knights. Our baggage was protected by the crossbows. Our numbers had been swollen by the survivors from the ill-fated expedition. I asked John of Nottingham, as we rode, "If there are five other castles, why could their garrisons not reduce the one they did capture?"

"Numbers. They keep small garrison here, Captain. I think there must have been treachery, else Bourg Neuf would never have fallen. I know you are confident in what we can achieve, but Gaston de Béarn has large numbers of men behind his walls."

I nodded. "Do you gamble, John?"

"I have been known to wager."

I took out a silver sixpence. "I will wager this, that Gaston de Béarn is not inside Bourg Neuf."

"A bold statement, Captain, what makes you think thus?"

"Last night, you all said that he was cunning and that he was thoughtful rather than reckless. Why trap himself inside a castle, where he could be captured and end his war? That is why I am confident. It will not be their leader. It will be some bold warrior who seeks to make a name for himself, and when we begin to kill his men, he will want to strike back. You have seen these two castles. How far apart are they?"

"A hundred paces at the most. They share a wall."

"And if we hide behind the crenulations can their crossbows hit us?"

"No."

"But we can hit them. The secret will be to keep up a steady rate. When we stop, I want them to think we have run out of arrows. We will not. We will just be resting."

When we reached Tarbes I saw why they had the defences that they did. Nestling in the foothills of the Pyrenees, the six towers formed an east–west axis with the centre resting on the cathedral. The walls were not ridiculously high, but they would need ladders to scale them. However, when we finally saw Bourg Neuf, I became almost numb with anger. The heads and genitals of the men who had been captured were on the top of spears. I looked down the line of heads. Some were unrecognisable as men. This would be my fate if I was captured. Then I saw one that was familiar. For some reason the face had not been disfigured. I saw Harry. My friend was dead. My archers also saw friends who had been killed. Their anger was obvious.

Lord Edward took off his helmet and rode with Roderigo and John to within hailing distance of the walls. "I come to demand the surrender of my castle. My father is the rightful ruler of Gascony and I am here to see that his property is returned to him."

Their leader laughed. "I am Count Alfonso of Valencia! The heads of your men show what I think of you. When my lord brings all of his forces here, then we will rid Gascony of all Normans and Angevins once and for all."

Lord Edward was remarkably calm. "Is that your last word?"

"It is."

"Then hear my terms." He raised his voice. "I speak so that all may hear my words. You have one hour to surrender. Any enemies of Gascony who remain after that time will be given no quarter." He said nothing more and silence swept over the castle. He rode back and conferred with his knights. They began to organise their men and he came to me. "Come, Gerald, bring your archers into Bourg Crabé. We will see if your plan can succeed. For now, I see my enemy's."

John, his squire, asked, "Which is?"

I had seen it too. "They wish to make us waste our men on the walls while Gaston de Béarn brings more men here." Lord Edward pointed to the Pyrenees. "They will come from that direction, and it will negate our horsemen. We need to reduce this castle and then make him break upon these walls."

Each of the castles had their own entrance so that they were self-contained. They were small. Whoever had built them had thought that they would be able to mutually defend each other. This had failed, but I was now even more convinced that there had been treachery involved. If I was Lord Edward, I would be looking for a traitor when we took the Bourg Neuf.

The castellan was an old Gascon. He recognised the three lions and bowed and scraped. Lord Edward was annoyed with the burghers of Tarbes. He was short with him. "These archers are here to help destroy the Bourg Neuf. You will assist them in any way they wish. You obey Captain Gerald's commands. Is that clear?"

He looked at me and opened his mouth to say something. It would probably have been that I was too young, but he thought better of it. Lord Edward's tone was warning enough. "Aye, lord."

"How many men do you have?"

"There are four men with crossbows and six others."

Eleven men to guard a castle. It was no wonder that the other had been taken so easily.

Lord Edward recognised that too. "Is there no knight who commands here?"

"Lord Gilbert prefers life on his estate, lord."

"Then we will have to see Lord Gilbert when this is over."

I had learned that each of the castles was supposed to be manned by a knight as part of his fealty. It was a good system. It provided a good garrison. However, the system depended upon knights doing their duty.

Lord Edward turned to me. "It is in your hands now. Begin when you are ready, and have a man come to tell me when you think the castle is ready to fall."

Abruptly he left and I turned to the castellan. "What is your name?"

"Juan, Captain."

"Well Juan, I need a number of things from you. Do you have tables in here?"

"Tables?"

"Where do you eat?"

"Oh yes, Captain, we have tables."

"Then I need them all on the fighting platform, but first tell me, are all the castles built to the same design?"

"Exactly, Captain."

"And where is the highest part?"

"That would be Tower Crabé. I will take you." He led us through a narrow door and up a spiral staircase. The more I saw, the more I wondered how the castle could have fallen. The narrow entrance would have made the keep a death-trap for any who tried to enter. My shoulders barely fitted through the door and I had to duck my head. When we reached the fighting platform I saw the men crouching beneath the crenulations. As I stepped out with my bow, behind Juan the castellan, I saw a crossbowman about to say something. When John and the others followed me, he thought better of it. The Tower Crabé was square. It rose to the height of seven men. We entered another narrow door and this time we ascended a ladder to the square top. There were just two men there.

"Juan, I want the tables brought up here."

"Here?"

I silenced the question simply. "Lord Edward told you to obey my orders. Do it, and we will not need these men here. I will send them their instructions when we are ready."

I laid down my bow and went to the embrasure. The tower at the Bourg Neuf was just two hundred and twenty paces from us. Each tower appeared to be to the west of the main entrance. Even as I stood there, a bolt flew at me from the walls of Bourg Neuf. It clattered off the stone and flew into the air. I saw men on the other tower pointing at me. That was where the danger lay. I would use our crossbows to keep down the heads of their men on the walls. The men in the tower had a flat trajectory. They could reach us.

John said, "That is why you want the tables."

"Aye, if the enemy is coming here then we need to clear their tower quickly and we do not have time to make some pavise." I risked another glance over the top. The gate of the Bourg Neuf lay fifteen paces below us. I could see a large number of men on the fighting platform above the gate. Lord Edward would never be able to enter through the narrow gate. He would have to use ladders. I saw smoke rising from the Bourg Neuf. They were preparing pig fat or water. Lord Edward might take the outer wall quickly but not the tower.

I turned to John. "See if you can count how many men are at the gate."

"Captain."

"David, go and tell the crossbowmen to use their bolts against the enemy crossbows."

"I have to talk to crossbowmen?"

Stephen Green Feathers said, "Pretend they are sheep!"

He descended, grumbling. John of Nottingham said, "I counted twenty men in mail and another twenty besides. They have vats of something bubbling, Captain. I would wager boiling water."

David returned. "They weren't happy, but they are doing so."

I heard the sound of a cry from the walls of Bourg Neuf. The bolts were flying and they would keep the defenders occupied. Our danger lay in the tower. Once they realised we were archers then every crossbow would be brought there. They would be able to stop us releasing our arrows.

"Gather round." They joined me. "We have one chance to surprise them. One hundred and twenty paces below us is their gatehouse. When I give the word, we rise and kill as many of their mailed men as we can. When they realise what we are doing and send crossbows to their tower, we will stop until we can erect our improvised pavise. After that, we will be sending arrows blind, so mark where they are."

"Aye, Captain."

I saw each of them select what they deemed to be their best six arrows. We had climbed the ladder and knew how long we had. A crossbow was unwieldy to carry. It would take them longer to load and send the bolts. Once they reached the top of the tower, then the stone embrasure would give the crossbow support. They would be accurate. They would be slow but accurate. I hoped that by having our own crossbows engaging theirs, it would delay them reaching the top of the tower.

"Ready?"

"Aye, Captain!"

"Then let them know they have archers to contend with!"

I rose and aimed at a knight who was exhorting his men on the outer wall. At a hundred and twenty paces and from a lofty perch I could not miss. My bodkin-tipped arrow penetrated deep into his back and flung him forward. Five others in mail fell. The defenders were disorientated. They looked to our walls first, and in that heartbeat, we sent another six arrows, and another six men in mail fell. We released a third before I heard an order given, and shields came up. For four of their men it was too late. We each chose another target and sent arrows towards them. One man at arms did not have a good helmet. Stephen Green Feathers' arrow penetrated the metal and the man died. I saw a shield wall. While they had a shield wall, they could not defend against Lord Edward and his men. They could no longer support those defending the outer walls.

"Switch to the tower! Aim for the crossbows."

I chose a good arrow. It was one of my father's that I had dyed red. I aimed at an empty embrasure. This was a longer range, but I was confident. I did not make a full pull. That would tire me. I quarter pulled and I waited. When I saw a head I pulled back, and, as the crossbow appeared, I released and nocked another. The crossbow fell to shatter in the inner bailey as the crossbowman died. I nocked another arrow and sent it towards the crossbow which rose above the wall. My arrow hit the crossbow and then spiralled into the air. The crossbow was knocked from the crossbowman's hands, and it fell to the bailey. An archer always had a spare bow. A crossbowman could not afford a spare.

Suddenly a bolt cracked into the wall. "Down!" We had done enough until the pavise came.

Juan and his men at arms huffed and puffed as they struggled up the ladder with the tables. They were six feet by three feet and perfect. "Take them from them. You know what to do!"

My men took them and lifted them easily from the Gascons. They held them before them and jammed them into the gaps between the stones of the crenulations. Even as they placed them there, bolts like angry hornets cracked into them. The crossbows' first bolts had been ranging ones. Now they had the range. The could send their bolts on the same trajectory all day if necessary. We were now protected, and I knew from my father that crossbows were prone to damage with repeated use. The more bolts they sent, the sooner they would break and require repair.

Five of us lined up behind the protection of the tables. Robin of Barnsley was our first spotter. He crouched and peered around a table. The angle meant that crossbow bolts could not reach him, and yet he still had a view of the gatehouse. He nodded, and we all pulled as one. We raised our bows together, and when we released it was a single crack. It was so loud that I knew the enemy would hear it. We waited.

Robin said, "Short."

We all adjusted our aim and I ordered, "Release!"

The five arrows flew, and this time, after the crack I heard cries.

"Perfect!"

We nocked, pulled and released steadily until we had each sent ten arrows towards the enemy. Then Robin took the place of Peter Crookback. We sent another ten missiles. Gradually, we were all relieved until Robin returned to his duty. When that happened, I said, "Robin, find Lord Edward, tell him now is the time to strike, for they are weakened."

"Aye, Captain."

"Eat, drink, you did well." We had all spotted. Our plunging arrows had thinned their ranks. Not every arrow found mail or flesh. Some hit shields and some found good helmets. One arrow had managed to smash into the vat of boiling water. Its contents had spilled along the fighting platform. It did not kill, but it did make the defenders move, and arrows found men who were trying to avoid boiling water.

John of Nottingham drank from his ale skin. My archers preferred ale when they could get it. When this was gone, it would be a long time until they got more. "They will think we are out of arrows! They are in for a shock."

David the Welshman said, "We have forty more each and that is all, Gerald War Bow."

I tore off a piece of bread and smeared it with the goats' cheese. "And that will have to be enough."

We waited until Robin returned. We needed a spotter. "They have taken the outer wall. Lord Edward is waiting for you before he begins the assault."

"Then let us begin."

My arms and shoulders were aching. This was the most prolonged period of releasing arrows I could remember. I had practised for longer, but then I had not had the cacophony of crossbow bolts striking the wood just three feet from my head. The rain of bolts had slowed, but they were still there.

"Short, but you still hit one knight!"

We adjusted and again heard cries. The cries of the enemy dying were augmented by the sound of the men of Gascony and England assaulting the walls. We were down to our last four arrows when Peter Crookback shouted, "I see Lord Edward on the walls!"

"Cease!" I noticed that the bolts had stopped hitting the pavise. "Take down the tables, let us see if we can help."

We dared not risk sending arrows blindly when our own men were attacking but we could still make a difference. I nocked an arrow, aware that I was down to a handful. I saw that Lord Edward and John were leading men towards the Count Alphonso. I levelled my bow and half pulled. I did not have a clear line. Suddenly I saw Lord Edward slip on blood, or guts; it was hard to see. Count Alphonso raised his sword to end the life of my new lord. I now had a target, and my arrow struck him in the neck. It tore through his ventail and entered his shoulder. He slid to the side and that heralded the end. Men threw down their swords. I saw John help Lord Edward to his feet, and Lord Edward looked at the arrow. He raised his sword in salute. We had won.

John of Nottingham laughed and handed over sixpence. "Here Captain – you were right. Gaston de Béarn was not within the walls, and I believe that it is you who have earned your gold coin!" He raised his bow and cheered, "And we did not need to use fire arrows, let us hear it for Captain Gerald!" My men joined in the cheers. It was a victory and I enjoyed the sound of it.

CHAPTER 7

The first act that we did was to remove the heads of our dead from the spears on the walls. Some had been damaged in the fighting and that made us even angrier. The defenders who had surrendered cowered as we passed. Lord Edward had promised death to the defenders. They would do nothing to remind him of his promise. There were just sixteen survivors. No knights survived, and of the others, only six were unwounded. Once we had seen to our dead we retrieved as many arrows as we could. Only a few were totally usable, but the heads on some, the fletch on others and some of the shafts could be made into arrows again. We would need them for the attack which we knew was coming.

As we were collecting them Lord Edward's squire found me. "Lord Edward is pleased with you, archer. Once again, you saved his life. His gold is reaping a fine investment. He would have you and your men in the centre castle, by the cathedral. That will be the point of the enemy attack."

I was curious as to how he knew. "Why do you say that?"

"One of the prisoners agreed to talk in exchange for his life." Even as he spoke I heard the snap of ropes as the others, wounded and whole, were hanged.

"What if he lies?"

John gave a cruel smile. "Matthew watches him. If the attack does not happen as he has told us, then he will be emasculated, hanged, drawn and finally quartered. I do not think he lies. Besides which, the centre castle lies close to the cathedral and has the best approach for engines of war."

"If he thought we would still be attacking Bourg Neuf then he would not need siege engines."

"Lord Edward is like you, archer, he is young but he is clever. On the morrow, he leads the knights out to find Gaston de Béarn. He will draw him to the walls."

I nodded. "It seems a good plan." I turned to my men and shouted, "When you have your arrows, come to me. We have a new place to defend."

I knew why there was a delay. While they were retrieving arrows, my men were also relieving the dead of anything they had which was of value. When they eventually arrived I led them back to our horses. It would be better if they were with us in the castle. The castle was the count's castle and had two towers and higher walls than the surrounding ones. There were stables and we would use them. I now had a scabbard for my saddle. With Roger's two swords and scabbards across my back, the one on my horse became a spare. I still had my packs on my sumpter, and so we walked our animals to the stables.

The count was meeting with Lord Edward and the other leaders. The sergeant at arms was expecting us. "You are fine archers. We saw your fall of arrows. I thought there were more of you."

"There will be, eventually."

The sergeant seemed an affable man, and as he led us to the fighting platform we chatted. "Tell me, sergeant, how did the enemy take Bourg

Neuf so easily, and why did the rest of the garrisons not attempt to retake it? I mean no offence but we retook it easily enough."

"None taken. There were many of us as angry as you. A message came from Guy de Montfort, telling us that the men of Béarn were racing for Bayonne. The count took men and knights from the castles to thwart them. Guy de Montfort agreed to stay and watch our town. It was he and his men who allowed Count Alphonso to sneak in. When Sir Richard arrived they were ambushed. We tried to help, but with only a dozen or so men in each castle..."

The de Montforts reared their heads again. Simon de Montfort was bitter about the loss of his governorship. I could see why Lord Edward wished to return to England with all haste. The two had been close friends, but now they were moving towards a hatred which would consume England.

This time we had the fighting platform above the gate. There was a tower on each side. We would not need pavise. If they had crossbows, we would have the crenulations to protect us. They would be below us. A crossbow worked best when it had elevation. It made it a good weapon to use in a castle. We were now using arrows which had been kept at Tarbes. They were not as good as the ones we made ourselves, but until we had access to some good wood and a blacksmith and could find the right goose feathers, we would have to make do. It was all a matter of confidence.

That night we ate at a table and we slept in beds. To an archer used to campaigning it was luxury. The others were interested in my swords.

John of Nottingham asked, "Why two swords, and why are all your swords longswords? Most archers use a short sword. It is good enough for us."

I told them the story of how I had come into the possession of my first sword. I showed them the scabbard my father had made. "When my friend died, he asked me to take his weapons and his coins. I did as my brother asked me." I held up my purse. "It is no secret that I hold a large purse of gold. If I die then, as I have no one else in my life, I ask my brother archers to share it equitably."

Peter was the most thoughtful of my men. He said, quietly, "If Guy of Sheffield was here, then you would wake with a second throat."

I smiled. "I choose my brother archers carefully! Lord Edward wants a whole company. You are the first. The others will have to match your standards. When we return to England, we will be attired in a livery."

"We return?"

I nodded, "Aye, we do." I said it with a smile, but my heart was heavy. I would have to speak to Lord Edward before we left Gascony. I would not leave with a lie between us.

We heard the knights ride out in the early morning. Lord Edward had forty knights and squires with him. They were not all the knights; we had twenty more in the castles. In addition, every castle was well garrisoned with men at arms and crossbowmen. We then waited. I had taken to wearing my hat again. This time it was not for the cold, as it was in England, but for the sun, which burned down. David had fair skin and he wore a brimmed straw hat to keep off the sun. We were almost in the land of the Moors, Spain, and although winter approached, it was still hotter than an English summer's day. While we waited I went to the blacksmith and used his wheel to sharpen my two swords and my dagger. Roger had made a good scabbard. I barely felt the weight, and they were easy to draw over my shoulders. I would only need them when I was close to an enemy or had run out of arrows. I knew that I would need to practise with both of them. If I did not use a shield, I would have to compensate by using a sword.

Noon arrived, and we ate at the fighting platform on the wall walk. My men were vigilant. They enjoyed being well paid, and more importantly, they enjoyed the honour they had been given. We had the most dangerous position to hold.

Robin of Barnsley had good eyes, and it was he who spotted the banners of the knights as they galloped down the road from the mountains. He shouted, "Ware the gate! Riders approaching."

Roger de Mortimer, one of Lord Edward's closest friends, was at the gate nearest to our castle with the best knights and men at arms. They would hold the gates while Lord Edward and his men entered. They would then defend the outer wall. We would be able to send arrows over the heads of our men. Crossbows could not do that. Crossbows lined the lower wall, along with men at arms. I wondered if the ruse had worked. Was Gaston de Béarn coming to take Tarbes from Lord Edward?

"Robin, can you see who pursues?"

He had no fear of heights, and he stood on top of the crenulation and peered south. "There are riders and many men on foot, Captain. They wear bright clothes, that is for certain." He jumped down.

"Then perhaps Lord Edward has drawn them here. Remember, we aim for their knights and their mailed men. Choose your targets carefully."

Waiting was always hard for me. I did not mind the wait of the hunt when you stalked your prey. This waiting was different. You could see your enemy. He grew in numbers, and he grew in the threat he posed. The unknown became known. When you hunted, you looked at the tracks and knew what you would find. When I had spoken with the sergeant of the castle, I had asked him of our enemies.

"The worst are the Basques! They are not Moor and they are not Spaniard. They are neither French nor Gascon. They are like some mongrel who squats in the corner of this land. They are fierce fighters and they are tough fighters. If you defeat them, Captain, make sure they are dead. And watch out for their trick of jumping! They are like fleas. In their mountain country, they can jump from rock to rock like mountain goats. I have seen good warriors die to their jumping tricks. The others are those you may have fought before; knights, men at arms and Arabs."

"I have never fought Arabs."

"You did not crusade?" I shook my head. "Do not be deceived by the flimsy clothes they wear. Their cloaks, they call them bisht, have many layers and are almost as good as mail at preventing wounds."

"Our arrows can penetrate mail."

"Aye, but your swords, should you have to use them, are a different matter. Go for any flesh you see. It matters not if it is a hand or a finger. They are an easier place to hurt than the body or the head. They wear fine helmets beneath their garments."

It would be new and unknown warriors we fought. I wished we had more arrows.

I saw the gates open and the knights and squires rode in. I saw that some were wounded. They did not stop in the outer bailey but carried on beneath our gate. Lord Edward lowered his ventail and raised his arm to me. The seven of us had an important job to do. We all hoped that the knights with Roger de Mortimer would stop the men of Béarn, but we all knew that it was unlikely. Robin of Barnsley said, "I see ladders. They are well prepared, Captain!"

"So are we."

I nocked an arrow and waited. The outer wall was just a hundred paces from us. We could see men who were one hundred and fifty paces, but we had too few arrows to waste. When they scaled the walls, then we would make it a killing ground. I was able to watch the men with crossbows. They were a powerful weapon, but once they had released it seemed to take an age to reload them. While the crossbowmen did so they had to stand upright, and I saw some struck by lead balls as the enemy slingers hurled their deadly missiles. The men of Béarn also had archers and crossbows. Their bows were not as good as ours and their arrows were more like hunting arrows, yet they could still hurt a warrior who did not wear mail. The knights were safe, and most of the sergeants and men at arms, but the others began to fall.

I saw ladders raised and knew that the crossbows had failed to halt the enemy. That was confirmed when the crossbowmen left the outer wall and sought sanctuary within the main castle. I saw a black-faced warrior stand on top of the wall. He had a mail shirt on. I released. The arrow threw him from the wall. It seemed to be the signal for the enemy to leap over in even greater numbers and for my archers to pick their targets. We kept the wall around Roger de Mortimer clear of enemies. The longer he and the other household knights held out, the more of the enemy would die. He and the other knights slew many who tumbled over the battlements, but further along the wall men were cleared.

Lord Edward appeared next to me with John. "John, sound the fallback!"

"Yes, Lord Edward!" He sounded the horn three times.

"Captain, I rely on you to ensure that my household knights survive."

"They will."

That was easier said than done. As the knights began to descend, the walls were filled with a mass of men. We could no longer pick and choose enemy knights to kill. We had to kill those closest to our knights. We could not miss, but there were only six of us. Sending an arrow every few heartbeats, we soon made the enemy respect our arrows. They slowed and used their shields for protection. David and Peter concentrated their arrows on the men attempting to open the gates to allow in the rest of their army. Twelve men died before they managed to do so. By then, Roger de Mortimer and the other knights had entered the gates safely, which were slammed behind them.

Lord Edward clapped me on the back. "Nobly done! I will go and speak with my knights."

I shouted, "Choose your targets now! Our men are safe!"

I heeded my own words. I ignored the half-naked warriors who raced ahead of those with shields and mail. I aimed at the gap between the ventail and helmet of the warrior who had a red shield with a blue cross. He fell dead. My men did the same to other targets. They were fewer than fifty paces from us. To archers using the long war bow, this was almost point-blank range. As I aimed at the next knight who had a ventail, I could have chosen an eye and still managed to hit my target. Another fell dead. I saw another knight wearing a full helm. There was no ventail and no gap. John of Nottingham sent an arrow through the mail of his shoulder. As he dropped his shield, Robin of Barnsley sent one into his chest. A full-face helmet meant he was a rich knight and had experience. It was worth two arrows to end his threat.

I heard shouts from below as the men who had just reached us were sent to the walls. Lord Edward, his squire and ten knights and squires joined us at the gatehouse. Already the enemy was bringing its ladders to try to take our walls. We were higher at the gatehouse. Their ladders would not reach us, but they could reach the walls which joined ours. As I sent arrow after arrow into mail that was just thirty paces from me, I saw the sea which threatened to engulf us. Had Lord Edward made a mistake by spreading his men out in seven castles? Our enemies were concentrating everything at us. Had he gambled and lost?

I put my negative thoughts from my head and continued to send my arrows into the mailed bodies. I reached for an arrow but there were none. I looked around and saw that only Stephen Green Feathers had any remaining.

"Lord Edward, we are out of arrows."

He nodded."I have been counting. There are almost a hundred and fifty men who are dead thanks to you. If we lose this battle it will not be your fault."

I could not help but think that it would not make a deal of difference to us. Our heads would be on top of spears and Lord Edward would be ransomed back to his father. Henry might lose Gascony, but his son would live. I would die a rich archer. My father had died a poor archer, but he had lived his life. I had yet to do so. I had not even planted seed!

"Archers, we fight as men at arms today!" Of course, we had no mail. We had no helmets and we had no shields. All that we did have were a pair of quick hands and a mind to match. They would have to do.

I drew my two swords and moved towards the door which led from the walls below. That would be where the enemy would emerge. I saw that now our arrows had ended their rain it was left to the few remaining crossbows, and they too soon fell silent. The men to our sides would be at arms on the fighting platform. It was wide enough for three men to walk along but only two to fight upon. With a fall to the inner bailey, if you slipped, there was no mercy to be found on the wall. We had the luxury of a rectangular floor. It was eight paces by six paces. Would the extra room suit the attackers or us?

It was then that I saw a chance. I had never fought on a wall before. I saw that the men who came along to fight us had their shields on their left arms. Their right arms were next to the walls. They would find it harder to swing their swords. It was a small advantage, but an archer learned to use any he had.

Lord Stephen and his squire stood to block the enemy who came through the door. They slew the first three, then I saw a pair of spears jab through and strike them both in the calf. The spears were twisted and the two men fell to the inner bailey. Although Sir Walther and Sir Ralph ran to seal the breach, they were too late. A veritable flood of men ran towards us. I was no hero, but I charged at the half-naked man who ran next to the wall. I saw blood on his sword and on his shield. His helmet, which had a nasal, was also spattered with blood. This warrior had killed this day. Even though he had a long sword and a shield I thought I had a chance to defeat him. I was wrong about the wall. It did nothing to stop him swinging. It just meant his sword came down across my body. My strength came to my aid. I used the sword in my left arm to block the blow. I saw the surprise on his face when his sword did not strike flesh but, instead, sparked off steel. I lunged with my right hand at his head. His shield came up to deflect the blow.

As our bodies closed I saw his head begin to move backwards. I knew what was coming; a headbutt. I had suffered them in fights before, but this warrior had a helmet. We were so close that neither of us could use the edge of our swords. I turned my head as I punched at his head with the hilt of my sword. I knocked his head to the side and the pressure was released. As we both stepped back, I stopped thinking as a man at arms and began to think as an archer. I looked for the flesh. I brought my right hand from on high. Still reeling from my punch, he brought up his shield again. I stabbed upwards, under his shield, with my left hand. He was naked from the waist up. I guessed he was a Basque. I remembered the sergeant's words. My sword travelled diagonally through the ribs on his left side. I kept pushing and twisting until I saw the tip emerge at his shoulder. Then I tore the sword from his body. He was dead, and his bleeding body fell to block the fighting walkway.

Behind me, I heard Lord Edward shout, "John, make the signal!"

A horn sounded four times. I had no idea what it meant. More men ran towards us. I ran towards them. I would use my speed and agility. I jumped the dead man to run at the next warrior. I was aware of my archers and knights to the side and behind me. It was a maelstrom of swords, shields and bodies. An Arab faced me. Enclosed in cloth he looked an easy target, but I harked back to the advice I had been given. His hood was down and he wore a pointed helmet with an aventail. He had, however, no ventail. I could see his face. I could see his hands. His armour was beneath the cloak and bisht. His shield was smaller than the ones our warriors used and his sword thinner. I was under no illusions. The smiths of Spain made the best of steel. His sword would not bend.

He initiated the fight with a stab at my head. I could see why. I had no helmet and no armour. Once again, I deflected it with my left hand, and this time, did the unexpected. He anticipated a blow to his head and his shield flicked up. I brought the sword in my right hand over and chopped off his right hand. His sword and hand tumbled to the outer bailey. He looked at me in surprise and I backhanded him across the face with my sword. The blade smashed across his face. It tore deep into the flesh and the bone. The power of the blow knocked him across others, who were hurrying to get to us. With his spurting blood, he made the platform slick. He was going to be a dead man. His lifeblood pumped from his severed arm.

Some of the enemy slipped. I heard Lord Edward shout, "Now, at them!"

The knights rallied behind Lord Edward, and, with shields held before them, they began to march towards the enemy. There were Basques amongst them, and they tried to run and jump at Lord Edward. It was a mistake, for the blood and the gore made them slip. They were hacked and chopped as they lay writhing like beached fish.

Then I heard a cheer from my left. I was next to the wall and I risked a glance. The men from the other castles had been summoned, and they were slaughtering the men who were trying to climb our walls. The signal from Lord Edward had been to initiate his trap. It was not over. Thanks to Roger de Mortimer and his knights, who had guarded the gate, none had gained entry, but we had our gatehouse to clear and then the fighting platforms. I fell in behind Lord Edward and his knights. I had realised that I was out of my depth, and my luck might not last.

I found myself behind John, Lord Edward's squire. I saw the advantage of his mail when a sword came from nowhere to hack at his shoulder. The mail held. As we closed with the door, the press became tighter. It was hard for either side to swing their weapons. Our own castle walls were working against us. It held them. I saw that John was face to face with a bearded Spaniard. I insinuated my sword between John's body and Lord Edward's. I angled it upwards and then I pushed. I saw the bearded face as my sword bit into him. His eyes widened and then blood came from his mouth. I pulled out the sword and his body went limp.

John shouted, "Gerald, reach in and pull his body away!"

I sheathed my right-hand sword and put my hand between Lord Edward and his squire. I found sticky blood and a baldric. I pulled. John and Lord Edward turned their bodies slightly, and the Spaniard popped out like a cork from a jug. I fell backwards with his body on top of me. That allowed the two of them to stab the man in the door, and they were through and onto the fighting platform. Pushing the corpse from me, I stood. In the moments that had passed, the knights and the squires, along with the sergeants, had left the gatehouse to pursue the survivors. There were just my archers, the wounded, dead and the dying left on the charnel house that was the gate.

I saw that John of Nottingham knelt by Peter Crookback. I hurried over to them. I could see that Peter was dying. I could see his stomach laid open. He gave me a wan smile. "I did not get to serve you long, Captain. I envy John and the others. They will become famous."

John of Nottingham said, "Hush, Peter. They have healers."

He shook his head. "Do not lie to a dying man, John of Nottingham. You are a good friend, and I have served alongside you these two years. Watch over the captain. He is a good man to follow, and give my…"

He said no more. The light left his eyes and my first archer had died. John closed the lids on his eyes. "He was a quiet man but there were none better."

"Captain, come, Stephen Green Feathers needs help."

I hurried to Robin's side. Stephen had a wound to the leg. He had lost blood and already he was pale. I went to the Arab I had killed and hacked a long piece from his bisht. I ran back and made a tourniquet above the wound. My honey and vinegar were in my quarters. "Robin, carry him. We will find the healers. John, take charge here. You know what you must do."

"Aye, Captain." The enemy wounded would be given a warrior's death and their bodies searched. It was what archers did. I went first with drawn sword. The sound of fighting had moved towards the outer walls as Lord Edward led our men to eliminate all opposition. My caution was rewarded. As I stepped off the last stone step, a Basque ran and leapt at me. He had been feigning death. My hunting experience came to my aid. I had once been helping Sir Henry as a beater when a wild boar had leapt at us. I had dropped to my knee and held the boar spear before me. The boar had impaled himself. I did the same with the Basque. I held my sword above me with two hands and it entered his groin and his own weight drove it deep within him. I then used his weight to throw the body over my shoulder. It cracked into the wall of the gatehouse but he was already dead. I rose and led Robin to the cathedral. There were healers in there.

There were many men being tended to. The priests all looked busy. I shouted, "Aid, I have a wounded man!" Robin faithfully followed me.

The nearest priest looked up and, seeing that we were archers, turned back to his ministrations. "You can wait until your betters are healed."

I know he was a priest but I was tempted to use the flat of my sword, which I still held, to teach him a lesson. However, it was not necessary for I heard Lord Edward's squire John say, "You will tend to him priest, or I will whip you myself. Those archers are the reason we won!"

"Yes, lord!" The priest hurried over to Stephen.

I walked to John, who lay on the floor. He too had a bandaged leg. He shook his head. "It was a lucky blow. I had felled a Basque, but the man was not dead and he stabbed me as I passed. It will hurt in the winter for he nicked the bone."

I nodded. "I was told to kill the Basques twice. It is good advice. We lost an archer."

"Then that is a grievous loss. You and your men broke the back of the attack. Lord Edward said that you would. In fact, he relied on it so that he could draw them to the gatehouse and then launch the surprise attack."

"It worked."

"Aye, and now we return to England. It may be a month or so before we leave, but we will be going home, and then you will have to find more archers. Lord Edward has seen their worth, and he wants twenty."

I nodded. I now had a dilemma. How did I go back to England without telling Lord Edward what I had done?

CHAPTER 8

In the end I decided to tell Lord Edward myself. I waited until we were at Bayonne, preparing to take ship. That way, if it went badly, I could leave quickly and head north to France. Both my archer, Stephen, and John, Lord Edward's squire, had healed while we had awaited ship. I had been trying to find an appropriate time to catch the prince alone. This was not the sort of news to speak in a public place. However, there were other matters which prevented a meeting. They were nothing to do with me. Other lords came to Bayonne to speak with my master. I learned much through John the squire. Whenever he was sent on errands to the camp he always passed our tents and spoke with us. From him we learned that not all was well. Lord Edward had allies who had promised funds for his campaign. The money had not been forthcoming. I knew nothing of Lord Edward before I had helped to rescue him, but from John, I learned that he had played a dangerous game. He had allied himself with his father's enemies. Now it had come to a head. Those enemies wanted him to join them in taking power from his father, King Henry.

My chance to speak came when Lord Edward and John rode into our camp. My men were in the town. I had given them the afternoon to enjoy themselves. I was alone, sharpening my sword when they approached.

"Gerald War Bow, are your men healed and ready?"

"Aye, lord, whom do we fight?"

"No one yet, but I have had enough of this treacherous place and the intrigues. We sail home for England, two days hence. Sell your horses, for we have no room for them on the ships. We will buy new, if we need them, in England."

I nodded.

He frowned at my lack of enthusiasm. "What is wrong Gerald? I had thought you would have been delighted to leave this disease-ridden, pestilential hole!"

I approached and dropped to a knee, "Lord Edward, I have a confession to make."

The young prince laughed. "I am no priest. God's blood but I have committed more sins than enough myself. Rise, you look ridiculous on your knee!"

I rose and forced myself to speak. I had committed the crime, and I had to take responsibility. "Lord, before I came to France I killed the knight I served."

The smile left his face and even John looked shocked. "An accident, Gerald?"

I shook my head. "No John. I wounded him with one arrow and slew him with a second."

Lord Edward's eyes narrowed. "You do not appear to drink too much, so you were not drunk. Was it murder?"

"No, lord, it was justice. He had hanged my father for no good reason. My father had killed his hunting hounds. The hounds killed his dog and threatened him. He did what he did to protect himself, and I did what the law should have done but did not."

"And who was this lord?"

119

"Henry of Clwyd."

John said, "He serves under Sir Ranulf. He is a knight of Chester."

I saw something akin to relief on Lord Edward's face. "I know this Sir Henry. He was a lout of a man, and as far as I can recall, averse to fighting." He picked up the sword I had been sharpening. "You have given me a problem." He balanced the sword in his hand. "If Sir Henry had been a lord anywhere else in England, then I would have had to take you back to stand trial for murder. You would be hanged."

I spied hope in his words.

"As he was one of my lords, then, as Earl of Chester, it is for me to mete out justice. Tell me, was the baron unarmed?"

"No, lord, he had his sword drawn and was advancing on me."

"Then it seems to me that it was self-defence. Your punishment for that crime is to make pilgrimage on foot from London to Canterbury. You must beg forgiveness at the tomb of Thomas Becket." He gave a grim smile. "If my ancestor King Henry had to do so, then so can you."

I nodded. "Thank you, lord."

"What would you have done if I had had you arrested?"

I looked him in the eyes. "I would have escaped and run, lord."

He stared at me and then burst out laughing. "God's blood, but I bet you would! You are an honest fellow, I will give you that. I am guessing that Gerald is not the name with which you were baptised." I shook my head. "Grow yourself a beard. You have been forgiven, and there is no longer a crime for which you have to answer, but I would not have you upset my knights when we return home."

They left, and I felt as though a weight had been lifted from my shoulders. It was as though I could breathe once more. When my men returned, I gave them the news that we would be going home. "Sell your horses and anything else that you cannot carry. From Lord Edward's words, space will be limited on the ships."

Some of the men were sad. They had become attached to their horses. That was especially true of me. My own horse had served me well and I felt guilty about leaving him, although, in truth, I had little choice in the matter. As luck would have it, we were able to sell them in the camp. There were other mercenaries there. They were part of the retinue of William de Valance, Lord Edward's uncle. They were about to leave and needed horses. John of Nottingham discovered this and arranged for them to come to inspect the animals. We knew we had to sell them, but the men of de Valance did not.

"These are fine animals. You must be desperate for money. Are you sure you do not want to hold onto them? We will all need them when we head north to fight in Aquitaine."

"Aquitaine?"

"Did you not know? Our lord is going to take some of King Henry's castles. There will be coin for everyone."

I looked at John of Nottingham and gave a slight shake of the head. "We did not know. We will still sell them. Silver is silver."

We agreed a price, and John and I shared the money equally between our men. We purchased that which we needed for the voyage and moved into the port. We bought supplies. We were all warriors for the working day. Who knew when food might be in short supply? We bought a ham and some of the spicy sausages that came from Spain. We found some hard cheese which would last the voyage and some of the oranges which could be bought at the local market. Finally, we bought two jugs of wine. We shared them out in our bags.

The coins meant we could afford a night in an inn. Thus it was that we witnessed, on the quayside, the argument between Lord Edward and his uncle. We were too far away to hear the words but it was acrimonious.

I could tell that from Lord Edward's red face. His uncle and his knights stormed through the streets, scattering market stalls in their wake.

Captain William, the leader of Lord Edward's men at arms, followed them. He approached our table. He was grinning. "Well Gerald War Bow, you had best get your men and their war gear to the quay. It seems we are no longer welcome here, and we sail for England. Yon cog, *Maid of Portsmouth* is your vessel. I should get aboard and find the best berths. It will be a crowded ship!"

I nodded. "Thank you, Captain. I am grateful." As he hurried off I said, "John, get our gear. I will pay our bill." We had been ready to move at a moment's notice. Our bow staves were in their cases, as were our arrows. The spare clothes we had were in canvas bags. By the time I had paid the innkeeper my men had carried our war gear to the quay.

When I got to the ship there was a large sailor blocking the gangplank. John of Nottingham was arguing with him.

"What is amiss, John of Nottingham?"

He jerked his head in the direction of the sailor. "This no-neck lowlife says that we must pay to board."

I used a reasonable voice, for I thought that the sailor had misunderstood. "We are Lord Edward's men. His captain, William, told us that we had berths on this ship."

He smiled. I noticed that his front teeth were missing. That was a sure sign that he was a brawler. He had the knotted arms of a sailor and the gut of a drinker. "I don't give a tinker's curse who you serve. Captain Alfred sails the ship, but I, Guthrum of Akethorpe, am the man who is in *charge* of the ship. You want an easy voyage, then you pay me."

I walked a little closer to him so that I could speak quieter. "Friend, we are coming aboard this ship, and if you try to bar our way, you will taste the sea! We are warriors, and we are not men to be crossed."

"You are mercenaries with pockets full of gold! Pay! One way or another you will pay me!"

"You will get out of my way, now!" I had pulled my dagger from my belt and I held it to his groin.

He looked down as I pushed it a little harder. He stepped out of the way. He spat into the sea. "One way or another, you will pay!"

When we reached the deck there were two men waiting for us. They must have seen what had happened and yet they said nothing. "I am Captain Alfred. My first mate, Jack of Lothnwistoft, will show you where you can stow your gear. It will be crowded. The men at arms of Captain William will be joining you."

As we followed the young sailor he said, "You should not have crossed Guthrum. He is an evil man."

"The captain saw what occurred?"

He nodded as we ducked below a small door and climbed down a ladder. "Guthrum keeps the crew in order. He is the captain's cousin."

John of Nottingham said, "If he tries anything with us, he will regret it."

I saw that we were in the hold of the ship. It had carried sheep, for there were still droppings on the deck. The sailor said, "Guthrum would have had this swept if you had paid him."

I laughed. "I think we can sweep a few sheep turds away!" I looked around the hold. The worst berth would be by the ladder. Men would be using it constantly to make water and to go on deck. There was a bulkhead at the bow end. "We will use here. Right boys, let us get rid of the sheep turds and make ourselves comfortable." I heard raised voices from the quay.

Jack of Lothnwistoft grinned. "I think your comrades have met Guthrum."

It did not take us long to clean the area of deck which was close to us. We used our bags with our war gear to create our own area. Our bow staves and arrows were placed close to the bulkhead where they were safe. I heard footsteps above us and then heard feet coming down the ladder. I recognised Ralph Dickson; he was, like Matthew, a sergeant at arms, and he was Captain William's lieutenant. As he came down I saw him wiping blood from his nose.

John of Nottingham said, "This looks like it will be an interesting voyage."

I had to walk with a bent back to reach Ralph, for the deck was low. "I am afraid there is sheep shit all over the deck. We have to clean."

He nodded. "I would like to clean it with that big bastard. He asked for money!"

"He asked us too. You did not pay him, did you?"

"No, and I have a bloody nose for my pains. He had better watch out."

"I think that the crew are afraid of him. We will watch out for each other, eh? How many of you are there?"

"Twenty. The captain sails with Lord Edward and the knights."

"There are just two ships then?"

"Aye. He paid off the rest of the men."

I pointed to the ladder. "We had best keep a clear passage to the upper deck. We may have to move in a hurry."

While the men sorted themselves out, we headed for the deck. This would be our last view of land until we struck England. Captain William was on the quay. Guthrum was glowering at him. I strode down the gangplank. For one moment, I thought the sailor would try to stop me leaving, then he thought better of it and stepped aside.

As soon as I stepped ashore, Guthrum strode back up the gangplank. Captain William was an old warrior. He had served with King Henry before following his son. He frowned. "Trouble? I saw he had a bloody knuckle."

"He seemed to think we had to pay to sail this ship. He struck Ralph Dickson."

"That is not good. Perhaps I should sail with you."

I smiled. "If you have a berth with Prince Edward, then I would say take it. This one is overcrowded as it is. It stinks of sheep."

"Aah. Then it will be a long voyage."

"Where do we land?"

"Lord Edward wishes to get to his father as soon as he can. We will sail up the Thames to Windsor. That may be why you had trouble. There is not as much profit for them. There will be no trade for them at Windsor. But Lord Edward has paid them well."

"It is not the captain who is the problem, just someone who thinks he can bully us. Fear not, we have faced worse in this campaign than a handful of sailors!"

He clasped my arm. "Fare you well. I will see you in Windsor. We will be at the castle for a while." He leaned in. "I think the son goes to make peace with his father."

I nodded. My thoughts were with my own father. I had not had the opportunity to say farewell to him.

We were ready to sail long before the other ship. I saw more supplies being taken aboard the larger ship, commissioned by Lord Edward. Jack of Lothnwistoft was walking by as I joined John of Nottingham at the ship's waist. "What about food on this ship?"

John of Nottingham asked, "And ale?"

The sailor looked around to see if Guthrum was close by. "It is cold rations. We have ship's biscuits. We call it 'hardtack'. We have oats, and there is water to make a cold porridge. We have two barrels of water and one of ale."

John of Nottingham said, "That is it? No meat? No hot food?"

He shook his head. "Fire is dangerous on a wooden ship, and you did not pay Guthrum." He grinned. "A little tip before you eat the hardtack. Tap it on the deck. There are little weevils that live within it."

He went off and I called, "Robin of Barnsley, watch our gear. Come, John, let us go ashore."

"What for?"

"We will buy bread. Even stale bread will be better than the hardtack he spoke of."

We found a bakery close to the port. I knew its prices would be higher than those in the town. They relied on people such as we, who had to buy bread for the voyage. We bought ten four-pound loaves. It cost far more than it should, but it would last us for at least a sennight. Even when stale, we could dunk it in the ale and soften it. As we stepped aboard, Ralph Dickson and his men at arms were taking the air. They looked at the bread.

"Do we not get fed?"

I nodded towards a grinning Guthrum. "It is cold porridge and hard biscuits we eat. This was not cheap but..."

"I hear what you are saying, Captain of Archers." He waved to two of his men. "Come, let us copy the archers."

It was after dark when we sailed. We followed our larger consort. Lord Edward's standard, with the two lions on the red background, fluttered from his masthead. It told the world that the heir to the throne was aboard. We stayed on deck, where the salt spray made it unpleasant. The sea became even choppier, and we soon retired below deck. With the hold filled with men and their war gear, it was crowded and it was dark. We had a candle but it was secured in a box, which kept it safe. It was a glow rather than a light. During the day some light had drifted down through the door, which we left open, but at night...

Two ship's boys brought our food. It was cold porridge and water.

There were no beakers and no platters. My archers all had their own. We had made them from wood when we had been in the camp. It had passed the time, and now we were grateful. Some of the men at arms had their own, but half did not, and they had to either share or do as I saw two men do: use their helmets.

We declined the porridge. We had supplies, and we would only eat it when those ran out. We took the water for it would eke out our wine. As we ate Ralph Dickson came over. "I can see we have much to learn from you archers."

I nodded and sliced a piece of sausage for him. "Aye, I am guessing that Guthrum and that baker work together, but at least we all have bread. We will not starve."

Ralph pointed to his men. "We did not bring as many loaves as you. This voyage cannot be over soon enough for me."

The first night was, in many ways, the worst. Some of the men at arms had been in Gascony all of their lives and had never sailed. The night was filled with the sound of footsteps racing up the ladder and then men emptying the contents of their stomachs over the side. I did not get much sleep.

When dawn broke I went on deck. The seas were rough. The other cog disappeared in troughs and then rose on waves as we ploughed north. I saw that the helmsman was the grinning Guthrum. He had cost us money but he had not beaten us. When my men awoke they joined me. "Let us eat up here. Some of the men at arms did not make the ladder last night. Until they clean it, this will be the sweeter place to eat."

We broke our fast beneath grey skies and on a deck which canted and rolled in the grey seas of Biscay. I had endured worse conditions in Wales. At least it was not raining! The men at arms joined us but many did not eat. That would be a mistake. The ship's boys brought round the porridge and the water again. I tried the porridge. A man would have to be desperate to eat it.

Archers need to exercise their arms each day, and after we had eaten, we fetched our bows and drew them. We each had our own regimen. Mine was to pull the string all the way to my ear and hold it for a count of twenty. I would release and then count ten. I did this action thirty times. Then I would unstring my bow and restring it. By the time I had used all six bowstrings, my muscles burned, and I knew that I had exercised. After two days the men at arms joined us. They had the wooden staves they used to carry their war gear. They practised with those. It was to stop boredom more than anything else. When we were not practising, we spoke of our lives before our service with the prince. We came to know each other better. There were still secrets. They knew about Delamere forest and that I had been an outlaw but not the crime. I would tell them one day.

Six days into our journey, we had a break from our boring routine. Our consort stopped. Our captain reefed his sails so that we did not career into her stern. I wondered if there was a problem. Then I saw a ship approaching. I could not make out the standard, but if Lord Edward had stopped, then it was a friend and not a foe. The two ships bobbed at hailing distance and we endured the uncomfortable motion as our cog rose and fell. We were smaller than the other two ships and the motion more accentuated. I was relieved when we were able to lower our sails and continue our journey.

As we neared the coast of England our supplies of bread finally ran out. We had shared our last two loaves, our ham and cheese with the men at arms. Some had been so ill in the first half of the journey that we feared they might not survive without real food. It meant that, for the last two days, we ate porridge and drank stale water. I thought, when we began to sail down the Thames, that our ordeal was over, but it was not. We tacked back and forth up the twisting, turning Thames. Ironically, we could have sailed the river faster, for we were smaller, but we had to sail behind our consort. It added to the agony of the four men at arms who had suffered the most.

We passed the White Tower. No standard flew. The king was not there. Then we left the city that was London and sailed the last few miles to Windsor. It was King Henry's favourite castle and he had done much to make it a palace. For myself, I just wanted to be off the cog. We had to wait, for there was only space for one ship at a time, and Prince Edward had priority. Now that we were in England we would call him "Prince". Captain William had told us that before we left Bayonne.

When it was our turn, we were all ready waiting with our war gear. Ralph and I had agreed that the four sick men at arms could leave first. We waited at the waist while the ship was tied to the quay and then the gangplank lowered. The prince, the knights and their servants had departed by the time we were ready to disembark. Only Captain William stood waiting for us.

Guthrum stood at the gangplank. Whenever he had had the chance he had made our lives hard. It was not just the food. He had had his sailors leave ropes and handspikes lying to trip the unwary going to make water in the dark of night. He had not caught my archers, but two of the younger men at arms, who had been the most unwell, had fallen and suffered sprains as a result. His leering face invited a fist. As the four most in need left, he put out a foot and, after tripping the third, pushed the fourth, so that all four tumbled down the gangplank. Their war gear fell into the river. I had had enough. I was bigger than Ralph, and I was a captain of archers. Handing my gear to John of Nottingham, I strode up to the laughing Guthrum.

"Go to the river and fetch their war gear."

His face darkened, "Puppy, you may order these arse lickers about but not me. Go to hell and fetch them yourself!"

He stood belligerently with fists bunched. I half-turned to Ralph, "I tried, Ralph!" Before he knew it, I had swung and hit him in the gut with all the power in my left arm. It was a mighty blow and he doubled up. I brought back my right arm and smashed it up into his face. I heard his nose break. His head jerked back and he flew over the side of the cog. There was a splash as he hit the water. Our men cheered.

I turned to the captain who was standing by the stern and I shouted, "Captain Alfred, you are a piss-poor captain. You were paid good money by Prince Edward. We were treated worse than slaves. If I ever see you again, pirate, you will receive worse than Guthrum."

"You threaten me on my own ship!"

I was angry. This was the culmination of the privations of the voyage. Before I could race to him, Ralph and four of his men had run the length of the ship. They picked him up and dumped him over the stern.

I glared at the rest of the crew. "Anyone else wish to voice a complaint?"

Jack of Lothnwistoft shook his head. "No archer. I think the lesson has been learned."

We stepped off the ship. The four men had retrieved their war gear when it had caught on the bank. Guthrum was pulling himself one-handed up the bank. His other hand lay at an awkward angle. It had broken in the fall.

The captain also pulled himself ashore. He stood dripping and waved a hand at us all. "You will pay for this!"

John of Nottingham walked up to him and said, quietly, "Do you really wish to make enemies of us?" He took out his dagger. "Your

Guthrum might frighten your sailors, but believe me, if we wished you harm…"

He left the rest unsaid. We strode along the road towards Captain William. He had a bemused look upon his face. "I can see that you have taught my men at arms some bad habits."

I smiled. "It is never a bad habit to punish bullies and thieves. That is what they are. You, Captain you ate well?" He nodded. I pointed to the four men who had come down the gangplank first. "Let us hope that we do not need these men to fight anytime soon. They are in no condition, and the rest of us will need time to recover."

He leaned in to me. "You may be prescient, Gerald War Bow. When we stopped in the channel, the ship brought news that Simon de Montfort and his allies are back in England, and they are stirring trouble against the king."

I remembered what the men at arms, to whom we had sold our horses, had said. Was this the same plot? "And the prince? You know him better than I do."

He looked around to make sure that we were not being overheard. "There are some who think that the prince sides with the king's enemies. For myself, I do not believe it. When he was growing up, he was led astray by uncles and cousins, who sought to use him against his father. I have seen a change. I have served them both. Prince Edward is the better warrior. If he turned against the king…" He looked up at me. "You saved his life, and his squire says that he likes you. What do you think?"

I rubbed my chin. My beard had grown and it still felt uncomfortable. "I do not think he is a traitor. He would fight for the king. Will he have to?"

"De Montfort is a good leader. He is ambitious. We will have to fight them." He turned and waved his men forward. "Come, we shall sleep under a roof this night." Then to me he said, "Keep this counsel, eh Gerald? One warrior to another."

"Of course."

The castle was most impressive. Built for William, it had been added to by successive kings. Now that Henry had made it a palace, it would be the preferred home for the royal family. It was away from the unpredictable mob that was London. They could be bought and bribed. The people of London did not care about England. They cared about themselves first and London second. I thought that the king had been wise to make this choice.

We had quarters in the lower ward. The king and his knights were in the upper ward. We settled into a routine while we awaited orders. I had butts set up in the lower ward and we practised each day. Better fed, we soon recovered from the voyage, and I saw that our skills and strength had not diminished. It was ten days after our return that Prince Edward and John, his squire, came into the lower ward. Captain William and his men at arms were practising too. The prince called over the captain and me.

"I am pleased to see that you are practising. We may need your skills soon enough." He glanced at me. "It seems that when I am not there to watch you, then you get into trouble."

"Trouble, my lord?"

"Breaking a sailor's jaw and arm do not constitute trouble?"

There was little point in explaining and so I just bowed my head. "Sorry, my lord."

When I looked up I saw the hint of a smile on his face. "Good, we understand one another. We have been set a task. We are to go to Wales. Llywelyn ap Gruffudd needs to be taught a lesson. Each summer the Welsh raid for six weeks. It is, apparently, a tribal tradition. They have laid waste to parts of the land around the Conway." He looked at me. "You know the area, I believe?"

I shifted uncomfortably. "Yes, lord. I was raised there."

"Then you have one month to hire another fifteen archers. I would have twenty archers and twenty men at arms in my retinue."

I nodded. "Do you care where they are from, lord?"

I saw Captain William cock his head to one side and the prince frowned. "What do you mean?"

"Do you want good archers?"

"Of course."

"Then I shall seek them in the forests of Yorkshire and Nottingham."

His squire, John, said, "Outlaws?"

"I was an outlaw in Delamere Forest. I have not asked, but I would guess that John of Nottingham and Robin of Barnsley would know of good archers who live in the forest, even if they were not outlaws themselves."

I saw Prince Edward taking the prospect in. "When you saved my life it came at a price, archer! Very well. They must swear to be honest men; on a Bible. I will have John fetch one along with a warrant. You are on my business. Come to the stables on the morrow and get horses." He turned and left.

I shook my head. "A month only!"

Captain William said, "Aye, and if they are men who live beyond the law, why should they choose to serve the next king?"

"Because the life of an outlaw is not a good one. All of the outlaws I joined are now dead. Life is short in the greenwood. Do not believe all the songs from troubadours." I nodded. "At least we have something to do. All of this practice dulls my men's fighting edge. A trip into the dangerous world of outlaws may be just what we need."

CHAPTER 9

We headed up the Roman Road which led to the north. My guess had been accurate. Both John of Nottingham and Robin of Barnsley had served in outlaw bands. They had both been very young, and, like me, their time with them had been brief. The prince had only sent money for the journey. He had not sent coin to hire archers. I thought that a bad idea. I had brought some of my own coins with me. It would be a good investment. We travelled light, with just one spare sumpter. Any men we hired would have to walk back to Windsor, where we were mustering the army which would march to Wales.

"Where is the best place to begin, John of Nottingham? The forest?"

He laughed. "From what you told us of your time in Delamere forest, Captain, that would be the worst place to start. There is a tavern built into the stone upon which Nottingham castle sits. They brew fine ale there."

"We have a month! The less time we spend drinking, the better."

"You misunderstand me, Captain. It is an alehouse which is frequented by those who know the outlaws. Outlaws cannot exist for long without help. They are outlaws, but they are also men, and that is how we will find them. I know not who they are now, but the alehouse will be a good place to begin."

As we now wore the livery of Prince Edward, we did not look like ruffians. It meant that we were not closely questioned as we rode through the towns which had walls and gates. Our bows and swords did not attract attention. However, they were the only benefits. Prices for food and ale were higher, as traders thought we could afford it. The feed and stables cost us more too. England is an expensive country.

When we reached Leicester we were in de Montfort land. Simon de Montfort was Earl of Leicester. We were within half a day's ride of Nottingham. We found an inn with a stable and were enjoying a meal when we were approached. I did not recognise the livery. It was a rampant white lion on a red background. I learned later that it was the sign of Simon De Montfort. The oak-like arms of the man and his broad chest told me that he was an archer. He wore a wrist-guard which confirmed it. He had a jug of ale with him.

"May I offer you lads a drink? I too am an archer; Wilfred of Melton."

I nodded. "I have never yet refused ale. I am Gerald War Bow."

He smiled as he topped up our beakers. "I have heard of you. I am Hugh of Bolsover. I am captain of the earl's archers. You serve Lord Edward?"

"Prince Edward."

"My mistake. I forgot he was in England. The Earl of Leicester is also in England. I would make you an offer. Serve my lord and I will double whatever the prince is paying you."

"You know not what we are paid. We could make up a figure."

He supped his ale and shrugged. "Whatever you say, we will pay. I can see that you are all experienced archers. You look young, Gerald War Bow, but I have heard of your reputation. The earl was in Gascony, and your exploits were told around our campfires."

"Then you know that we are Prince Edward's men. I thank you for your offer, but we must decline."

He looked at the others. "Does your captain make all your decisions?"

John of Nottingham nodded. "He does. But know this, Captain of Archers, we agree with all of them!"

The captain snatched up the jug and stormed off.

"We have made another friend, Captain."

"I know, Robin." I had watched the man as he had spoken. I did not like his face, which looked shifty. "I think that he just wanted us away from Prince Edward. There is a war coming, and this Earl of Leicester seeks to make the board suit his pieces. It is even more urgent that we hire archers now."

It took three days to reach Nottingham. In the days of King John it had been a much more important castle than it was now. Even so, it was as busy a place as I had seen. We arrived on market day and there were many people in the city. For the first time we were able to eat cheaply. We found a stable not far from the alehouse. It was called "The Saddle". An old saddle hung above the door. We did not go in. With our bows in their cases, we walked the markets. That was my idea. I wanted other archers to see the five of us wearing livery and with our bows. When we spread the word it would travel quicker. We visited the stalls and spent a few copper coins. Though the food that we were able to buy was cheaper than that in the inns, it was of dubious quality. The rabbit we ate looked remarkably like rat to me! We found a room for the five of us. It was next to the stables. For that reason it was cheaper than the others, for it was a large stable and there were many horses. The smell filled our room.

It was getting on for dusk when we headed back to the alehouse. The market had finished and traders were heading home. We had spied cutpurses and charlatans at the market and they now headed for the alehouses and taverns to spend their gains. They would steer clear of five archers. We had swords and muscles. There were easier targets than us.

The alehouse had food. It was not the best food we had ever eaten. It was pea and ham soup with barley bread. I suspect they had shown the soup the ham bone, for I could find precious little evidence of ham in the soup. It was, however, filling. The ale was better. The brewhouse also served the castle and was in the sandstone rocks behind the alehouse. That first night was a scouting expedition. We were looking for signs of our prey: archers. We saw none, but the lures we laid would, hopefully, reap rewards. We asked if there were any archers who were seeking work. We could not afford to spend more than a couple of days in Nottingham. If this failed then we would move further north, to Sheffield. Each mile we travelled further north made our journey home that much longer.

As we walked back to our inn we were followed. If we had turned around we would not have seen anyone, but an archer who is a hunter has a sense of such things. Once we were in the room we would share, David the Welshman confirmed that we were being followed. "There were two of them trailing us. I didn't see them but…"

John of Nottingham seemed satisfied. "That is what I thought too, Captain. They probably suspected we are from the castle and the sheriff's men. Tomorrow we will see if the fishes bite."

Even though I was not worried we took precautions. Robin of Barnsley slept behind the door. No one was getting in without waking him.

The next morning we went to see to the horses and then we split into two groups. I went with Robin of Barnsley. The other two went with John. I thought it more likely that we might be approached if we were in a smaller group. It took until the middle of the afternoon. We had been to the centre and waited outside the church. Pilgrims had been entering and leaving for most of the day. It was often that way after a market day. Those who travelled a long way frequently stayed the night and then visited the church before leaving for home. When you lived close to the mighty forest, then God's help, and whatever saint you could summon, was always welcome.

We were about to turn when two cloaked figures approached. Both had the build of an archer, albeit an underfed archer. They kept their voices low, and as I looked them up and down, I saw daggers beneath their cloaks; they were pointed at us. I saw that there were few people around. They had chosen their moment well. I liked that. One was a taller man, almost my height. I could not see his face, for he was hooded. The other was slightly shorter, but I could see that his nose had been split by a blade. It looked deliberate. It was normally the punishment for poaching rabbits.

"Do not move suddenly or summon help. If you do, then you are both dead men." It was the hooded man who spoke.

I smiled. "Why would we run? We have been seeking archers, and you have found us. Besides, if we wished it, then we would have those daggers and you would be our prisoners."

They both started at that. "Cocky! And a Welshman too!"

I feigned outrage. "Do not insult us! I am Gerald War Bow and I am English. This is Robin of Barnsley. We come here looking for archers to serve Prince Edward."

"How do we know that you are not the sheriff's men?"

"Firstly, we wear the livery of Prince Edward, and secondly, you followed us last night and know where we slept. We would not pay for lodgings when we could sleep in the castle. I am Gerald War Bow and I am the captain of Prince Edward's archers."

The one with the split nose said, "It sounds right, Peter."

"I told you, no names! I do not trust them."

I smiled. "Then let us go our separate ways. You are obviously too fearful for us. You would rather hide in the wood and eat short rations. You prefer a damp greenwood to a roof and a bed. You would rather make your own clothes than have the money to buy them. I am sorry to have wasted your time, Peter, although, as you accosted us, I suspect that there is an interest in our offer."

Split Nose smiled. He pushed his hood back and I saw that he was an older man. He was losing his hair. "Peter is the suspicious type. The sheriff hanged his brother for poaching two years since." He put his dagger in his belt. "I am Jack of Lincoln. We would get paid?"

"You would."

"But we are outlaws."

"As was I. You would swear to be honest." I took out the warrant. I doubted that they could read, but the seal would impress them. "This is my warrant. Now I need an answer. I seek more than one man." I looked pointedly at Peter. "And we would be gone from here by tomorrow."

Peter said, "That could be true. Your eyes do not lie and you are no coward. I wondered at the sheriff sending one so young. His killers are older men." He sheathed his dagger. "You need more archers?"

"We do."

"Then we may be able to help you, but not here in Nottingham. The sheriff has his spies. If you say you head home tomorrow, where would home be?"

"The prince's army musters at Windsor, so it would be south."

"Then we will meet you on the road to Leicester."

I took two coins from my purse. "Then here is the metal to seal the agreement."

"We could run and never see you again."

139

"Then I would have lost a couple of coins, and you would have lost the chance for a new life, free and clear."

Jack nodded. "Until the morrow."

We headed back to the alehouse, where we had said we would meet the others. "Two is not fifteen, Captain."

"No, and I do not think that we will find the number we need on the morrow. We will have to seek the rest elsewhere. It is a start. If we are heading for the land of the Clwyd and the Conway, then we might get some from there."

"The prince wants them now, Captain."

"Then he should have given us longer."

The others had had no success. I said, quietly, "There are spies of the sheriff watching us. See if you can see them, and do not talk of our quest until we are in our room."

John answered me straight away. "There were two men by the door. I saw them yesterday. They drink little and they watch everyone. When you and Robin entered, then one left. Do you want us to do anything about them?"

"No. It will not serve us. Let them watch. We leave in the morning."

David the Welshman cocked an eye. "When we are in the room, then all will be revealed."

John of Nottingham nodded. "We spent the day enjoying the delights of Nottingham. David here must have a woman he has an eye on. He bought some lace in the town. He paid a pretty price too!"

Nottingham was famous for its lace, but it was not cheap.

David shook his head. "You are a fool, John of Nottingham, it *is* for a woman, but it is for my mother."

Stephen Green Feathers remarked, "Your mother!"

"You say 'mother' like you think I was hatched from beneath a rock!

Of course I have a mother, and if we going to the land around Conway, then we will be passing close by Wrechcessham. My mother lives there."

"Wrechcessham is in Powys. We lost that land twenty years since."

"Unless Prince Edward plans on a longer march north into the land around Nantwich, then he will have to pass by Wrechcessham. I have not seen her this twenty years."

Stephen said, quietly, voicing what we all thought, "Then she may be dead."

Equally quietly Stephen said, "Then I will leave the lace upon her grave."

We left the alehouse after some more of their food, with its dubious meat. Once in the room I told them all about our latest recruits.

John of Nottingham said, "This Jack of Lincoln, did he have a split nose?"

"Aye, he did."

"I know of him. I never met him, but it is said he led the outlaws for a time." John shrugged at our questioning looks. "I told you, I ran with outlaws for a while. We were not the same band, but he was said to be a fine archer. He had his nose split by the Constable of Lincoln when he was but seven summers old. He had poached rabbits to feed his family. When they died he joined the outlaws. If he is considering leaving the forest then these must be desperate times."

I felt more hopeful. We paid our bill and saddled our horses. I had Robin buy plenty of food for the journey and we made sure that our ale skins were full. We headed out of town, using the south gate. I knew that we would be followed by the sheriff's men. I did not wish to alarm our would-be archers, and so I had David the Welshman leave us at the first crossroads. We made an act of saying farewell. We rode another half mile and then stopped at a small wood. The road had bent around the wood, and we were able to shelter in its eaves. We heard the hooves of the sheriff's men's horses as they hurried to catch us. With arrows nocked, the four of us stepped out. We took them by surprise. One tumbled from his horse and the other tried to whip his horse's head around to make his escape. David the Welshman had his sword at his throat before he had travelled twenty paces.

"Whom do you work for, and why do you follow us?" They were silent. I looked up and down the empty road, exaggerating my movements as I did so. "This is an empty road. You have two horses and, I have no doubt, fat purses. What is to stop us cutting your throats and taking what you have?"

To emphasise my point David pricked the skin of one of them and blood dripped down. It had the desired effect.

"We are the sheriff's men and if you kill us you will be hunted. He knows that Prince Edward's men were in the town."

I realised then that this was something bigger than just curiosity. "Answer this question, and we will let you live." They both nodded. "Were the Earl of Leicester's men in Nottingham in the last month?"

The one with the pricked neck said, "Aye, the earl himself led them! How did you know?"

I tapped my nose. "Get you back and tell the sheriff that treachery comes at a price. Now turn and ride back. If you follow us then you will die."

They needed no urging and they left. John asked, "What was that about, Captain?"

"There is a plot here. The Earl of Leicester returns to England at the same time as the prince. He has had a falling out with the prince. It is known that the Earl of Leicester is no friend to King Henry. I see a conspiracy. This is de Montfort land. We must tread carefully. We will avoid Leicester. We were seen heading north to Nottingham. Wilfred of Melton will be waiting for us."

The outlaws were good. We neither saw nor smelled them. They just seemed to materialise from the scrubby, overgrown hedgerow by the dilapidated hut. There were ten of them. Jack of Lincoln was the oldest. There were some who were younger than I was. One looked to be barely fourteen summers but he already had an archer's chest. Five bows were aimed at us.

I spread my hands. "We are here, Jack of Lincoln. There is no need to aim arrows at us unless your intention is to rob us."

"Just being careful, Gerald War Bow."

A man appeared behind us; eleven. He shouted, "No one following, Jack." His voice was heavy with suspicion. It was as though he did not believe us.

"How did you get out without the sheriff's men following you?" Jack asked.

"They did follow us," I smiled. "We discouraged them." He nodded and waved his hands so that the bows were lowered. "Have you thought about our offer?"

"The ones you see here are willing to think about it, Captain, but not all are convinced. For myself, I am getting too old to sleep on soggy leaves. I have joints which now ache in the cold. I will swear on your Bible. As for the others, they are here. They will listen."

I slipped from my saddle and took out the Bible. I handed it to John, who nodded. I turned to the others. "It is simple, lads. If you will swear on the Bible to give up your brigandage, then I will give you a coin, and you will join my company of archers. We fight for two things: Prince Edward and for ourselves. Whatever we take from the battlefield we share equally. If one of us dies then the others share his coin. It is no more complicated than that. Prince Edward will clothe you, feed you, house you and I will pay you." I spread my arms. "Decide now. If you wish to follow, then welcome, and if not, then fare ye well."

They looked at each other. I heard Jack of Lincoln as he swore.

Turning to my men, I said, "Let us take off our livery and don cloaks. I fear that the next part of the journey may be hazardous."

They dismounted and did as I did, slipping off my surcoat and rolling it up. With just our old cloaks we would be anonymous.

Jack of Lincoln laughed and pointed at the others. "You wait? Where is another offer? Peter of Wakefield, you spoke with this captain. Did he strike you as dishonest?"

The suspicious man we had met shook his head and nodded. "I will swear. Like Jack of Lincoln, I have had enough of a life without bread."

It was like a dam being broken. The others all joined him. I pointed to the sumpter. "I thank you Jack of Lincoln. You can ride the sumpter."

He laughed. "You think me old and I will slow you down."

"I will not lie; that was my thinking."

"You may be right. Tell me, Captain. How did you become a captain when so young? I mean no offence."

"And none is taken. I saved the life of Prince Edward. My companion, who was also an outlaw, died. The men who follow me were chosen by me."

He gave me a shrewd look. "And if we do not meet your standards?"

"Those who are not made of the right wood will be paid off. They will have more money than they do now."

"That is reasonable. And our route?"

"We will head south and west to avoid Leicester. Such a large body of men will be noticed on the Great Road. We will head through the back roads south of the Trent. It is quieter there and the roads frequented less."

"Six days then."

"To get to Windsor?" He nodded. "With men walking, aye."

John of Nottingham said, "They are all sworn, Captain."

"Then give them all some food, for our journey is a long one. Stephen Green Feathers, take us down the road to Ashby. David, ride a mile behind us."

Jack had a hunk of bread in his hand and a piece of cheese. "You are a careful man."

"I am."

We made good time and travelled almost thirty miles. We camped in the woods north of the small town of Hinckley. We were still deep in the heart of de Montfort country, and we made a defensive camp in a dell, deep in the wood. There was a stream and enough wild brambles for us to cut and make a barrier which would warn us of any danger.

I watched my new and old men get to know one another. John spoke at length with Jack of Lincoln. Jack did not remember him, but they had acquaintances in common. This was how bonds between warriors were made. We had done the same with the men at arms when we had been aboard the ship. When we fought, it would be fighting for more than the lions upon our chests. We would fight for the men with whom we had shared ale and bread.

I set sentries; I would have the middle shift. I was about to roll into my blanket when Jack of Lincoln came over. "You did not tell us the whole truth, Captain."

"I did not lie."

"No, but you did not tell us the scale of your deeds. Your youth made me doubt you, but I can see now that your fresh beard hides more than a youthful face. The men I brought will not let you down. Even Dick, son of Robin, the youngest of our band, is a reliable warrior."

I nodded. "I never doubted it, but as we both know, Jack of Lincoln, the proof will come not on a ride through England but when we face men on horses who try to kill us."

He nodded. "Good night, Captain."

Trouble found us the next day. John of Nottingham and Ralph, son of Richard, were the scouts. They hurried back to us when we were north of the village of Rocheberie. I had been contemplating buying food there, for we were short on supplies. The arrival of my scouts drove that thought from me.

"Captain, there are men waiting for us. Some are in the village and others hide in the woods along the trail we would take if we wished to avoid the village."

"Are they hiding in the village?"

"No, Captain, the six men there are openly walking about. The ten in the woods are hiding. They have an ambush prepared. I saw, beneath the cloak of one of them, the livery of de Montfort."

We had a dilemma. If we turned back or tried to head east we risked running into more of them. If the sheriff had been one of de Montfort's men, he would have sent a message to his master. The captain of archers already knew of us. My reputation and my name had brought us into danger.

"We need to set off this trap. Jack of Lincoln, remember that of which we spoke last night?"

"Aye, Captain."

"These men know not of you. They are waiting for five archers and six horses. We will give them that. I wish you and your men to get ahead of us and ambush the ambushers."

"You trust us to save you?"

"When we fight in the wars, Jack of Lincoln, we will do that each time we fight. Our lives are in your hands."

He dismounted. "We will not let you down. Give us to the count of two hundred, Captain."

As they trotted off, I said, "We will use swords. Ride in twos. Stephen, drop the sumpter when we are attacked."

As we set off I slipped my sword in and out of its scabbard. It was sharp. John pointed at the trail and we left the road and entered the wood. It was a mixture of elm, rowan and oak. There were hawthorn, elder and blackberry bushes. It was perfect ambush country. The trail twisted and turned. If these were archers we faced then that helped us. They would have to wait until a straight part of the trail before they could attack. The trail was barely wide enough for two horses. That meant John and I were a big target. The waiting made me nervous. I was waiting for the sound of a twang which would tell me I was about to die. When the twang came it just told me where they were. Twenty paces from me one of my men cried out and fell to the ground with an arrow in his back. I dug my heels in and jerked my reins. I went to the right of the trail and John the left.

My sudden movement took one of the ambushers who was armed with a sword and shield by surprise. He looked at his comrade for help. I swept the sword from behind me. I was not a skilled swordsman. I did not need to be. With my powerful arms and the speed of my horse, I smashed the shield into the air and the edge of my sword tore through the man's face. I wheeled left and rode at the archer who was trying to aim at me. Behind me, I heard John's horse and then the cry of the man I had wounded as Robin despatched him. The archer released but it was hurried, and I was already jinking to the side. He had no shield and I brought my sword down on his unprotected head. My arm jarred as I split his skull.

In the distance I heard the sound of men fleeing. I whirled around, but all I could hear around me were the moans of dying men. I reined in. "Is anyone hurt?"

My archers, old and new, called out their names. We had caught them by surprise. Already the bodies were being stripped. David and Stephen led four horses. "We have their mounts."

I nodded. A plan was forming in my mind. "Dick, son of Robin, head towards the village and watch for the rest of de Montfort's men. David, take the five spare horses down the trail. Do not worry about making noise. I do not need you to be hidden. Halt when you reach the edge of the woods."

They looked at me quizzically but they did not argue. I dismounted and picked up the body of the archer I had slain. My men had already taken his arrows, dagger and coins. I saw that he had de Montfort's livery beneath his cloak. I lifted him up and draped his arms through the branches of the elder before me. I put his bow in his hands.

"Put the other bodies like this one and then hide. I want them to attack their own dead when they come."

Peter of Wakefield said, "You think they will come?"

John of Nottingham laughed. "Do as he says. You will learn to trust his senses."

There were six bodies, laid in the trees by the trail. Dick, son of Robin, ran in. "They are coming. Four horsemen and the rest on foot."

I slapped my horse and it galloped off behind me. It was a good horse, and when its reins fell, it would stop. I drew my sword and stood behind the body of the archer I had killed. The men of Leicester were loud as they hurtled through the woods. They still thought there were but five of us. An arrow thudded into the body before me. It must have touched the bow the corpse held, for the weapon fell to the ground.

A voice shouted, "They are waiting here! No quarter!"

A rider galloped towards what he thought was a corpse. It was, but it was a corpse with a sword behind it. As the rider rode past the dead archer, I stepped out and swung my sword two-handed into the rider's back. He had no mail and my sword hacked through to his spine. Arrows flew, and two other riders fell from their horses. A figure suddenly leapt into the air and knocked the last rider from his horse. Peter of Wakefield drew his dagger and slit the horseman's throat. With the riders dead, the rest fled. This time they would not stop running until they reached Leicester, and that would be after dark.

I lifted the cloak of the rider. He was one of de Montfort's men. He had a healthy purse, and his leather boots suggested that this was a sergeant at arms. I took his dagger and his sword. Jack of Lincoln approached. I threw him the sword and the belt. "Here, I am guessing you know how to use this."

"Aye, Captain. That was as neat an ambush as I have ever seen. You know the greenwood."

I nodded. "I do."

We quickly recovered our horses. We now had nine. With men riding double we could make better time. David the Welshman was waiting at the edge of the road. The road from the village passed nearby.

"Come, let us ride. I want as much distance as we can twixt us and Leicester. If we ride the road our trail will go cold."

CHAPTER 10

We reached Windsor three days later. Riding the horses along the road had helped, and then we had taken to the trails through the woods. I had sent John of Nottingham into Aylesbury to buy food. We had fewer than forty miles to go but we needed nourishment. It was dark when we entered the lower ward. We knew the guards. They had been on the ship with us from Bayonne.

Tall Alan cocked his head to one side. He took in the new men and the horses. "I can see there will be a tale over the table this night, Captain."

"There will indeed." I turned to John of Nottingham. "Take the horses to the stables and then the men to the guard room. I will go and inform the prince that we have more men."

The sentry said, "Begging your pardon sir, but Lord Edward is not here. Captain William went with him and half the men to London." He leaned in conspiratorially. "From what I heard, Captain, some of the barons are getting above themselves. They are challenging the king. The prince went to sort them out."

It sounded like gossip but there could be a nugget of truth in it. It seemed I had arrived back just in time. I went to the upper ward to speak with the constable. Sir Hugh D'Avranches was an old knight. He had been wounded in one of King Henry's campaigns in Wales. He was now the castellan. I liked him. He reminded me of my father. He had been a warrior all of his life. Like my father, he had expected to die on the battlefield. He was at the entrance to the upper ward and he saw me approach. He frowned when he saw that I was not wearing my livery.

"Captain Gerald, where is your surcoat?"

"I am sorry, my lord. When we were in Leicester we were attacked by the Earl of Leicester's men. It seemed a good idea to hide our identity."

He stared at me as though I had spoken a foreign language. "Come, I would hear more of this." He led me to an anteroom by the Great Hall. He nodded to the sentry. "We will not be disturbed."

I told him all, including the attempt to recruit the four of us. "I know the prince asked for fifteen archers, but it seemed better to come with what I had, rather than lose them all."

"You made the right decision. I confess I worried that appointing such a young captain of archers was a mistake. Perhaps I was wrong. And you have eight horses too?"

"Yes, my lord. The prince wants us to be mounted archers."

"A good idea. I will find another two for you and send over the surcoats and breeks for the new men. You will be needed by the end of the month."

"It is getting onto autumn, lord. I lived in that part of the world. It is hard enough campaigning in summer. In autumn and winter it is almost impossible."

"Nevertheless, Prince Edward is determined to show his mettle. For myself, I approve the change wrought in him. Something in Gascony changed him."

"Perhaps it was his brush with death, lord. Near death can have that effect."

He smiled. "Wise too. I shall watch you, young Gerald. Next time, change into your surcoats before you enter the castle. Make an old curmudgeon happy, eh?"

My new men had all been allocated a bed. The rest of the garrison was eating in the refectory. John of Nottingham looked at the new recruits and said, "Welcome to your new home. You will all be issued new clothes." He looked at me and I nodded. "I have lived in the woods and know what it is like. Without meaning offence, you lads need to bathe! We are lucky here, there is somewhere for us to sluice down."

A few of the new men glowered belligerently at him. I wondered if he had gone too far. Jack of Lincoln said, "And I for one am grateful, brother. Come, let us bathe. It will be like a baptism and we will be reborn anew!"

When they had gone I said, "The castellan said there would be surcoats and breeks for them, go and fetch them eh? It wouldn't to do have them put on their stinking old clothes!"

I did not have my own quarters, but I had a bed which had more room around it. I also had a chest with my war gear. I took out the coins we had collected. The men had handed them over to me. I divided them into sixteen equal piles. I placed them on the table we had in the middle. There had been little else I had wanted from the dead. The new men had taken swords and daggers. One had taken a silver cross he had found on one of the bodies. I had enough money for myself. I had barely spent a tenth of that which I had been paid by the prince.

I felt dirty and sweaty. I went down to the room with the water trough and the rough, homemade soap. I took an old, clean cloak that I used to dry myself down. The new men were all there in various stages of undress. Some of the younger ones looked a little embarrassed. I just stripped off and stepped into one of the troughs. Others had been in there before me but it would be emptied at the end of the night and refilled in the morning. I rubbed the soap all over and then sluiced the water off me. I stepped out and began to dry myself.

Jack of Lincoln nodded. "It must be twenty years since I had soap to wash myself. We must have stunk, Captain."

"Don't worry, we all stink worse than this normally. Riding horses, blood and sweat are a combination of smells which tell others we are coming."

He laughed. "And we ride horses?"

"We do. We are Prince Edward's retinue. He has twenty-one men at arms and us. We have to move at his speed. If you are not horsemen yet, then you soon will be. The horses we brought today are ours, and we have two more coming tomorrow. I noticed that you have few arrows."

"We can all fletch, but staying alive in the forest is a greater priority than making arrows."

"We have a good supply here, but my men prefer to make their own."

"As do we."

We were both dressed and we headed back to the barrack room.

I gestured behind me with my thumb. "Will they all adjust to such an ordered life?"

"They will, Captain. None of us chose the life of an outlaw. Some lord or the sheriff forced us into it. I had a family. My wife died and then my sons were taken and hanged for poaching." He shook his head. "The bastard who murdered them is dead, but I ended up an outlaw. I do not regret my actions but I wonder what life I might have had. The others all have similar stories. You have given us a chance."

"When first we met you let Peter do all the talking."

"That way I could watch you and seek the lie in your eyes. There was none. I do not think we have made a poor choice."

The castellan had ordered the kitchen keep us some hot food. To the new men it was the first real meal they had had in years. It was not the best meal, for it was largely what the rest of the garrison had left, but as they sat, in their new surcoats and breeches, drinking ale and eating hot food, it confirmed that we now had a company of archers. I had fewer than fourteen nights to make them fight as one.

We began the next morning. I brought the practice arrows and we set the butts up outside the walls. The knights were with the king and his son in London. No one was hunting in the park. It was perfect.

I spread the four senior archers amongst them. The outlaws were raw clay. They needed moulding. They had not had discipline. They would need it now. I remembered every lesson my father and Ralph had given me.

"There are many differences between your life in the forest and your life here. The main difference is that you obey orders. When I say 'draw' then you do so at once. When I say 'release' then you release and nock another arrow. We do not worry about how many arrows we carry. We might each send twenty arrows in as many heartbeats. You may not have the strength yet, but by the time we march to Wales, you will."

We spent all morning sending arrows into the targets. I was impressed with their accuracy but not their rate. John of Nottingham saw me becoming agitated. "Captain, this is all new to them. Give them time. Their fingers are bleeding."

"Aye, you are right."

We broke for food. We ate in the hunting park. I continued my lessons as we did so. "I notice you all have just one bow. You need at least two spares. You need six spare bowstrings. We will have just thirteen more nights to prepare. When we leave here, we will be living on the backs of horses and we will be carrying enough arrows to slay a thousand Welshmen."

The older archers such as Peter and Jack nodded. The younger ones like Dick, son of Robin, looked a little overawed. It was at that moment that I truly appreciated my father. I had been younger than these and yet I had had more awareness of what was expected of me.

The afternoon was spent practising with the swords they had acquired or been given. Every archer had the strength to wield a sword and to hit it hard, but few of these had the skills they would need. Jack and Peter apart, the rest had no idea at all how to fight with a sword. I asked some men at arms to help me to teach them. By the end of the afternoon we had made progress, but all of us were tired.

After two more days I could see clear progress. That proved to be all that we had. The prince returned with his father, the king. We were in the hunting park when they arrived. It was not yet time to finish but we did, for I knew that the prince would wish to see those whom I had brought.

The army did not follow the prince and the king into the ward. They began to erect tents. My new men noticed. "They do not have the roof we do?"

"No, William of Derby. They are the retinue of knights who serve the prince. There will be many more than this waiting for us at Chester. These knights will hope that we have success and that they can win a manor. That manor will come at the cost of a dead Welshman."

"Each banner is a knight?"

"It is, Hugh. Some of these knights will have a squire and twenty men to follow them. They will not have horses. They will be marching. It is a long way from here to Wales. Two hundred or more miles. The last part will be through land which the Welsh call their own. Think yourself lucky that we have horses and we ride."

The prince did not come to see me until after we had eaten. I had begun to think that we had been forgotten. He had with him his squire John, and there were two young warriors with him. Both seemed to be my age.

The prince smiled when he entered the barracks. My men all stood and bowed. Edward seemed pleased. He nodded and then waved them down. "You have done well, Captain Gerald. The constable has told me what you did. I approve, and it proves that de Montfort is up to something. The army I brought today will leave on the morrow for the Dee. Sir Roger de Mortimer will lead them. We leave in five days' time. Are your men ready?"

"Another seven days would be useful, my lord, but they will do."

"They had better. Along with Captain William and his men, you will be my only protection."

John said, "There will be us as well, my liege."

"There will indeed, Sir John." I must have shown my surprise. "Yes, Captain, Sir John has won his spurs. Geoffrey is my new squire. Richard is Sir John's. You will be seeing much of them for they will be passing commands to you." He dropped a purse on the table. "Here is your pay for this month. I have added extra for the horses you captured. That was clever." He turned to the squires. "I would watch yourselves around these men! Most of them were outlaws!"

The two young sons of nobles almost recoiled and Prince Edward laughed. Sir John said, "Fear not. They appear to be honest a bunch of men as you will ever meet. I would put my life in their hands any day."

I nodded my thanks for the compliment.

The training and the practice were forgotten as we threw ourselves into the task of preparing for the campaign. The knights and their retinues, who had arrived with the prince, left. The bulk of our forces would come from Chester and the land around the Welsh border. I was not looking forward to that. Sir Ranulf was still there. Would he recognise me? Worse, Hugh of Rhuddlan would most definitely recognise me, and he had a grudge to bear. My saving of his life would be forgotten.

The prince would be taking servants with him. They would erect the tents when necessary and cook the food. We, along with Sir William's men, would be responsible for our own spare arms. In our case that was not too onerous. Two sumpters could carry the arrows and one the bow staves. The rest of our war gear would be on our horses. The new men had been amazed to be issued blankets and cooking pots. We had one pot for every four men. To men used to eking out a living in the woods, it was luxury.

Sir John seemed to be taking over as a sort of quartermaster for the prince, who spent hours these days closeted with his father. I had learned that this had not always been the case, and it confirmed Sir Hugh's view that the last months in Gascony had changed the prince from feckless to loyal. Richard sought out me and Captain William. "My lord wishes conference with you in the Great Hall."

As we followed the young squire, Captain William said, "I have much to tell you when time allows. London proved a most interesting experience."

I nodded. We did not know Richard yet. Until we did, we would be wary loosing our lips in his vicinity. Sir John had with him a map on the table. "Our journey north will be relatively easy until we reach Wrechcessham. You know it, Gerald?"

I shook my head. "The Clwyd, that I know. The Welsh hills which abut it were as familiar as my bow stave but…" I hesitated, "when I served in that area, I had no cause to venture there. I know that the castle was built in the conquest but the Welsh hold it."

"Thank you for an honest answer. Then we will be giving it a wide berth. Once we are close to that stronghold and the borders, then you and your archers will form a screen before us and act as scouts. That means that you, Captain William, will have to guard us, our servants and our baggage."

He looked at the map. "We could go further east, where there would be less danger."

Shaking his head, Sir John said, "The prince is keen to get north and to quickly deal with this threat from the Welsh. We have work here in the south which is also important. First, we travel north to Wales. We have to secure the land around Chester."

I knew the Welsh. They were tough warriors, especially in their mountain stronghold. "I would not expect this to be swift, lord. The Welsh are cunning fighters."

Sir John smiled. "We have over a hundred knights. There are two hundred men at arms. I think we can deal with the barbarians who inhabit those hills. They are not the French, nor are they our own rebellious people. We will be back here within two months."

I thought about speaking again but knew that it would be a waste of time. I merely nodded my compliance. As we headed back across the wards Captain William said, "You did not agree with Sir John."

"It is not horse country. The Welsh have archers who are the best I have ever seen. I think my men are their equal, but there are but sixteen of us. They will have hundreds. They will not risk an open battle. They will ambush. They will lay traps, and they will hamstring animals. In short, they will wear us down and bleed us to death."

We stopped. We were in the middle of the lower ward, and we were alone. "Tell me of your time in the Marches." I hesitated. "Gerald, be honest with me. You and I are the prince's protectors. I know there is a secret. I know the prince knows of it. Do not let it be a wall between us."

Part of me wanted to keep the secret safe, but another part knew that I had to tell him. I had no doubt that the secret would be revealed as soon as Chester's men joined with us. I nodded. "I served Baron Henry of Clwyd. He had my father hanged for no good reason, so I killed him. I was an outlaw. Prince Edward knows of this."

"A heavy burden. I have known many barons who deserved such punishment. You are the first to have meted it out. I thank you for sharing. Know you that your secret will remain locked within me. I can tell you a little more of what I learned in London. Our master plays a dangerous game. He met with Henry de Montfort while in London. He knows him well. They were childhood friends. I was not privy to that meeting, but both seemed pleased with how it went."

"That should be a good thing. Simon de Montfort is King Henry's implacable foe. The prince is making allies of a potential enemy."

William shook his head. "Henry de Montfort is loyal to his brother. I fear our master is playing a dangerous game and we are caught in the middle. Keep your ears and eyes open. You and I must share that which we discover. There will be civil war. Of that, I have no doubt. What I fear is treachery whilst we are on campaign."

"We have good men who serve us. No matter what our betters do, we are brothers in arms."

Forewarned is forearmed, and although I had no one to confide in, I was able to prepare better. Now that I knew what was expected of me, I would plan accordingly.

King Henry himself came to say goodbye to his son. The embrace told me that they were now close. My father had never embraced me that way. It had not been in his nature. I thought back to all of the goodbyes I had had, and I regretted not saying more. Sir John carried the prince's standard but it remained furled. It would be unfurled when we fought, and so long as it flew, none would retreat. For many men, that unfurled standard would be like a death warrant. We were Prince Edward's protectors. He might use us in battle, but ultimately, we were there to guard his person.

We rode faster than I had expected. We stayed at the king's subject's castles as we progressed along the Roman road north and west. I listened to the men who manned those castles and learned that barons were taking sides. The castles in which we stayed were loyal to King Henry. That made me wonder about the ones we passed. Were they foes?

We stopped at the border town of Oswald's Cross. It had a wall around the town but no castle. Prince Edward sought me out. "Tomorrow we will close with Wrechcessham. We will have to leave the road. You must find us a safe way around it."

"Yes, lord."

"I would make Chester in one day."

I did not know Wrechcessham well, but I had an idea of the land to the north of it. As I went back to my men, I tried to form a mental picture of it. The River Dee was a barrier. It was the old border. The Normans might have captured large swathes of it, but they had had to cling onto it. Any knights would now be gathering in Chester. I intended to cross us at Bangor on the Dee. As I remembered, it was an uncontested crossing, and the road thence was a good one. I gathered my men and gave them their instructions.

"Tomorrow, we ride early. We will leave before the main body. David the Welshman and Dick, son of Robin, will accompany me. John of Nottingham, you will lead the archers, and you will be half a mile before the prince. We will head for the Dee. Dick will act as messenger. If you do not see him then all is well. If he comes, then we have deviated. You will ride with a strung bow. I care not if the string is ruined, but I want you to be ready to dismount and send arrows at an enemy."

"Yes, Captain." We had not been a company for long, but they were becoming one, and I had confidence in them.

I told the prince and Captain William my plans and left before they did. I wanted to ride slowly and cautiously. If there were enemies about, then this would be the perfect opportunity to harm the king's cause. The road was a local one. It had stone, but it was not the well-tamped roads which the Romans had built. Nor was it straight. It twisted and turned. Parts of it were hedgerow and parts were open. Some farms and houses we passed had frontage along the road.

When the sun rose, we were just two miles from the Dee crossing. We had ridden with the sun to the south of us. We would soon find a crossing point. My men and I could have forded it but princes preferred bridges. Four villeins trudged along the road ahead of us. They were going to work in the fields. At the sound of our hooves, they stopped. Horsemen rarely brought joy. They knew that flight was impossible and so they crowded to the side, beneath an old elm tree. I could manage a few words of Welsh, but we needed accuracy and so I deferred to David.

He rattled off a mouthful of Welsh. The only words I caught were "soldiers" and "bridge". The rest was too fast for me to understand. They talked amongst themselves and David listened. While they did so, I was able to examine them a little more closely. They had wooden-soled shoes and homespun breeks and tops. They wore a hat woven from straw. They looked emaciated. These were the poorest of villeins. They would have been given a few ploughs of land. In return, they would give half of their crop to their lord. It was a parlous existence. Grain for bread would be ground by hand and eked out. I had known many such men when I was growing up. My father had been an archer. He always had coin. We ate simply but we were always well fed.

David turned to me. "Captain, they say that there are Welsh warriors at the bridge. The bridge is fewer than two miles from here. The warriors came there two days since. They arrived the day after an army marched north across the bridge."

"They would be the men who left us days ago. How many men?"

"He says there are six."

I nodded. "Give them some bread." I reached into my purse and brought out four silver pennies. They had been taken from de Montfort's men. I tossed them to the men. "Tell them thank you."

The four men knuckled their heads gratefully.

"Dick, ride back. Tell John of Nottingham I need half the men, and then ride to Sir John and tell him that the bridge is held, but I will clear it."

"Aye, Captain." He dug his heels into his horse and galloped back. As we waited for my men, I watched the four of them divide up first the money and then the bread. I knew, even without speaking to them, that they would have shared the work on their ploughs. I heard hooves. The four men looked up at me and I nodded. They scurried away.

My men, led by Jack of Lincoln, comprised of five archers. He said, "John of Nottingham thought you might like to see us in action."

I nodded. "We will ride a little closer." I looked at the five archers. Ronan was the youngest, although not by much. "Ronan, you will watch the horses when we stop." He looked disappointed. "I will whistle when you are to bring them up. Can you manage eight horses?"

"Aye, Captain."

We did not gallop, but walked our horses the next three quarters of a mile. When I saw the smoke of the huts and the cross on the top of the church, I stopped. We dismounted and took our bows. Ronan took the reins, and I waved my arm to signal my men forward. They showed their skill by finding cover and moving from bush to bush, tree to tree. I dropped into the drainage ditch and walked along it.

I heard the men before I saw them. Their sing-song voices carried across the bridge and the river. I nocked an arrow. Looking around, I saw that my archers each had one nocked already. I nodded, and we moved forward. I stepped from the ditch when I was a hundred paces from the bridge. The bridge itself was just forty paces long and three paces wide. As I pulled back, I saw the Welshmen. They were at the far end of the bridge and oblivious to our presence. I released my arrow and then dropped my bow. Drawing my sword, I ran. There were seven other archers who could rain death upon them. I wanted to make certain that none escaped the arrows. The stone and timber bridge had places to hide, and just twenty paces from the bridge was an inn. There might be horses there.

As I ran, I saw that my arrow had struck a Welshman. It had not been a clean kill. He was writhing around on the ground. My arrow had entered his shoulder and emerged above his ribs. He would die. The others appeared mesmerised. A second and a third fell, even as I broke cover. One turned to run towards me, and a white-fletched arrow – David the Welshman used those – struck him in the chest. The others turned to run, but it was too late. One fell with two arrows. By the time I reached them, they were all dead. The one I had slain was surrounded by an ever-widening pool of blood.

I turned to whistle and then ran across. I reached the stables just as a seventh Welsh warrior mounted his horse and tried to leave. He saw me and tried to ride me down. It was not a big horse. It was one of the large ponies the Welsh favoured. I had no hesitation. I swung my sword, two-handed, at the pony's chest. As my blade bit into the animal the warrior tried to pull its head away from me. All that he succeeded in doing was pulling his wounded pony over, and that allowed my sword to slice deep into his thigh. Blood spattered and showered me. He gave a scream, and as he fell off, his head cracked into the door frame. It gave him a quicker death. I ran out and saw people emerging from the inn. Others peered out from their huts and houses. They saw me with my bloody sword. I shouted, in Welsh, "Get back inside!" I was not certain I had used the exact words, but the sense was clear, and when horses galloped across the bridge, they disappeared.

Ronan and Peder were searching the bodies of the dead. I heard splashes as they threw the corpses into the water. David the Welshman nodded. "Quick thinking, Captain."

"I do not think any escaped, but go and question some of those in the village." He nodded and left. I waved over Jack of Lincoln. "There is a wounded pony. Put it out of its misery. See if there is a haunch we might cook."

He slung his bow. "You are no slouch, Captain. That was as pretty a piece of killing as I have ever seen."

He left, and I went to the dead Welshman. I cleaned my sword on his kyrtle and then took his purse and his short sword. Ronan brought my horse, and I tossed him the sword. "Here, Ronan, for your trouble. Next time, you shall come with us and someone else will watch the horses." I examined the rest of the stables. There were six other ponies.

By the time I had finished, Prince Edward and the rest of my men were arriving. "Did any escape?"

David appeared as the prince spoke. He shook his head. "No, my liege. These were the only ones. From what I can gather, the Welsh were alerted when our men marched north."

Sir John said, "I know not why they were here. What could a handful of men do?"

"Warn whoever placed them here. Their job was not to stop us, my lord; it was to bring men and attack us in numbers."

"Then we had better move. We are close enough to Chester now so that I can almost smell it." The prince leaned down from his saddle. "Perhaps it might be better if you and your archers did not enter Chester. I would rather explain your presence to Sir Ranulf before he sees you."

I had thought he had forgotten my confession. It had seemed a lifetime ago. "As you wish, my liege, and where would you have us go?"

"Once you have escorted us to the castle, then cross the Dee. Mold castle has fallen to Llywelyn ap Gruffudd. They took it from the Montalt family two years since. From what I hear, he has made it something of a royal residence. It will be the first place that I intend to attack. It will make a statement. I need you and your archers to scout it out. You have a good eye for these things. Find us somewhere we can camp. If you can come up with any ideas to take it then so much the better."

As we were now in what was supposed to be English territory, we stayed closer to the rest of the column. When we spied Chester in the distance I prepared to leave the prince. "When will you be arriving, my liege?"

"I speak with my knights tonight, and we leave tomorrow at noon. We will be with you soon after."

"That is not long, my lord!"

He gave me a thin smile. "Then you had better move now, archer!"

CHAPTER 11

We skirted the castle and crossed the bridge. The gatehouse could have sent crossbow bolts and arrows our way had we been foes, but this was Prince Edward's castle, and we wore his livery. We clattered over the wooden bridge. There was still a stone Roman one, but this was closer. I waved David the Welshman forward. As we rode, we spoke.

"What do you know of Mold?"

"Nothing, Captain. I thought that you would know it better. You lived around here. I lived further south." He was right. As we had passed within ten miles of his own home, I had allowed him to visit his mother and give her the lace he had bought. It was he who had brought us news of Welsh forces gathering there.

I nodded. "The lord I served did not get on with the Montalt family. I have never seen it close up. That will make our task harder. Take Ronan, he seems keen enough. Ride to the castle and find us somewhere to camp this night. Tomorrow, we will begin to examine it more closely."

I rode alone, at the head of the column. John and Jack must have realised I wished to be alone, for they rode behind me, chatting about Nottingham and some of the characters they had known. I thought back to the killing of Sir Henry. I knew now that I had thrown a stone into a pond, and that the ripples went further than I might have expected. I wondered if my killing of Sir Henry had allowed the Welsh to take Mold. A sudden fear filled me; what of Denbigh? Had that fallen too? I had not asked. Denbigh and Mold, along with St Asaph and Ruthin, controlled the Clwyd valley. Mold was the gateway. Once Mold was captured, then there was a high ridge and the three castles spread along the valley. Now I understood the reason for this campaign. King Henry had lost all of the land to the west of Chester. The Welsh raids had done more than yield food and treasure. They had gained land. What I did know about Mold was that the river, the Alyn, was small. The castle was not near to it. It relied on its position above the road from Chester; that was where its importance lay.

A whistle alerted us to Ronan and David. We had not yet reached the river. In fact, I could see it just a hundred paces from us. We entered the wood. I saw that my two archers had dismounted. I followed suit. "John, take charge. This looks a likely place to camp. I will go with David."

I followed David, and he went along a hunter's trail through the woods. When the trail headed west, he took out his short sword and cut us a path through the wild blackberry bushes. I saw why when we reached the riverbank. There, just over five hundred paces from us, stood the castle. The Montalt family had used an existing piece of high ground and built a motte and bailey castle. The Welsh king's standard fluttered from its keep. I walked up and down the riverbank to examine the walls from the safety of the undergrowth. There was a curtain wall with a strong gatehouse. A ditch ran around the walls. When I had seen enough, I headed back to the others.

The horses were tethered. We would take them to the river for water after dark. There was grass for them to eat and we had grain to supplement it. I waved them around. "Tonight we explore the houses and the castle. We do not get caught! Examine the ditch. Are there traps within? How many men are on the walls? How many are in the houses? I will go with Robin of Barnsley and David the Welshman. We will scout out the roads which lead to the castle." They nodded. "We eat first and then leave when it is dark. Dick and Peder, you guard the camp and the horses."

Jack of Lincoln had brought the haunch of pony. He rubbed salt on it and then put it into a large pot with some river water and wild garlic. When the main army arrived we would cook it. The salt would tenderise and the garlic would flavour it.

As we left the camp we did not take our bows. At night the advantage of a bow is lost. We carried our swords and our daggers. The bridge was in darkness, and we slipped across. The river was so narrow and shallow that we could have crossed it if we had needed to, but dry feet and clothes were always preferable. We slipped around the back of the huts. The three of us had the longest journey. The rest would be back in camp long before we were. We kept well away from the walls of the castle. Others would investigate those, but I saw from the burning brands that they had sentries at the gate, and it was barred. I wondered if they had a second?

Once clear of the castle we made speed on the road. This was well worn. Horses and men would make the short journey to Ruthin. Half a mile down the road I had seen all that we needed to see. There had been no paths or tracks leading from it. A relieving army would have to come down this road. Rather than walk back to the castle, I led us north, across the ploughed fields. They were the sorts of fields the men we had met had farmed. The barley was just knee high. It would get higher. We found the road which headed north-west. We had only gone four hundred paces down it when I recognised it. This was the road to

Denbigh. We were just a few miles from my home. It was strange that I had not visited a place so close.

I circled my hand and led the other two back. Prince Edward just needed to seal off the two roads and Mold would be surrounded. A motte and bailey castle could be quickly reduced or even left alone. We could push on to Ruthin and then Denbigh.

As we neared the road from the west I heard the sound of hooves. They were coming along the road from the west. The castle was a mile away, and we ran to the road junction. There was the crossroads sign. I saw Robin of Barnsley make the sign of the cross. Suicides were often buried beneath a crossroads with the post through their heart. It was supposed to stop their restless spirits wandering.

I pointed to the other side of the low wall on the far side of the road. David the Welshman nodded and went behind it. I pointed to the other walls and Robin did the same. After taking out my sword and putting it beneath me, I lay down close to the crossroads sign. A rider would slow down and, more importantly, his horse would baulk at a man lying on the ground. I heard the hooves slowing as the rider approached the crossroads. It had to be a Welshman, for he was coming from the west. It had to be a warrior, and he had to be going to the castle.

The horse slowed to a walk, and I heard a voice say something in Welsh. I did not recognise the words. Suddenly, I heard his horse neigh, and I knew my two men had leapt from cover. I jumped up and grabbed the horse's reins. The rider lost his balance. He tumbled from its back, and I heard his head crack against the stone wall. Robin ran to him and then shook his head.

"Search him. He may be a messenger. Then throw his body over the wall. We will take his horse back with us."

While Robin searched him, David the Welshman calmed his horse. "Through the village?"

"We might as well. The prince will be here by noon tomorrow. It is a gamble, but it is worth it if we can find out information."

We led the horse. It made less noise that way. Once we neared the castle it would be heard, but the sentries would not be able to leave their post. By the time someone was summoned, we would be over the bridge. The only danger lay in a villager coming out. We walked with drawn swords. As we passed through, I heard a door creak, but whoever opened it merely peered out. No alarm was given. Perhaps the sight of the swords made them wary. As we crossed the bridge, and the hooves clattered on the wood, I heard a shout from the castle walls. We hurried down the road and Robin led the horse down the trail. David the Welshman and I quickly climbed two oaks which lay just three paces inside the wood. We waited.

I heard feet on the bridge and Welsh voices. I could not make out what they said. I hoped that David would. Then I saw them. There were eight men at arms. They passed us and walked down the road. Their voices faded and then they returned. When they neared the trail, they halted, and a debate went on. They were arguing. Suddenly one of them struck one of the others. There was silence. It was when he spoke that I felt shivers down my spine. A shaft of moonlight illuminated his face as he spoke. It was Hugh of Rhuddlan. He had changed sides!

The blow had ended the debate, and they headed back across the bridge.

I waited until I had heard them cross the wooden bridge before I descended. When David joined me, I said, "What did they say?"

"They were confused, Captain. They heard the horse, but they could not understand why it crossed the bridge. One of the men said it might have gone into the woods and the man who was in charge told him to stop being stupid. The horse had thrown its rider. He was sending them back up the Ruthin road to find him."

"That means that when they do they will come back down here. Let's get to the camp."

With men watching for us we could not afford a light. John of Nottingham had searched the horse and discovered the leather message pouch. There was a message, but it was in Latin and we could not read it anyway. Even had we had that skill, the light was too poor. I had a dilemma. The prince needed the information that was in the pouch, but if I sent a rider with it, we risked the garrison finding it. The rewards outweighed the risks.

I asked my men, "What did you discover?"

"There is but one main gate. They have a sally port, but it is on the north wall. A horse and rider could get out, but it would take time to evacuate the whole garrison."

"There are no traps in the ditch. It is steep, but a man could climb it."

"Dick, son of Robin, saddle your horse. I want you to ride to Chester and give this to either the prince or Sir John. Tell him that there is one gate and a sally port and no traps in the ditch. The rest of you, we will go to the edge of the woods. Bring your bows."

By the time he was ready we had strung our bows. He walked his horse to the edge. I whispered, "Walk him for half a mile and then ride as though the devil himself was after you. If you hear fighting, ignore it. The message must get through."

"Aye, Captain. I will not let you down."

I thought the hooves of his horse sounded loud, but I knew that they were not. Then I heard a cry from the north. They had discovered the body of the messenger. Perhaps we should have dropped it in the river.

"Move back into the woods. They may come here."

Jack of Lincoln laughed. It was not a pleasant laugh. "Then if they do they will never leave. A forest at night is where we do our best work, Captain."

"I believe you. If they come here, then we lead them away from the horses."

Roger Peterson said, "And kill them?"

"Of course we kill them."

I had an arrow nocked, as did the others. I knew that we could not be seen, but we would be able to see our foes for they would be on the road. I heard hooves clattering over the bridge. "We stop them following Dick! If you have to then kill the horses."

I did not know how many horses they had, but if Hugh of Rhuddlan was leading them, then the men at arms would know how to ride. The hooves drew closer. I could not see them yet, but I estimated it to be no more than six riders. I pulled back. The road was just thirty paces from me, and I had a clear line between the trees. I saw the first horse and waited a heartbeat. Then I released as the rider passed between the two trees. He was not wearing mail, but it would have made no difference. My arrow went through his neck and knocked him from his horse. The horse galloped off. I heard the thwack of arrows as another three hit their mark.

I heard Hugh of Rhuddlan's voice. He shouted, in Welsh, "Back!" Then he shouted something I did not understand.

David the Welshman exclaimed, "He is calling out the guard!"

"We have stopped the pursuit. Let us fall back and wait for them to come closer."

Jack of Lincoln said, "Captain, this is knife work."

I slung my bow. He was right. We could only see two or three paces before us in the dark woods. We could hide and use the trees for cover.

They would have no idea how many of us were hiding in the woods. We would come as a shock to them. We heard their feet as they clattered over the bridge.

When they came this time, they came on foot and in numbers. They did not have one point of entry but many. I saw that they had brought shields. That was a mistake. We would not be sending arrows at them. I stood behind a mighty oak. It was wider than me. I had my hood covering my head, and its shadow left my face in darkness. I had a dagger in my left hand and my sword in my right. I saw the Welshman. He had a metal coif instead of a helmet, a leather jerkin, a short sword and shield. He was walking carefully and not making a sound. That made no difference, for I had seen him.

I slid around the side of the tree as he walked on the other side. I stepped out behind him. I brought my dagger up under his left arm. His head turned at the last moment, and I put my sword hand across his mouth. I struck something vital and hot blood gushed over my hand. I lowered his body to the ground. A movement behind me made me turn. There was a man at arms four paces from me. He ran at me. A voice shouted something in Welsh. He pulled his shield up. I used my dagger to pull the shield forward and rammed my sword into his throat. He tried, as I did, to swing his sword in an arc. That is a mistake in a wood. He died with his sword embedded in the oak.

I turned and parted from the two bodies. I headed deeper into the woods. I could hear more shouts and cries now. The shouts were in Welsh and my men were silent. I moved quickly into the forest. I heard another scream and then a gurgled shout. Hugh of Rhuddlan's voice boomed out, "Back to the castle!" There was another cry, and then I heard the sound of flight as the survivors crashed through the woods.

I turned and slowly made my way back to the place I had killed the two men. I took their swords, mail hoods and purses. When I reached the road I risked peering out. I saw two men being helped towards the bridge. They were beaten. Would they return in the morning? That bridge would have to be crossed. We had done our job, and if we had to, then we could evade them. I made my way through the woods. I found Rafe Oak Arms, one of my new recruits, stripping a body of weapons and valuables. He was laughing. "Something amuses you?"

"Aye, Captain. When I did this in Sherwood, I was breaking the law. Here, the heir to the throne is paying me. It is a strange world."

As we headed back to camp we picked up others, and all were in high spirits. The mood changed when we reached the camp. Jack of Lincoln was kneeling over the corpse of Peder. We had lost someone.

"Is anyone else hurt?"

Jack looked around and shook his head. "The big old bastard did this. The one who was shouting the orders."

"Hugh of Rhuddlan."

"You know him?"

"Knew him. He was my sergeant at arms. Peder stood no chance."

Jack nodded. "Then this has become personal. Peder was my brother's son. I am now the last of my family."

We set guards and then we buried Peder. A woodland grave was all an outlaw would have expected. He was buried by those who had come from Sherwood. My senior archers stood a watch while we dug the hole, buried the young warrior and then piled stones on the body to stop foxes digging it up. I could not sleep, and so I took a long watch, along with Jack of Lincoln. It was just after dawn when we heard the hooves, but this time they were coming from Chester.

"Sounds like one horse, Captain."

I nodded. I stood and stretched. This would be a long day. I knew that later I would regret my long watch. Jack and I had spoken during the night watch. If Peder had been an older archer, one who had lived a little, then it might not be so bad. He had seen sixteen summers. He had not had time to begin to live.

Dick, on a fresh horse, galloped into the camp. "The prince is following me, Captain. That letter, it told the men in the castle that the Welsh king is coming. He will be here within the week! The prince was delighted." He showed us the gold coin he held in his hand. "This is my reward! Wait until I show Peder!" He, Peder and Ronan had been close.

"Peder was killed last night, Dick."

The young archer went from ecstasy to agony in a heartbeat. It brought home just how parlous our lives were.

CHAPTER 12

Now that the enemy knew we were close, there was no point in hiding. We lit a fire and put the salted horsemeat on to cook. I took eight of my archers and we rode to the bridge. I peered ahead to the crossroads, just beyond the huddle of huts which constituted the hamlet. The ground close to the crossroads was perfect as a camp. It effectively cut off the castle, and it was flat. The fields had walls. The walls would help to divide up the camp. I had learned, in Gascony, that was important. The horses had to be kept separate and the knights preferred to be away from the common soldiers. The three roads would allow that.

I had restrung my bow and carried it with me. Leaving our horses at the south end of the bridge, we crossed to the north. As soon as we did, we heard the alarm in the castle. A horn sounded and men ran to the walls. To my surprise, those who lived in the huts, house and farms of the village suddenly ran towards the castle. I saw them clutching that which they thought was valuable. There was just a handful of us, but they had taken us for the advance guard of an army.

I turned. "Stephen Green Feathers, take Will Yew Tree and Matty Straw Hair; fetch your horses and ride to the crossroads. Stop any who try to leave."

"Aye, Captain. Come on you pair. We will see how fast you can ride."

I knew that those in the castle would send for help, but it took time to saddle a horse. They had lost some the previous night. A couple had run off, and at least two had been struck. I nocked an arrow. My three men galloped over the bridge and, lying low in the saddle, galloped through the village towards the crossroads, half a mile away. The castle was three hundred paces from the village and the road. Even so, the men behind the walls had crossbows, which they used to try to hit my riders. It was a forlorn hope though. Crossbows were powerful, and if an enemy was approaching in numbers, they could be deadly. But at extreme range and against a moving target, they were wasting bolts and making it more likely that their crossbows would fail when they needed them.

The three riders passed the castle when I heard the gates open. Was this an attempt to move us from the bridge or to seek help? When the riders turned to head north to Ruthin, I had my answer.

Hugh, son of Hugh, another of the former outlaws, stood with me. "Will they get by our men?"

"Will and Matty are your fellows. What do you think?"

He grinned. "Then they are doomed Welshmen, Captain."

I turned to the others. "Peter of Wakefield, take Ronan and Tom. Search the houses. They may have left items we can use. I saw no animals with them. See if they have left fowl there. We can augment our rations eh?"

"Aye, Captain."

The crossroads was beyond our sight but not our hearing. I heard the neighs and cries as the three riders were intercepted. A short while later, one Welsh rider and one horse returned to the castle. They had learned that the English had archers too.

Hugh frowned. "Where are the Welsh archers, Captain? If they are as good as you have told us, then why did they not send arrows at our men?"

I had not thought of that. I nodded. "You are right, Hugh. That is a puzzle."

Shortly, Peter of Wakefield and my men returned. They each had a brace of hens with them. "Peter, take these men back to the camp. The others can stand a shift and you can eat."

"What about you, Captain?"

"I will eat when the prince arrives. He will expect me to tell him the situation. Now go!"

Thus it was that I was alone on the bridge when I heard the clatter of hooves and the jingle of mail behind me. Captain William led the men at arms towards me. He reined in.

"Guarding the bridge on your own, Captain Gerald?"

I pointed to the distant crossroads. "Some of my men hold the crossroads. That is the best place to camp. The village is emptied. They have left their homes. None has escaped with news of our arrival."

"Good. The prince is pleased with your actions. He follows. He sent us ahead, for he feared for your safety. I told him that you would be safe."

I shook my head. "We lost one archer."

"We are warriors and that is the risk we take."

He led his men across the bridge. I walked back to retrieve my horse. As I mounted, I saw the banners of the army as it approached. Prince Edward was surrounded by those knights who would, over the next years, become his trusted companions: Sir Roger Mortimer, John de Warenne, William de Valence and Sir Ranulf. As they reined in I saw Sir Ranulf glaring at me. He had been told of my presence and was not happy.

Prince Edward, in contrast, was delighted to see me. "The news you sent has given us the chance to end this quickly. How goes it Gerald War Bow?"

"The crossroads will be the best place to camp, lord. My men and Captain William hold it. The village is empty. They fled to the castle. No one rode for help. My men are camped in the woods and watch the castle."

"Then you have done well."

I watched the army as it passed. At first I was happy. I counted over a hundred knights and then fifty men at arms. Then I saw that the men who marched were just the ordinary men of Cheshire. They had no mail and few had helmets. Worse, I only counted twenty bows. Where were the archers? When the baggage train arrived, I saw that it was escorted by men on horses. I recognised them. They were the archers led by Captain Jack. He reined in and waved the baggage train forward. I saw my old comrade, Alan of Denbigh. He stared at me as though I was a ghost.

Captain Jack dismounted. "I heard that the prince had a fine captain of archers. I wondered who it could be for I had never heard of a Gerald War Bow. Now I see, and his lordship's ire becomes apparent. You slew your lord."

He said it simply and there was no point in denying it. His lord knew, and that meant soon it would be common knowledge. I had braced myself for the storm that would follow. The knights who served with the prince would not be happy, for a commoner killing a knight was unheard of. Certainly, a commoner killing a knight and living was something which had never yet happened.

I nodded. "He had my father killed for no good reason. The law would have done nothing. I did. The prince knows, and when I have made pilgrimage, I will be forgiven."

He looked at me, scrutinising my features. "I have known many bad lords who deserved to die, and certainly Henry of Denbigh was a poor excuse for a man, but I should warn you…" he smiled, "Gerald War Bow, there are men who will seek your death."

I pointed to the castle. "Hugh of Rhuddlan now serves the Welsh."

His eyes narrowed. "It is worse than that. He allowed the Welsh to take Denbigh without a fight. He opened the gate and let them in. The men you knew were killed by the Welsh. There are just three men left from the garrison: you, Hugh of Rhuddlan and Alan of Denbigh. I fear the castle was cursed." He looked to the north-west and then turned back to me. He held out his arm. "You are a good archer and you are a captain. We have the only archers in this army. We must, perforce, be friends."

I took his arm. "I was never anything else."

As I rode back to my men I wondered if the lack of archers might come to hurt us. We had fewer than thirty-five good archers, and I had seen perhaps twenty or thirty bowmen. I had no doubt that we could take their castles, but how would we drive the Welsh king back beyond the Conway?

I met my men in the woods. I circled my hand above my head. "Back to the camp. The army is here. We are now needed. Dick, go to the crossroads and fetch our men. This camp will do us. If the prince needs us close by, then we will move."

I sat by the fire while John of Nottingham ladled some of the horse stew into clay bowls. I looked up at him questioningly. He nodded towards Peter of Wakefield. "When they searched the houses he found them. They will break before long, but until they do then we will enjoy eating from them." He handed me some day-old bread. "And he found bread too. We eat like kings!"

I was hungry and the stew was hot. Tom handed me a beaker of ale. "God smiles on us, we found ale, Captain."

Stephen Green Feathers smiled. "The rest of the army will not be happy that we have plundered before them."

"They had a night in a castle. They would have been well supplied. We took the risks; we take the reward."

Geoffrey, the new squire, came for us in the middle of the afternoon. "The prince would like you camped by him, Captain." He hesitated. "He is not happy that you tarried here."

I gave him what I hoped was an innocent look. "We were awaiting orders, my lord."

When we crossed the bridge, we saw the siege works. The levy was already labouring. Men were cutting down trees. The prince had to strike quickly and take Mold before the Welsh arrived with their army. He did not want to be trapped between a relieving army and a castle.

Captain William waved to me as we approached the prince's standard. "We have saved a piece of ground for you yonder. Sir John wishes to speak with us when you can."

"That means now."

He laughed, "Aye, you are learning. We wait on our betters, but they demand instant obedience."

I dismounted and handed my reins to Tom. I also gave him my bow staves and arrows. "Put them somewhere safe."

The tents were already erected, and Sir John and his squire were there with a map. "Well done, Captain. This is a perfect camp and chosen with a good eye." I nodded. "We begin our attack this afternoon. We need fire arrows. Captain Jack and his men are preparing theirs. This afternoon we rain arrows on their walls and this night we turn them to fire. Our men at arms will storm the walls." I glanced at Captain William who shrugged. Sir John saw my look and sighed. "Captain

Gerald, we need to save our knights for the time we meet the Welsh in the field. It will be our knights who win this land back."

I knew he was wrong, but I could not argue with him, "You are right, my lord. Sorry!"

"As soon as the castle is reduced, then you and your archers will scout out Ruthin and give us notice of the advance of the Welsh."

I looked at the map. Had I not known the area, then it would all have been squiggles and colours. I recognised, however, the blue line that must have been the Clwyd. The red little squares with the flags had to be the castles. I pointed to a line of brown. "Lord, this is high, rough ground. It is perfect ambush country. I know it, for I have hunted Welsh brigands there before. Their archers can rain death upon the road."

He looked at the map. "It does not look high to me."

"It may not be high, lord, but it is covered in trees, bushes and rocks. We were unable to use our horses there. We had to go afoot and winkle them out one by one."

"I will tell the prince, but I do not think it will be a problem. Once we have met the Welsh, shield to shield, then they will sue for peace, and we can return south and deal with a more serious problem." He looked up from the map and smiled. "Fire arrows then, and you, Captain William, had better prepare ladders."

We both bowed and left. I looked at Captain William, "A night attack?"

"It might work." He did not sound convinced. "And fire arrows? Do they work?"

"They are a waste of a good arrow. We cannot send them far, and to be certain that they work, we need to send many into the castle. They will, however, distract the defenders. I was in a garrison at Denbigh, and we were always fearful of fire."

"Then I pray that you and your archers make our attack unnecessary."

I did not think that would happen, but I set the men to making fire arrows. We chose the arrows that were not our best. It galled me that we would have to leave the valuable arrowheads on them. They had to stick in the timber in order to burn. I had each man choose twenty such arrows. We mainly used the ones which we had not made or we had captured. We gathered cloth taken from the huts and oil and soaked the cloth in it. The oil-soaked cloth was wrapped around the end of each arrow. Then each bundle of arrows was left in a pot of oil. That way the oil would seep into the wood. We needed something which would burn for as long as possible. The walls were stone, but the buildings each had a roof which was not, and there were many wooden buildings within.

Captain Jack wandered over. He had with him Alan of Denbigh. The captain saw what we were doing and nodded. "I see you have had to make fire arrows too."

I stood. "If we could be certain that they would work, I would not mind, but in my experience, they often fail to ignite the buildings."

The captain gestured to Alan. "My archer wished to speak with you. Do not keep him long, we have much to do before the attack this afternoon."

He wandered away and Alan approached me. He seemed nervous. "I thought you dead! When we heard what you had done, and that you were hunted as an outlaw, I felt certain that your life had been ended."

"No, Alan. It seems that someone or something has plans for me. Harry is dead. He died in Gascony."

"And you are now a captain."

"As I said, I have been lucky." I gestured at the walls behind me. "When we attack, watch out. Hugh of Rhuddlan is within those walls."

"He owes you a life."

I shook my head. "That ended when I slew Sir Henry."

He nodded. "I had better go. I wanted to know that it was still well between us. I am glad that you are alive. You are the best archer I know."

I had little time to dwell on his words. Captain William and his men arrived. They had broken down some of the palisade around one of the buildings in the village. They had made large shields. "It is time, Captain Gerald, to begin the assault."

I had made all of my arrows. One or two of the outlaws had yet to finish theirs. "Leave the ones you have not yet made. We begin our attack." I pointed to the shields being carried by the men at arms. "Use the shields. Nock your arrows when standing behind them. Stand and release. Duck back behind the shield again. They have archers and crossbows. Rely on speed. We are trying to thin their numbers so that our brothers in arms can assault the walls tonight." I had already spoken to Peter and Jack, as well as my senior archers. They would each watch over one or two of the less experienced archers.

We followed them to within a hundred and fifty paces of the walls. Arrows and bolts were already thudding into them. The men at arms had made a bracing arm for the shields. They took their own shields from their backs and held them aloft too. We would have some protection. Just on the other side of the gate, the men at arms and archers of Chester were doing the same.

I pulled out an arrow and nocked it. I shouted, without raising my head, "Ready?"

A chorus of "Aye, Captain!" was reassuring.

I pulled back and shouted, "Draw!" You could hear the sound as the bows creaked. "Release!"

I stood and released an arrow before dropping down. Next to me, Ronan was almost too slow. An arrow from the walls took the cap from his head.

"You cannot dawdle. That could have been your head."

He looked behind us where the arrow had pinned the cap to the ground. "These Welshmen are good."

I pulled back and shouted, "Draw!" I rose. "Release!"

This time there was a ripple of cracks as the enemy sent arrows at us, anticipating our action. Ronan was quicker this time and came to no harm. We continued for twenty more flights. It was infuriating. We could not see the effect our arrows were having. We had to rely on Prince Edward and the knights who were watching it like some sort of show. They were beyond bow and bolt range.

After twenty flights we stopped. I laid down my bow, unstrung it and wound and stored the string. I took another bow. I picked out a fresh string and strung the new bow. I could see that the men at arms were confused. I said, "We need a rest after twenty flights, and a fresh bow and string will be more effective. It also helps to unnerve those we are aiming at. They wait for the next flight."

The two men at arms who were near to me nodded. Part of the mystery of the archer was gone. We sent, in all, eighty arrows each. I then called a halt. If we were to send arrows again at night, we needed a rest. "Time to go back to the camp." I stored my bows in their covers.

Captain William asked, "Are you ready?" We had to get back to the camp without being hit by arrows and bolts from the walls.

"Aye, Captain." We now had the difficult task of running out of range with a man at arms protecting us. Our time on the ship came to the fore. The men at arms knew us. We trusted them, and we made it back to our lines unhurt. The men of Chester were not so lucky. One archer was slain and a man at arms had a bolt sent through his leg.

"Thank you, Captain William."

"You can repay us by setting fire to their castle."

"We will do our best." I turned to my men. "Those who still have fire arrows to make, finish them. The rest of you, let us eat and then get some rest." The muscles in my upper back and my arms were burning from the exertion. The night attack would be even harder. We might not have as many arrows coming in our direction, but when our own arrow was ignited, we would not have long to release it. More than half of our men had never used one before.

Sir John came over to speak with me. He had his squire, Richard, with him. "The archers did well. We think you slew or hit at least twenty men."

I gave him a wry smile. "And it cost us almost a thousand arrows."

Richard said, "You can always get more!"

I shook my head. The squire was young. "We have to make them, young master. We need ash and we need goose feathers. We need metal for the tips. We can fight or we can make arrows. We cannot do both." I pointed at the castle. "If we can take this castle, then we might be able to salvage some shafts and arrowheads. If we are really lucky, then we might find a cache of arrows in the castle. Unless, of course, we are too good and burn it down!"

The young noble looked crestfallen.

Sir John smiled. "Watch these men, Richard, and you will learn much. They may be base-born but they know their trade and that trade is war. They wear a little leather armour studded with metal. They have neither shield nor helmet, yet they can defeat knights on horses!"

I saw his squire looking at us as though for the first time.

Sir John asked, "Tell me, Gerald War Bow, what think you of our chances this night?"

I stood and licked my finger. I held it up in the air. "The wind is behind us and that will help. If Prince Edward wishes truth then this is it: we can keep the Welsh distracted and fighting fires; of that I am certain. If we manage to fire the buildings then the Good Lord favours our enterprise."

He patted my broad back. "Then that is all we can ask." He was about to leave when he said, "Do you require supplies? I am aware that you have had to live off the land."

I smiled, knowing we had the six fowl we had collected the night before. With the stock from the horsemeat and some greens David the Welshman had foraged, we would eat well. "We have enough supplies, lord."

I saw Jack of Lincoln and Peter of Wakefield as they approached. They stopped and stood together as the two nobles left. They knuckled their foreheads. Sir John smiled, bemused. When he had gone, they turned and lifted the barrel of ale that they had managed to liberate.

"Where did you get this?"

Jack adopted an innocent look. "I have to say, Captain, that it came into our possession somewhat fortuitously."

"You stole it."

"Not exactly, Captain. It was by the tents of some Cheshire knights, that much is true, but it looked lonely and lost. We thought it empty and took it to use it for our water. Imagine our surprise when we found it still had some inside."

"You stole it!"

He shrugged. "Captain, if you will hire outlaws, then what do you expect?"

I suppose if I had asked Sir John, he would have provided us with ale. I confess that this was better. Something stolen was much better than something given. Something given implied a return gift. We ate well, and we drank well. An archer always had an unquenchable thirst.

When darkness fell we made our way to the shields unaccompanied. The enemy could not see us and it was less dangerous. Captain William and his men were there already. I had no doubt that the men on the walls would know something was afoot. They would hear the fyrd and the men at arms milling about. We had pots of burning coals. John of Nottingham had come up with this method. He had used it before in Gascony. An archer nocked an arrow. He dipped the arrow into the fire and in one motion, lifted, drew and released. I had never tried it, but John assured me that it minimised the risk of burning your own hand. I could see that the younger archers were both fascinated and worried in equal measure.

Captain William checked that his men were ready and then came over to me. He was leading his own men at arms, twenty from the men of Cheshire and fifty of the levy, the fyrd. They would follow. He had confided in me that the fyrd was not reliable. They would only follow if the walls were taken. Their numbers would merely swell the ranks of those within. "Whenever you are ready, Captain!"

"Godspeed, my friend." As they slipped into the dark to wait close to the ditch in the darkness, I called, "Ready!" Once I gave the first order, my men would not wait for me. They would send arrow after arrow until their supply was exhausted. "Draw and release!" I leaned forward and dipped the oil-soaked arrow in the fire. Alarmingly, it flamed immediately, and I saw tongues of fire begin to eat up the shaft. When I pulled back my fingers were scorched by the burning arrow. I released and watched it arc. It sailed over the wall, and I saw it hit the roof of the keep. It was a lucky strike, for that was the hardest place for the Welsh to extinguish the flames. I saw more arrows from my right as Captain Jack and his men sent theirs. One or two of my men had not reached as far as me and their arrows had struck the wall.

I learned from my first. I dipped my next arrow quickly and trusted the oil to make it burn. Consequently the fire did not lick down the shaft. My second arrow followed the arc of the first and joined it amongst another four which had lodged there. Even as I looked I saw the flames taking hold. From within the keep came cries as men left the walls to extinguish the fire. I saw that the men at arms were scaling the walls and there appeared to be little opposition. The wind from behind us fanned the flames. The flames caught and the fire grew. I switched my aim. I sent my next arrow deeper into the castle. This time I did not see where it landed, for it arced over the wall. There were buildings there, and there were men. As I sent my last arrow over I saw that the gatehouse was on fire, and flames were leaping into the air from around the north-west corner of the castle. Captain Jack and his men had done that.

We had done what we had been ordered. "Well done archers. Let us head to the horses. We have to move north."

Our camp and our horses were close to the road and close to the sally port. Sharp-eyed Ronan shouted, "Captain! Riders at the sally port."

They were fewer than two hundred paces from us, but it was night. "Kill them!" We did not want word of our attack reaching the Welsh king. I had three arrows left. In the dark I stood little chance of hitting a man and so I aimed at the leading horse. I hit it but, as with all horses, it staggered on. As my archers sent their arrows towards the men who were leaving, I sent a second. It hit another horse. My last one struck a horse in the rump. It might run for a long way. I dropped my bow and drew my sword. "Dick, get your horse and catch any who escape us." Dick was our best rider. Others had heard the commotion, and men began to filter from those attacking the walls. The Welsh closed the gate, and I saw that there was just the one rider who had evaded us. Dick would catch him, but there were twelve men who had escaped the walls.

As I ran, I saw that there were not twelve. Three had been hit by arrows. Those three were either wounded or dying. The men we would be facing were either knights or men at arms. We needed knights, but ours were busy watching the walls. It was up to us. Some of our levy had been closer than us. They had been standing by the wall and waiting to ascend. Ten of them ran at the fallen men. We were close, and they thought themselves supported. I saw that Hugh of Rhuddlan was one of those who had escaped. I wanted to shout to the farmers and labourers to flee but my voice would have been lost. The men at arms used their swords with wicked efficiency. Only one of the nine men at arms who survived fell, and the levy was butchered.

Their sacrifice enabled us to close with the Welshmen. I was aware that I had young archers with little experience and no sword skill. I shouted, "Ronan, Tom, Matty Straw Hair and Roger Peterson, guard our backs!" I saw them look at me, and then they nodded. The blood had rushed to their heads but my words had calmed them. "These are cunning bastards! Watch for tricks and kill them! The old one is mine!"

I approached Hugh of Rhuddlan. I surreptitiously drew my dagger. I would still have a spare sword across my back if I needed it, but Hugh of Rhuddlan was a wily old wolf.

I saw him laugh. "The murderer returns! I will enjoy killing you; you cost me a good lifestyle! Sir Henry was a waste of skin but he made me coin. You will die, and I will reappear somewhere else."

I said nothing. I would need all of my strength and my skill just to survive, but I could not allow one of my men to face this killer. I heard the clash of steel as my experienced warriors closed with the Welsh. Some would be fighting two on one. If they won then the odds would swing in our favour. That might come too late for me. The man I faced was a traitor. He had changed sides. That gave me both heart and hope.

I did not charge in. That would have been a mistake. I was much younger than he was. The longer it went on, the more chance I had. More of my men could come to my aid. I saw his grin. He had seen me fight and thought he knew me. I had improved since we had last met. I had killed men with my sword and with my dagger. I was not afraid of him. I feared his skill, but that was different.

He feinted at me with his sword. He had his hand behind his back, and I knew that he held a dagger in it. I did not fall into the trap of blocking the blow and then being gutted. I saw him frown. There was a cry behind me in Welsh. One of his men had been killed. Each Welshman who died meant more who would come to my aid. I saw that he was not as confident as he had been. I had fought good warriors before. I had slain Sir Henry, but this was a sergeant at arms I was fighting. He was a grizzled veteran. I might not have the skill. He suddenly launched himself at me. He used his dagger and sword so quickly that they were a blur. I simply reacted, unaware of taking a decision. My body took over, and I blocked sword and dagger with my own weapons. I felt blood trickling down my chin. He had slashed my cheek. I saw the look of joy on his face.

I had not spoken yet, but I did then. "If you think a cut on the cheek means victory, then you should have given up war years ago!"

He came at me again. I suddenly realised that I had a strength which he did not possess. When he launched himself at me, I spun around suddenly and brought my sword across the back of his mail hauberk. I had limited skill, but I had strength, and my blade tore through his mail, his gambeson and came away bloody. He cried out. It was not in pain but in anger. He whipped around and I lunged with my dagger. He was quicker than I was expecting. My dagger merely tore across the back of his right hand. Blood spurted. I was close to him, and I slipped my right leg behind his and pushed. He began to tumble backwards. As he sprawled I swung my sword. It sliced across his thigh, which had no mail to protect it. Blood gushed. I stepped forward and swung my dagger, almost blindly, up and under his arm. I saw the tip protrude from the top. He tore away and I lost my dagger. I used two hands, raised my sword and brought it down. I hacked through his coif and into his skull.

I slew Hugh of Rhuddlan.

I found myself out of breath. I looked around and found my men were cheering. We had stopped them escaping. I turned around and saw Dick, son of Robin, galloping up. In his right hand he held a skull. We had done our duty. We had contained the Welsh.

CHAPTER 13

We collected the mail, swords and coins from the dead men at arms. We would divide it later. We left the bodies where they lay. The delay had not been of our making, but Prince Edward would want us to complete the task he had given us. We would have to scout out the road to Ruthin. We could leave nothing at the camp. We would be needed to fight the next battle. Even as we were packing the horses, we heard the cries of victory from within the walls. The night attack had worked. I wondered how many of Captain William's men had fallen. It was almost dawn by the time we headed along the road to Ruthin.

Peter of Wakefield and Dick, son of Robin, rode ahead of us. They were unencumbered. We had spare horses with our supplies and what we had taken. We had had to leave the barrel of ale. There was little left in it anyway. The high rough ground, which I had said was ambush country, was just four miles from Mold. My scouts examined the ground carefully before they waved us forward. The sun was climbing in the sky. It would be a hot day.

Sometimes things happen which you cannot explain. Rafe Oak Arms was a good archer, but he was not the most careful of men. He was leading one of the horses with our spare arrows and he had not secured them. As the horse slipped on a stone, the arrows shifted and spilled. They would take some time to recover.

John of Nottingham rounded on him. "You useless excuse for an archer! We will need those arrows before long. Sorry, Captain."

I, too, was annoyed. "John of Nottingham, make sure that all of the sumpters have secure loads. Drink. I will ride ahead with Peter and Dick. Wait here until I return."

"Aye, Captain."

The road twisted and turned through scrubby undergrowth and untidy clumps of trees. We were just coming to the edge when something glinted ahead. I stopped. Hunting men was just like hunting animals. You needed to be patient, and you needed to be still. I saw the glint again and I shaded my eyes against the sunlight. Dick, son of Robin, had even better eyes. "I see them, Captain. There are knights and mailed men. If I were to hazard a guess I would say it was the Welsh. I count more than a hundred banners."

As my eyes narrowed I saw that he was right. I spied the banners as the army snaked along the road from Ruthin. They were coming to the aid of Mold. Had another message been sent, or had this always been planned? It mattered not. "Dick, ride to the prince or Sir John. Tell them that the Welsh army is six miles away."

"Yes, Captain." He turned and galloped off.

"Come, Peter." We rode back. John of Nottingham had secured the packhorses. "Each of you, take a spare quiver. Rafe, lead the packhorses back to Mold. We have a Welsh army heading down the road. We will try to delay them while the prince makes his dispositions." Rafe and the other three archers leading the sumpters turned around and rode after Dick.

John of Nottingham said, "There was a likely place just back there, Captain. The road rises and twists. We can hit them there."

"Good. Take half the men and go to the south side of the road. I will go to the north. Do not risk the men. When we have stopped their scouts, we mount and ride a mile or so. We will ambush them again."

I led my men back up the road and we divided. We rode our horses up into the scrub and tethered them. As we went back down, I shouted, "Hide yourselves in the undergrowth, and wait for my first arrow! Did you hear, John of Nottingham?"

"Aye, Captain! We will await your orders!"

I chose a spot between two young ash trees and a hawthorn bush. The bush would hide me and I could send my arrow beneath the lower branches of the ash. My trajectory would be a flat one. I would aim at one of the knights. Knights did not ride with shields protecting their sides; they hung from their cantles. Their mail might stop an ordinary arrow but not ours. We would be releasing at fewer than fifty paces. Nothing could stop our arrows at that range. I could hear the horses and their riders as they ascended the slight slope. It was dead ground and we could not see them. That also meant that they could not see us. The first they would know would be when they began to die.

I saw the banners first and then the heads of the riders. This was the vanguard. From my experience, I knew there would be eight or ten knights and men at arms with their squires. Their task would be to spot an ambush. We used my archers for such a task, and we were better. I saw that some wore helmets while others hung them from their cantles. I waited until the knights were just twenty paces from me. I aimed at a large knight in the second group. He had a full-face helmet. There were holes to help him breathe as well as eye holes. A sword would not be able to harm him, but a well-struck arrow could easily pierce the eye-hole. The Welsh used hunting arrows, and they were not as effective against our knights.

Many men at arms and knights believe that the bow is a silent weapon. That is not true. Some bows creak when you draw them, but all make a sound as the arrow is released. There is a thrum from the string and then, almost a hiss, as the wind whistles through the feathers. My men heard those sounds, and their arrows were released before mine drove through the eyehole and into the skull of the large knight. His head was driven back, and he fell from the back of his horse. My second arrow was sent at the knight who wore no helmet; he was twenty paces from me. He had drawn his sword, but it would avail him nothing. My arrow drove up through his neck and into his skull. The knight fell dead. Eighteen had been hit by our arrows, and it was only then that a horn sounded. My arrow struck his mouth, went into his skull and came out of the back. Pieces of bone showered the squires behind. The survivors turned and rode back to the main body. I had no doubt that Welsh archers were already hurrying up the road to deal with us.

"Horses!"

That was all I needed to say. I joined my men in hurrying back to our horses. Welsh archers went to war on foot. They would be running to reach us and we would be gone. I was buying time for Prince Edward.

I mounted my horse and turned to head north-east once more. I saw that none of my men had been hurt. We had surprised them. I saw two of the Welsh horses galloping along the road. If I could, then I would take them. As the ground descended slightly towards the farmland, I halted and tethered my horse. "Here is a likely spot." It was the last place we could hide before the open farmland began. I nocked an arrow as I hurried through the scrubby undergrowth to the road. This time we would not wait as close to the road. I found a steeper part where we could send our arrows down and they would find it harder to get back at us. I also waved my men to echelon to the right. This time we had to cover the woods as well as the road. We had told them that we had archers. They would know the danger was coming. I found a hawthorn which overhung slightly. It would not impair my arrow and would afford me some cover. I waited. As I did so, I glanced around and saw my archers, each choosing the best vantage point that they could.

I knew that we would not hear horses this time. They would have archers scurrying through the woods and the undergrowth to find us. The ones who came along the road would be the lighter horsemen from Ireland: muntator. These rode smaller horses than knights and men at arms. Their mail shirts just covered the upper parts of their bodies and they were not noble. Many of them were wild Irishmen and were not to be underestimated.

Robin of Barnsley killed the first Welsh archer. It was such a good strike that it killed him instantly. Both sets of archers heard the arrow but the Welsh had no idea whence it had come. I left my men on the slight slope to deal with the Welsh archers. Most were ex-outlaws. They knew the terrain better than any. I heard hooves and readied my bow. The horsemen were looking at the side of the road. My arrow drove into the neck and then the body of the leading rider. The one next to him was thrown from his saddle by an arrow from John of Nottingham's men. These men did not run. They charged up, through the undergrowth towards us.

I nocked another arrow and it struck a man who was just twenty paces from me. I hit him in the chest and threw him backwards over his saddle. His horse came at me, and I flapped my bow before it and drove it south and west to clatter and crash through the trees and undergrowth. It would put off the Welsh archers. I just managed to nock and release another arrow as a second rider tried to get at me. It was a hurried strike, but the arrow went through his thigh and into his small horse. The horse reared in pain. The man was thrown from the saddle and the arrow tore open his leg. It was a mortal wound.

"Horses!" We had managed to slow them down again, and now was the time for discretion. As I was running to my horse, I saw a Welsh archer aiming at me. I was drawing an arrow and looked for cover even as he tracked my movement. I saw a beech tree. It would afford some protection. I lifted my bow and released just before I dropped to the ground. The Welshman's arrow hit the tree. I nocked an arrow. I was listening for movement. I spied a rock. Picking it up, I threw it high to my left. As it clattered, I stepped to the right. The archer had crept to within ten paces of me. His head was looking to his right when my arrow went through his back. I had been lucky. I made my horse and mounted. I nocked another arrow. The rest of my men were at their horses, all except Hugh, son of Hugh.

"Where is Hugh, Matty?"

"Dead, Captain. The Welshman you just slew did for him."

"Fetch his horse." When this was over we would come back and find his body. We would bury it. It would not be left for the carrion.

The steep slope we rode led to a field which had been planted with winter barley. We rode through it towards the road. We waited for a few moments while John of Nottingham led the rest of my men.

"We have done enough. Let us find the prince."

As we rode down the road towards Mold, I saw Captain Jack leading his archers. Dick, Rafe and my other archers were with them. Prince Edward had reacted quickly and decisively. The Welsh would not catch us unawares. Hugh had not died in vain.

I reined in and pointed behind me. "The Welsh are coming. We slowed them down. What are the prince's plans?"

Captain Jack shrugged. "I know not. He was organising the men as we left. He only has knights and the levy left to fight. The men at arms suffered wounded and dead in the assault. The castle is ours, but we do not have the army we would have hoped for. The good news is that we found a great store of arrows. Why they did not use them, I do not know. We can afford to use them without worrying about replacing them."

"And our orders?"

He smiled and dismounted. "Slow them down!" He turned in the saddle. "Horse holders!"

I dismounted too. "The wounded can hold the horses."

I saw that Roger Peterson and Matty Straw Hair had wounds. It would be better not to risk them. Between us we had thirty-six archers. It was not a large number, but we were the best. We had shown that already. We spread out in a long line. We all had an arrow ready. It would be nocked only when we had a target. It took some time for the Welsh to come, and when they did, it was the light horsemen again. They had spears, and these men wore the aketon: the padded jacket. There were thirty of them, and when they saw us they stopped. They might be fearless Irishmen, but even they would not willingly charge archers. They halted four hundred paces from us. They respected our range.

I saw one turn and shout something. A short while later, fifty or so Welsh archers ran from the undergrowth. They began to move forward. It would be a duel of archers. This would be a test of our skill and our bows. I believed we had a longer range, for we used a slightly longer bow stave. Captain Jack knew how far I could send an arrow. As the Welshmen moved towards us he said, "Try to hit one at your maximum range. I want them worried that we can all send an arrow as far as you."

I nodded and nocked one. The Welshmen were running now. They had run hard. Even at three hundred paces, I could see them huffing and puffing. At that range, and with them moving, I would be lucky to

199

be able to choose a target. Instead, I aimed at the knot of men running down the road. I pulled the bow back as far as I could. Even as it soared into the air I had another nocked, and I sent that after it, then a third. I had just released my third when my first arrow plunged down and hit an archer in the shoulder. My second went through the shin of another and pinned his leg. The third hit one of the horsemen, who had moved a little closer. He was also hit in the shoulder.

The Welsh archers stopped. The three wounded men crawled away. Captain Jack shouted, "Draw! Release!" The Welsh sent their arrows at exactly the same time. We were both finding the range. One of Captain Jack's men was hit in the leg by an arrow. The rest fell short. Eight Welshmen were hit. Two of the hits were fatal.

"Keep releasing!"

We could afford to waste arrows. I sent arrow after arrow at the Welshmen. They had realised that we outranged them and were trying to move closer. As they did so, they came within range of more of our arrows. Even more began to die. Once they were close enough they sent their own arrows at us. It was hard to say who might have won the contest, had the light horsemen not divided in two and attempted to outflank us.

"Mount! We have done enough! Fetch the wounded and the dead!"

We did not want our dead abused by the Welsh. As it turned out, none of my men had been killed, but Peter Wakefield was bleeding, as was Ronan. I could not assess the damage. When we ran to the horses we did not run in a straight line. That was a sure way to end up with an arrow in your back! We reached our horse holders. The light horsemen were galloping towards us. I mounted mine first and slung my bow. I drew my sword and turned my horse to gallop towards the advancing horsemen. I was trying to make them turn. I managed to take them by surprise. What I didn't realise, until we were close to each other, was that I was much bigger than they were. They had shields and swords, and I just had a sword, but I had a longer reach. When I saw them rein in a little I turned to my left and swung my sword, more in hope than expectation, across their chests. I struck none, but I had stopped them. I dug my heels in and followed my men.

Captain Jack had his bow ready and an arrow nocked as I galloped towards him. To some who were not archers, it might have appeared that he sent the arrow at me. But I knew that he was aiming at the horsemen galloping after me. I heard a scream and knew that his arrow had hit a man. Captain Jack gave a satisfied nod. "Between us, we have slowed them down. Well done, but that was reckless."

I could not help grinning. I felt excited. "I thought they might slow up. I did not expect them to stop."

He shook his head. "You and your men ride big horses, and every archer has a chest like an oak tree. You terrified them. I just hope that the prince uses the time we have bought him wisely."

We did not have far to travel to discover what was happening. There was now a barrier of men. The fyrd had moved up and was now in a three-deep line. There were two large woods, and between them there were farms and then the road. In all, the barrier of men was about twelve hundred paces across. As a barrier, it was hardly substantial, but the Welsh archers and the muntators would not charge them. They would wait for the men at arms and knights.

Sir John and his squire were ahead of the levy. Sir John was smiling. "That was well done by both of you. How many are coming?"

He meant, of course, knights. "We saw a hundred banners. They were strung out along the road."

"Arrange your men behind the levy. Our knights will deal with this."

Captain Jack looked at me and then Sir John. "My lord, Captain Gerald did well, but if he slew more than thirty archers it is still but a small part of the force of archers they can bring to bear."

"Then you will have to make sure that you kill more of them when the battle begins. Lord Edward is counting on you!"

We were dismissed. Sir John waved his arm and the levy opened up to allow us through. Once we were out of earshot Captain Jack said, "I do not envy you your master. At least Sir Ranulf values his archers. He would not expect us to do the impossible. We will lose archers."

I shook my head. "I have fought these archers more than enough. They are good, but because they are shorter, their arrows do not travel as far, and they like to target knights. They will send their arrows to the prince and his nobles. They will die."

"Are you certain?"

"There are many things of which I am ignorant, but Welsh archery is not one of them. My father taught me well."

Captain Jack raised his arm. "Dismount. Take the horses back to the crossroads. Fetch more arrows. We have our work cut out for us this day!"

As the horses were led back I began to assess the best place to stand. We were taller than the fyrd, but when the horses and knights came our view would be compromised. I pointed to the wall by the side of the road. "I will have my men on that side."

Captain Jack stroked his beard. "You will use the wall to let you see over the horseman." I nodded. "Good."

Just then, we heard the clatter of hooves, the creaking of leather and the jingle of mail, as Prince Edward led his knights. Sir Roger Mortimer, John de Warenne, William de Valence and Sir Ranulf followed the prince, and then there were another two hundred banners and bannerets. All wore the round helmet which completely covered the head. I knew that underneath would be an arming cap, coif and ventail. Their heads would be protected, but their vision would be impaired. The exception was Prince Edward. He had a bascinet with a small crown around it. As he passed me he slowed down. "You earned your pay today. Destroy the Welsh archers and I shall double it!"

"We will do our best, lord."

As they passed I clambered up onto the wall. I could see the Welsh. They were arraying for the fight. I saw that they had three battles. Two were of knights, and the third was men at arms, led by a knight. Before the horsemen were the archers and the levy. I counted at least two hundred archers. Their levy was the same size as our fyrd. The Welsh had put the muntators in two groups on the flanks. They would be able to filter through the woods and outflank us. Had we had the men at arms who were now in Mold Castle, then we would have had parity of numbers. As it was, the Welsh had the advantage. The archers and their light horses would decide this battle.

Prince Edward had his knights in three battles too, but they would be outnumbered by the enemy horses. He was relying on the great skill of the English knights. I was more worried about the Welsh archers. I saw that they were fewer than three hundred paces from our knights. They could send two thousand arrows at our knights before they would be able to close with them. The Welsh king was sacrificing his levy. His archers would run behind the knights at the last minute. The levy would break up the attack of our knights and the Welsh would destroy them.

I jumped down from the wall and ran to Captain Jack. "We are doing no good here! We are too far away."

"You are right. We need to be closer to the knights." He turned to the levy archers. "Follow us, and stand behind us!"

"Yes, Captain."

Captain Jack slipped his bow over his back. "These are men of Cheshire. They have to obey me. Archers, follow us. Levy, let us through!"

My men hurried behind me. We each had three spare bundles of arrows. We were burdened, but it would be worth it. As we passed Sir John he shouted, "You were ordered to stay behind the levy!"

"We have no targets, lord!"

Sir John did not know Captain Jack, but he knew me. "I hope you know your business."

"I do."

The two sets of knights were still weighing each other up. When they charged it would be too late. I knew that the Welsh archers would already be preparing to send their arrows into our knights. We would have to run after the knights and begin to send our arrows ahead of them. We would be releasing blindly, but the Welsh archers would not see us. If we could kill a quarter of their men, it would give our mounted soldiers a chance.

The squires at the rear of our lines looked over their shoulders at us. They each had a spare horse for their lord. I think they were surprised by our appearance. I heard our horns sound. I could not see it, but I knew that the banner now flew, and so long as it did we were honour bound to stay on the battlefield. I felt the ground shake as the horses moved. We ran and actually began to overtake the squires. They were struggling to keep their spare warhorses under control. As soon as we had covered one hundred paces, we stopped. I nocked an arrow and I pulled back. "Draw!"

I heard Captain Jack give the same command.

I shouted, "Release!" We would only have time for four flights. After that we risked hitting our own knights. I heard cries and screams from the front of the charging knights. The squires had a better view than we did, and when I saw eight of them gallop off, I knew that they had seen their lords unhorsed by Welsh archers and were racing to help them. Just then Tom shouted, "Captain! Horsemen!" He pointed to our flank. It was what I had feared: the light horsemen were charging us.

"Turn to face the threat! Kill their horses!" We needed to make the horses and their riders a barrier. There were too few of us to hold them. We did not want to be ridden down by stampeding, riderless horses. I nocked an arrow, drew back and released. The mass of horsemen was a big target. We were no longer fighting as one band; we were each in our own rhythm. However, because we had fought together so often, our training took over and our arrows soared at the same time. I heard the screams of wounded and dying horses. I saw horses and riders tumble over, and yet still they came. The secret was not to panic. We had to believe that we could slay them all. Nock, draw release; all the years of training had brought us to this point and the muntators died. Their horses were slain.

Inevitably some survived, and the closer they came to us, the more chance they had of killing us. One had been protected by whatever charm or cross he wore around his neck. As I drew another arrow, I saw him fewer than twenty paces from me. I nocked, and he was fifteen paces from me. I drew, and he was ten paces away. I could almost feel the breath of his small horse. I released. At five paces he was almost upon me. My arrow hit him so hard in the chest that he was thrown from his horse. His dead hand clung to the reins and the horse's head jerked to the side. Its tail flicked my face as it fell to the ground. I drew another arrow but the wild horsemen had had enough. The survivors were fleeing. I sent an arrow into the back of one. I saw the bodies of archers. Some would be the archers of Cheshire who had fought with us, but some would be my men. I forced myself to ignore that thought. The battle still raged.

I turned and looked at the knights. They were closely engaged. If we sent our arrows towards them then we might hit our own. Captain Jack came over to me. "That was close, Gerald!"

I looked at the dead man I had just slain and the horse whose neck had been broken in the fall. "You are right. And now we cannot help our lords."

Captain Jack turned to look at the battle ahead of us. The horses were no longer tightly packed. There was a melee. It was hard to see where one side began and another ended. All of our men wore a red cross on their surcoats. That was the only way to differentiate. The captain echoed my thoughts, "They are all closely engaged but we have arrows enough. We can go amongst them. What say you?"

I laughed, "I am game! Prince Edward's archers, rally on me!" My men surrounded me. There were ten of them. We would bury our dead when all was over. "We have some sport this day! Let us go amongst the men on horses and see what mischief we can make. Take no risks, just Welsh lives!"

I ran towards the thin line of squires waiting with remounts. If my men chose not to follow me then I would understand. What we were about to do was unheard of. I ran with an arrow nocked. Captain Jack had been right, there was room in which to move. I just needed to have quick reactions. Those reactions saved Sir Ranulf, for I saw a Welsh archer draw back his bow. The Welsh were doing as we were. My arrow hit him even as he began to release. Sir Ranulf did not know his saviour. I did, and that was enough. I nocked another and ran. I used the bodies of archers and horses to protect me. Their archers were more dangerous to our knights, and so I hunted Welshmen. It was almost too easy. They were trying to slay knights and did not see the winged death of my red-fletched arrows.

Horses and knights were becoming exhausted. My shoulders burned. Both commanders decided that they had had enough. Almost by mutual consent, horns sounded and both sides disengaged. I kept an arrow nocked. As our horses trudged back towards me, I saw a Welsh archer pull back. I released. My arrow flew so close to Prince Edward that he turned to look. My arrow struck the Welshman between the eyes. He fell back, as though struck by a war hammer. I nocked another and watched for more such treachery.

"Thank you, Gerald War Bow. Once again, I am indebted to you. I am pleased that you disobeyed orders. Your arrows, few though they were, thinned out some of the archers. Next time we will keep you closer."

"I am your captain of archers, lord."

I moved forward and began to search the dead who lay on the field. I kept my eye open for any enemy who might do the same. I took the good arrows from the dead Welsh archers and the purses from all the dead. I saw that the knights who had died had fallen to Welsh arrows. Their squires and their men were already taking them back to our lines. Many of the Welsh levy had been slaughtered, but they had little on them. I did not venture too close to the Welsh, and when I was burdened enough, I turned and went back to my men. I saw that some of them had profited too.

I reached the dead muntator I had slayed and his horse. My men wearily joined me. I looked at Jack of Lincoln. "Who was lost?"

"Roger Peterson, Rafe Oak Arms and Peter of Wakefield."

I looked up. Peter had been one of Jack of Lincoln's oldest companions. "I am sorry, Jack."

"Do not be, Captain. Since we joined you our life has had purpose. We are no longer just surviving day to day. We have lived. There is ale and there is food. There have been women and, occasionally, a comfortable bed. We would not have survived much longer in the forest. It was good that you found us. We will bury them."

We searched the bodies and collected the purses of the horsemen we had slain. We hacked a haunch of dead horse for that would be our meal. We trudged back to our camp. It was a sombre camp. Captain Jack brought his archers to join us. He too had lost men. He nodded towards the camp of the knights. Prince Edward had not gone inside the castle. He was wise enough to know that sharing his men's privations endeared him to them.

While the haunch was cooking, we collected and then divided the purses we had taken. We shared our dead comrades' goods too. We were a company. I had a leather sack for mine. It was quite heavy. Some of the others had less than I, for they had spent it. In the case of the ones who had been outlaws, it was goods which the rest of us took for granted: decent boots, a better cloak, a fine dagger. John of Nottingham brought over the ale skin and filled my beaker. "What do you plan for your treasure, Captain?"

I shrugged. "I need for nothing yet. However, I do not like carrying it around. When we return to Windsor or somewhere civilised, I will bury it. If our camp had been taken we would have lost it all." I swallowed the ale. "There will come a time when I am no longer needed. It happened to my father. I would do as he did and buy some land. The difference is, I hope to have more coin and buy a better piece of earth."

"Men envy good land. You might have to fight to keep it."

"Then I will sire sons to help me."

"Sire sons! First, Captain, you must find a woman, and the last time I looked there were few on the battlefield." He stood. "We will take the mail and swords we found and see if Captain William and his men wish to buy them. If not, there are other men at arms who may wish to be safer in battle."

Captain Jack came over and our men gave us some privacy. "There will be a truce and the prince will speak with the Welsh king. Their archers killed too many of our knights."

"Then all of this was in vain?"

"No, my young friend. We keep what we have taken. Mold is ours and we will have Denbigh returned to us. We may have lost knights and squires, but our men at arms were untouched. Many Welsh archers were killed. Winter draws on, and the Welsh cannot afford their men away from their fields. They have animals to bring in for the winter."

I was disappointed. "I hoped for a better conclusion. This was ill done."

"You will get used to it. Prince Edward did better than many lords. His father is less decisive. It bodes well. You know that the prince dallied with those like Montfort, who challenged the king?"

"I had heard."

"When we are done here, you will be returning to Windsor, for Prince Edward goes to the aid of his father. Things will come to a head. De Montfort has the backing of London and the Midlands. I fear that we will have to stay here to guard the Welsh border, but you my friend, will be in the thick of it."

"And I have lost archers. The prince seems to think that an archer is like a man at arms, they can be found anywhere. But I am well aware of the skills of my men."

"And that is why you watch over them. You are wise."

He was right; I did watch over my men. We left five days later. Ransoms had been paid for the knights we had captured and the two castles were garrisoned. We had shared out the money from the sale of the mail and swords. We had spare horses now, as we had lost men, and we carried all of the arrows we had taken from the castle with us. If war was coming then we would be prepared.

CHAPTER 14

We did not go to Windsor. King Henry was at Oxford Castle. Since the time of the war between Stephen and Matilda, the west of the land had been loyal to the king. The nearer to London lay the greatest discontent, and London itself was a hotbed of rebellion. There the people were self-serving and greedy. That was where the de Montfort clan had the greatest support. In the Midlands, the land around Northampton, Nottingham and Leicester, lay the wealth of the de Montfort faction. By choosing Oxford, King Henry was showing just how astute he was. He could reach those castles quicker than the de Montforts travelling from London. There was no war yet. I heard a rumour, begun by Captain William, who had been close to a conversation between Prince Edward and de Warenne, that King Henry had sent an embassy to the pope. He wished to be absolved from the Provisions. I had not heard of them and so I asked Sir John when we camped one night.

His face darkened. "Five years ago, the barons forced the king to accept a council of nine barons who would advise him and ensure that he ruled fairly. Over the intervening years, the de Montforts have taken control of this council. Do not worry Gerald War Bow, the pope has agreed to dissolve it."

210

What he meant was that we would have God on our side and the pope would instruct his bishops and archbishops to excommunicate the king's enemies. We would be absolved from sin. We spent much of our time close to death. That was a reassurance which we needed. If we died, we would go to heaven. It was the end of autumn when we reached Oxford. It was an armed camp. Neither my archers nor Captain William's men at arms could be accommodated within the walls of the castle, and we had to make other arrangements. We had coin and so we used it. I found a mean inn on the outskirts of the town. It was not in the best condition, but it had stables, and more importantly, it had three rooms which we could use. The owner, Dickon of Downholme, was more than happy for us to rent rooms and stalls. We did not pay an exorbitant rate, for he knew the value of helping the future king of England. His wife and daughter proved to be good cooks and we ate well.

Prince Edward seemed to forget his archers and his men at arms. Captain William and I had to visit the castle once a week to remind him to pay us. It was not deliberate. It was an oversight. When we visited the castle, we learned more upon each visit. Although we were in a haven of peace, all around was dissent. Prince Edward had not only left a strong army in the north of Wales, his father had left one around the Severn. There was no open war, but there were raids. Individuals who supported the barons' cause were ousted in royal areas, and royalists suffered the same fate in baronial England. It was like a pot on the fire. It was bubbling but had yet to boil over. That day would come.

Consequently, even though it was becoming colder and the days shorter, we practised each and every day. We had fought enough times to get to know each other. That made the releasing of arrows easier. We could get into the rhythm quicker. We gradually increased the distance we could send arrows. I confess that much of that was my doing. I had the greatest range and so the others watched my technique and emulated me. My frame and my build were the biggest assets I possessed, but by improving technique we were all able to send arrows further by Christmas.

I then pressed Captain William and his men to help train us to use swords. The attack of the muntator had worried me. That could have ended disastrously. All of my men now had a good sword. None was as long as mine, but they were well made. They all copied the way I wore my swords. They had theirs across their backs. Our belts were for our arrows.

It was Candlemas when I was summoned, along with Captain William, to the castle. There we were met by Sir John. He now had a title: Baron of Mold. His part in that victory had been recognised. He also commanded a conroi of knights, nine of them. Richard his squire was there, along with three of his knights. Sir John was no longer the young squire we had first met in France. He was now a seasoned and respected warrior. I wondered what the meeting would bring.

There was wine, bread and cheese on the table. We were the last to arrive, and I could see that the knights had already made inroads into the food and wine. "Now that our two captains are here, we can begin. The Earl of Derby, Robert de Ferrers, has been raiding Prince Edward's estates in Gloucester. We have suffered enough at his hands, and the prince has instructed me to lead a chevauchée into his lands in Derbyshire. Our aim is simple. We are to take as much plunder as we can. The prince wants de Ferrers punished for his audacity."

"It is a cold and harsh time of year to be raiding Derbyshire."

"I know, Sir James. I did not say it would be easy. Peveril Castle is subject to attacks from the garrisons of de Ferrers' castles. By raiding de Ferrers' lands, we ease the pressure on Prince Edward's castle."

The knights began to debate the military strategy involved. Captain William turned to me. "This is to provoke war."

"Truly?"

"If the barons allow the prince to do this, then they are accepting that the king has won. I cannot see de Montfort allowing that to happen. Why else do you think that the king has gathered his army at Oxford? These nobles can argue for the rest of time, but it will not change what we have to do. You have spare horses?"

"Aye, we have enough to carry our war gear and four remounts. And you?"

"We do not yet have enough. When we begin this chevauchée, the first thing we will need to do is capture more horses. Winter is terrible hard on horses. We need to strike and strike quickly. It is good that you have had your men practising with swords. They will need them."

"You are right. If it is wet then bowstrings do not send our arrows as far, and if there is fog we cannot see."

We were suddenly aware that the others had stopped talking and Sir John was giving me a wry smile. "It seems Prince Edward's captains do not need to hear our plans."

Captain William smiled back and then answered, "I am guessing, my lord, that we will be at the front, watching for foes, and Captain Gerald will be at the rear, guarding the baggage. As for where we will go first? I am guessing close to Peveril Castle. Makeslesfeld? Chesterfield?"

"Chesterfield. And thence the lands close by. Sheffield might be too large a castle, but we will see. Captain Gerald, you and your archers need to be familiar with the land. It may prove useful later." He nodded. "Very perceptive Captain William, for we will be based at Peveril Castle. At the moment, the garrison is ten old men. There should be plenty of room for us!"

With those enigmatic comments ringing in my ears, we left. We had two days to prepare. While we had been in the inn, we had become familiar with the innkeeper, Dickon, and his family. Dick, son of Robin, had become even more familiar with his daughter, Mary. There was a liaison there that promised something more than a quick dalliance in the stable. As a result, I had decided to bury my coin in the stables. When we returned from the meeting I set my men to prepare, and I took my leather bag. I took out enough coins for my needs and then buried the rest in the stable. I cleared away the hay and dug a deep hole. I used a stone to cover the bag and then filled in the hole with soil. When I returned, I would know where my bag was when I found the stone. I covered it with hay. Gratifyingly, as I led my horse back into the stall, it deposited some dung there. The stables were as safe a place as any.

David the Welshman had been on a chevauchée, and when we ate that night in our lodgings, he explained in more detail what was entailed. He was more than happy to do so. He had enjoyed the experience. It had been profitable.

"The idea is to annoy your neighbours. You say we will be based in a castle?"

"That is what Sir John said."

"Then so much the better. A chevauchée takes any animal which moves; kills any man; burns the huts and houses of all that they see and, hopefully, entices the enemy to send out their knights to stop you."

It all made sense now. "Sir Robert de Ferrers is busy around Gloucester and so his better knights should be there. I can see now why the prince does this, but I am guessing that it is we and the men at arms who will be doing the raiding."

David the Welshman rubbed his hands together. "And that means we get first pick of any weapons and coin. The people we are raiding will be poor, but they will have coins buried for their taxes."

I could not help glancing towards the stables. To cover my guilty look I stood. "It will be cold there. Snow may linger. Make sure you have warm cloaks and sealskin capes."

It was a long ride to the bleak, high land of Derbyshire, but Sir John had planned well. We were to stay halfway along our journey at Ashby de la Zouch with Sir Alan la Zouche. He was an old knight, but his family had served King Henry II and were loyal to the crown. We headed up the Great North Road. There were almost a hundred of us. The knights had brought servants and squires. Each had a small retinue of men at arms but I led the remaining archers. The men at arms who served the nine knights wore no mail, and their horses were not the best. I realised how lucky we were to have such a patron as Prince Edward.

We rode at the front, as William had predicted. We were not, however, scouting. We rode the main road, and we were a strong company. It would have taken a brave or perhaps foolish man indeed to challenge us. We wore the livery of the son of the king of England. We went with banners furled. Cloaked against the cold, we would look like what we were: ordinary men at arms and archers. Sir John wished the presence of the knights a secret.

The castle at Ashby was a wooden one. It was a motte and bailey. It had been expanded beyond the one built just before the civil war. The knights and squires were accommodated in the hall, but we had to make do with the stables. With so many horses we were overcrowded.

Peveril Castle had a commanding view. I could see why King John had liked it so much. The land around it fell away. It was sheltered by a huge rocky outcrop, and the road which reached it wound up the steep slope. An enemy would be subject to missile attack all the way up. I could see nowhere that could accommodate a war machine capable of reducing the walls. It was triangular, with a huge keep at the narrow end, furthest from the gate. The stairs to the entrance of the keep were outside of it, meaning it could be defended. Inside, however, it was run down. It showed neglect. It had been a royal castle since before the reign of King John, but following the death of that most unhappy of kings, it had fallen into disrepair. The castellan, and that was a grand title for someone who was, in essence, a caretaker, was an old sergeant at arms. Miles Beauchamp. He was older than even my father had been. He had rheumy eyes and had run to fat. He gave his quarters to Sir John, and he and the rest of the garrison joined us in the barracks. Despite his age he had a good sense of humour and, even more importantly, knew the land around.

Miles was not a noble and spoke easily with Captain William and I. "The de Ferrers family are nothing more than robber barons! They are both grasping and cruel. It is time someone took them on! I wish I was young enough to ride with you."

"What can you tell us about the castles around here?"

"Badequelle is the closest of the de Ferrers' manors. It has a small castle there and a church. Then there is Matlac. That is a rich manor. They have a fortified hall there. It is rich farmland. South of us is Buxton, which has a wooden castle. One knight is lord of the manor there, and he has twenty men serving him." He shook his head. "Piss-poor lot they are. They are only fit for raiding farms!"

"Is that it?"

"The land all about is de Ferrers' land. There are many farms, and there is much livestock. Sheffield, which is his, is the big castle on the other side of Stanage Edge. That is held by Thomas de Furnival. He supports King Henry, but he is away fighting with his cousin in the Marches."

I wondered why Prince Edward had not asked de Furnival to join this raid. Then I realised that it was a game they played and too complicated for a humble archer. We would just do what we had been asked. We were obeying our lawful lords and could not be held accountable for any wrongdoing. The pope himself had blessed King Henry's endeavours. Simon de Montfort and his allies, like de Ferrers, were trying to upset the natural balance and questioning the God-given right of the king to rule.

With our war gear stored and our horses stabled we prepared for our raid. Sir John had also spoken with Miles and knew almost as much as we did. I suspect Miles' language had been a little more flowery for the young noble. Captain William and I knew the calibre of men we would be dealing with. They were absolved outlaws! Sir John told us that we would be attacking the land around Matlac first. He had grown since I had first met him. I dare say I had too, but he now thought a little more about things.

"I want you two captains to take your men and raid Matlac. To get to it, you will have to pass Badequelle. There is a castle there. Just pass it on your way to Matlac. I want them to think that you are all that we have and that you are afraid of taking on their castle. With luck, they will send a rider to fetch men from Derby, Leicester or Nottingham; perhaps even Tutbury, which is Earl Ferrer's favourite castle. After Matlac we will take Badequelle, but I hope that we can keep the presence of so many knights hidden. When that is reduced we will head to Buxton, and our work should be done."

Captain William was more outspoken than I was. "With respect, my lord, you are asking a lot from us."

He stiffened. "These orders come from Prince Edward!"

I spread my arms. "What Captain William is saying, lord, is that while I can see why we should keep the knights and squires hidden, there are men at arms who could swell our ranks." I was talking about those who served the other knights.

I saw him relax a little. "You may be right. They do not look as smart as you, and if they accompanied you it would make you look less suspicious. After we take Buxton, then we take Chesterfield. We want de Ferrers' land to be a wasteland and draw him back from Gloucester."

The men we were to take with us were a mixed band. Some were solidly dependable men. We had spoken to those on the way north. Others were not. They were more like the men Miles had told us about – "piss-poor warriors". None were archers and so it would be Captain William who had to keep them under control.

We left after dawn. It was a grey day. Dark clouds threatened rain and the wind was in our faces, from the north-east. It was a lazy wind. It did not go around you, it went straight through you. Such a wind did not suit archers. It made hands numb, and archery was about touch and feel. Miles Beauchamp had told us where the king's land ended and that of de Ferrers began. The first farm we saw had a small field which was being used for crops. It was winter and none were growing but there were two pigs rooting in the soil. In another field there were two dozen sheep and a couple of cows. As farms went it was poor and I felt guilty. I saw the farmer and his family look up at the sound of our approach. They did the right thing. They ran.

Daniel of Tilbury laughed. "Right lads, let's have some sport! Who wants the women?"

William's voice was commanding. "Hold! Let them go. We are here for the animals and anything of value on this farm."

The man at arms, who served Sir Richard of Deal, laughed. "The most valuable things on this farm are those two pigs and that tasty young lass!"

Captain William drew next to the man at arms. "Let us get one thing clear. I give the orders. One more word from you and you will be sent back to Peveril!"

"Suits me! I did not know we were raiding with a bunch of priests!"

Captain William nodded. "I warned you! Back to the castle."

"But…"

Captain William turned his horse around. "I have wasted enough time with you. Go!"

Daniel of Tilbury's hand went to his sword but my hand was quicker and my dagger was pressed against his neck before the sword was halfway out. "Do as the captain says," I smiled. "Just to please me, eh?"

He jerked his horse's head around and galloped off.

There was precious little on the farm. The owner was a poor farmer. He was obviously a freeman. His lord and master, de Ferrers, must not have treated his tenant well. William sent two of his men and two others back with the animals, and we rode on to the next place. This time it was a small village. Eight houses and huts made up Badequelle. The castle was a small one, but the church was made of stone. As we approached, the villagers fled across the ditch and into the castle, driving their animals before them.

It was annoying to ride past the castle. It was poorly maintained. I could see the palisades showed wear and tear from the harsh weather of the region. I dug my heels into my horse's flanks and joined Captain William. "We could take that!"

"I know, but to be fair to Sir John, this is the right plan. We can take Matlac easily. Whoever is in that castle will send a rider for help. The message will say that a warband of men rode past the castle. It will not mention knights. That gives us the element of surprise."

In fact, Matlac gave *William* a surprise. It was just a fortified manor house, but it was defended. As we galloped towards it, men left the fields to flee inside the hall. Women grabbed their children and quickly followed. William sent the men at arms he did not know to watch the rear of the hall. We dismounted and he said, "We will use our men for this. Then whatever we find inside is ours."

I nodded. "Archers, string your bows." We tied our horses to the fence, which penned in the village pigs. It would be too far to drive them back to Peveril. We would slaughter them. Carcasses were more manageable. "How do we do this?"

"You and your archers keep your heads down. There looks to be just one entrance. There are steps up to it, but the cross-slits above might cause us a problem."

I nodded and waved my men to me. "We cover the men at arms. Hit anything that moves."

I saw the end of a crossbow appear from one of the cross-slits below the upper wall. A hand emerged to place a bolt. I aimed at the middle of the cross. It was only sixty paces from me and not a difficult strike. The crossbow disappeared. I had no idea if I had killed the crossbowman, but I had deterred them. I saw that there was a sort of balustrade close to the roof. I realised there must be a trapdoor when I saw a helmet moving along it.

"Look to the roof!" I nocked another arrow. My eyes had been tracking the helmet. As soon as I saw it rise, I released. At the same time John of Nottingham sent an arrow towards one of the cross-slits. My arrow struck the defender in the chest as he cleared the balustrade. He and his bow fell over the side.

Captain William and his men had wasted no time. They were already assaulting the door with axes. Robin of Barnsley sent an arrow towards a seemingly unoccupied cross-slit. Even above the sound of axes striking wood, I heard the scream. He nocked another arrow. "I saw a flash of something. I have used one of those arrow slits before. It is possible to use a bow if you stand well back. I took a chance!"

The blows on the doors intensified. My men sent more arrows towards the balustrade and the cross-slits. We had plenty of arrows, and when we captured the hall there would be some we could recover. A crash followed by a cheer told me that we had gained entry to the hall. Our work was done, and we moved a little closer to the hall. Screams, shouts and the clash of weapons told us the story of the battle for the hall. It would be an unequal battle. Captain William and his men at arms were seasoned warriors.

After a short time the sergeant at arms, Ralph Dickson, emerged. The other sergeant at arms, Matthew, had died at Mold. Ralph waved me over. "It is ours, Captain. Captain William asked that you slaughter the pigs and prepare to leave. I will go and fetch the others."

"Did we lose any?"

He laughed. "No! They had courage but no skill. Three of their warriors lie dead but the captain spared the rest. We are not butchers."

We had slaughtered the pigs and put them on the backs of the horses we had found by the time the villagers had been ejected from the village and sent on their way. They trudged north-east to Chesterfield. We fired the hall and the village, and with the cows and sheep, along with chests from the hall, we headed home. I rode with Captain William.

"He was a rich one, I will say that. I found a chest of coins." He winked at me. "I have them safe. We will divide them between our men at Peveril."

"Yours did the hard work."

"We are all Prince Edward's men! Besides, you and your archers slew as many men as we did. You did your part."

The village of Badequelle was still empty when we passed through it. The gates of the castle were still barred. The sight of us driving animals and with laden horses would ensure that the villagers would still be inside the castle the next day. They would not risk returning home while we were raiding. Miles Beauchamp looked happy as we dismounted. "Pigs! I hope you found salt, my lads!"

Captain William laughed. "This is not our first raid! Of course we did, and I hope you have someone who can do justice to these fine beasts! We would enjoy one this night."

"And this is not the first pig I will have roasted! We have the last of the windfall apples in store. I can promise that we will have a feast in the barracks this night!" Captain William went with Miles to choose the pig we would eat. It would be the biggest, and after another had been selected for the knights, we would have the rest salted and preserved.

Sir John emerged with Geoffrey as we began to unpack the horses. "A good raid."

I nodded. "See for yourself, my lord. Captain William set the hall and houses afire. The castle at Badequelle is barred, with the villagers within. It is all as you commanded."

"Good." He looked over at Captain William, who was leading a horse, along with Miles, towards the kitchens. "What of this man at arms? He said Captain William threatened him."

"No, lord, Captain William just sent him back. It was I who threatened him when he thought to draw sword against the captain. He wanted to use and abuse the girls and women from the first farm. We do not do that."

"He did not say that."

I laughed. "Of course he did not, lord. He ran bleating to his master, who came bleating to you. When you run with a pack of dogs, you must expect that not all are the beasts you would choose."

He nodded. "And the castle at Badequelle?"

"It is not well made, lord."

"Are the men able to ride again on the morrow?"

"They could ride again now. It was only Captain William's men who did any real work. The ones we ejected will be at Chesterfield soon, lord. They will probably bring more men to reinforce the castle at Badequelle. If we do not attack and reduce Badequelle soon, then it will be reinforced and our task will be twice as hard."

Richard seemed outraged at my impertinence. "Archer it is not your place to advise Sir John!"

"Nor is it yours to defend me! Captain Gerald is quite right. I was given a task, and if I am to complete it then I must be decisive."

My conversation had meant that the horses had all been unpacked by the time I led mine to the stable. Captain William was waiting for me. He handed me a bag of coins. "Here is the share for your archers. I did not count it, I weighed it."

I nodded. "It matters not. We did little." I put the bag in my tunic and we headed back to the barracks. "We attack Badequelle tomorrow."

He nodded. "I like not this way of war. I am a warrior and would prefer to make war on another warrior. These are poor people we fight."

"The lord we killed today was not poor, but you are right. It is winter and the people we sent north will suffer. We are just doing what our lord tells us. We have committed no sin."

I told him of Daniel of Tilbury's complaint. "Then I will have to lay down the law. We cannot have such divisions."

As we walked into the barracks we knew that something had happened. Daniel of Tilbury was rising from the floor. Two of his friends were helping him. His nose was spread across his face. I saw Jack of Lincoln with bruised knuckles and it did not take much imagination to picture what had happened.

John of Nottingham came over to speak to us. "That Daniel of Tilbury made threats against your lives. Jack has a short temper."

I nodded. Captain William shouted, "Listen to me! *I* command the men at arms here. *All* of the men at arms! You may serve a lord, but until this chevauchée is ended, if you have complaints then bring them to me." He glared at Daniel of Tilbury. "If you be men, then act like it. Tomorrow we go to take a castle. It will be the men in this barracks who have the task of taking those walls. We will all be shield brothers. There will be no more talk of vengeance. Is that clear?"

There was a murmur of approval. "I cannot hear you!"

"Yes, Captain!" they roared.

"And you, what happened to you?" He pointed at Daniel of Tilbury.

"I had too much ale and fell over going for a piss."

"Good." He took a silver penny from his purse and tossed it to him. "Here, this is for your troubles."

Daniel nodded.

I would not share the coin we had taken in front of the others. I would wait until we were alone. There was enough bad feeling without aggravating it.

When we rode forth the next day we had knights and squires with us. This time, we had my archers as scouts. Heading out first allowed me to share out the coins as I'd planned. It was an incentive for them to repeat what we had done the previous day.

We did not ride along the road. I divided my men and we rode across the fields and used as much cover as we could. Sir John would lead the main body along the road. He knew that if there was any danger then we would warn him. This way we would get close to Badequelle without being seen.

As we approached Badequelle I saw that men were in the fields. It was too good an opportunity to miss. I drew my sword and dug my heels into my horse's flanks. We galloped over the recently ploughed field. The hooves stuck a little in the sticky morass but that made our approach less noisy. We were two hundred paces from them before they saw us. A cry went up and women grabbed children and ran for the bridge over the ditch. The men ran too, but they found the muddy fields more difficult than we did. I did not wish to kill them. Using the flat of my sword I smacked it into the back of the head of the first villager I reached. He fell face down in the mud. Jack of Lincoln used his fist in the face of the man he followed, for the man he chased turned around. Five of the villagers were felled in a similar manner.

"Robin of Barnsley, secure the men! John of Nottingham, search the houses. The rest of you, to the bridge." We had caught them unawares. They had been forced to leave the bridge in place, for Matty Straw Hair had dismounted, and as one of the garrison tried to raise the bridge, Matty slew him with an arrow. The other three ran back into the gate, which slammed shut.

The castle was an old-fashioned motte and bailey. There was just one entrance, which we soon commanded. Once the rest of my men reached us they dismounted and, like us, nocked an arrow. The men in the castle had been too busy closing the gates to man the walls, but now they did so. The hall and inner ward were too far away from the gate to be able to support the men on the walls, and the men who would defend the walls ran through the outer ward. As heads appeared we sent arrows towards them. Matty hit one but it was hard to see if it was a killing blow or not.

I heard hooves coming down the road and saw Sir John leading the rest of the men. We had the upper hand. Had there been archers on their walls, or even crossbows, they could have made life difficult for us. As it was, we had eight bows aimed at the gate and the walls, which were adjacent. My men were the best. I doubted that the men inside the castle had practised, other than on a Sunday after church.

"Well done, Captain. You managed to secure the bridge."

"That was Matty, lord, he has quick reactions."

Sir John turned in his saddle. "Captain William. You may begin your assault." Sir John raised his arm and led his nine knights and squires down the Matlac road. Captain William organised his men into two columns. One was led by his sergeant at arms, Ralph, and was made up of the prince's men, for they were mailed. He led the rest. He looked over at me and shouted, "Whenever you are ready!"

"Just go, and we will cover you."

With shields held before them they tramped over the bridge. The defenders raised their heads. The first four did not live long enough to regret it, as they were plucked from the walls. Realising that we had made the walls a death-trap, they resorted to throwing stones over the top of the palisade. It did not work. The odd stone which hit its target was deflected by a shield. I heard a trumpet and wondered what it meant.

The axes of the front four of our men began to hack at the gate. They made short work of it, and when the gates burst asunder and they ran in, we saw the defenders fleeing across the outer ward towards the keep. Taking the keep would be harder, as they would have archers on the walls of the palisade, which protected it. This was also a higher wall. However, Ralph and the men at arms were in close pursuit, and there was little likelihood that the defenders would be able to raise the bridge over the ditch.

As soon as Ralph and his men had crossed, I led my archers the same way. Without armour we would be faster than Captain William and his men. Already Ralph's men had taken casualties. He had a shield wall, but sheltering behind it were two wounded men. Bolts or arrows had struck them in their legs.

I shouted, "Use the shields for cover and then clear those walls."

The men sending their arrows and bolts at us were part-time warriors. We were professionals. We did this every day. More importantly than that, all of us were highly skilled. I was pulling an arrow as we neared the men at arms. I nocked it and looked for a target. I saw an archer swivel, and I ducked. The arrow flew over my head. In an instant I had risen and sent an arrow back at him. Perhaps he thought he had hit me for he did not move and my arrow struck him in the face. His body hung over the palisade. We would have to eliminate them one by one. Captain William would use the other men at arms to break down the gates. They were fresher. We had to stop them being struck.

All of my men had joined me. The men I had sent to search the village had finished their task. We now had more archers and more arrows. It would only be a matter of time. It became a game of cat and mouse. We looked for movement, whilst they tried to catch us making a mistake. We made none. When the axes began to hack at the gate it became easier, for their archers tried to lean over the side of the palisade to hit the men at arms. As soon as they did so they signed their own death warrant.

The end, when it came, was dramatic. The gates burst open and every man at arms raced through. We cleared the walls and Captain William and his men hurried to the keep. This was not a stone one. It was wood and we had fire. Even as we hurried through the gate, I heard Captain William shout, "Surrender or burn!"

Before he could be answered Geoffrey galloped through the outer gate. "Captain, his lordship needs you. Enemy horsemen are approaching. He needs support."

"Archers, with me." As I passed one of the wounded men at arms, Tom, John's Son, I said, "Tell Captain William there are horsemen approaching. He should man the walls."

"Aye, Captain!"

CHAPTER 15

When we reached the village I saw the small group of knights and squires preparing to charge the approaching horsemen. They were outnumbered. I counted four banners. That meant four knights led them. They would have retinues. I estimated between eight and twelve men to a knight. There could be fifty men fighting the eighteen that Sir John was leading. They were over four hundred paces from us and I cursed Sir John. He should have drawn them onto our bows. This way, we would have to run to reach them, and by then they would be engaged.

We were just a hundred paces from them when we heard the crack of spears shattering on shields. Horses neighed and screamed and then there was the clash of steel.

"We have to get amongst them. Remember our men wear the red cross. Any with a white cross is a foe."

I saw a man at arms ride around the rear of the squires. I nocked and released in one motion. The men at arms were not as well armoured as the knights. Their mail was of poorer quality. My arrow drove through his left arm and into his body. He slumped but then turned his horse to gallop away. I did not care. It was one less foe. There was no point in sending arrows overhead. We had no idea who we might hit. This was risky, but I gambled that the knights and squires would be seen as more attractive targets than mere archers.

Already my men were having success. When an archer releases an arrow from thirty paces or so, it is almost impossible to miss, and there is no mail yet made which could stop our arrows. I released another, and my arrow hit a man at arms in the middle of his skull. The arrow came out of the back of his helmet. Some of my men had sent arrows into enemy horses. That was a clever tactic. The maddened beasts bucked and kicked. They caused more damage to the other horses. We stayed behind our squires.

One of the knights must have seen us. I saw him stand in his stirrups to shout an order. He was too tempting a target. My arrow hit him in the right shoulder as he raised his sword. His squire took his reins and led him away from the fray,

Having noticed, a dozen men at arms rode at us with lances poised to slaughter us. I shouted, "Turn and release!" Even though they were just thirty paces from us when we turned, they were doomed. In the time it took to close with us, I could send three arrows at them. Each of my men could send two. All twelve horsemen were hit. As one of the horses galloped at me I swiped it across the muzzle with my bow to make it turn. It did so. With half the men at arms dead, one knight and squire fled while the other three knights yielded. Only one of Sir John's knights had been wounded. That was the way when knight fought knight. It was rarely to the death. Often archers and men at arms were discouraged from killing them as they were worth more alive and ransomed.

I saw that Robin of Barnsley had been knocked over by a careering horse. He stood, somewhat groggily. "Bloody stupid horse!" He pointed to one whose throat had just been cut by Tom to put it out of its misery, "I shall enjoy eating that one tonight!"

Sir John took off his helmet and rode over to us. "Thank you, Captain, that was timely indeed. Did we take the castle?"

"We did, my lord."

"Good, then burn the village and have Captain William burn the castle. It will not be used by de Ferrers again!"

The next days were much of the same. We burned everything connected with the de Ferrers family. We all became richer. Even Daniel of Tilbury had realised the benefits of obeying Captain William. We ate and slept well. But it was too good to last, and when a messenger in Prince Edward's livery arrived, we knew that the chevauchée was ended. The weather was improving and we were needed elsewhere.

Sir John sent for me first. "Gerald, we have been ordered back to Oxford, but Prince Edward wishes you to scout out Northampton on the way back."

"Northampton, my lord?"

"The younger de Montfort, Simon, and Peter de Montfort are there. King Henry hopes to draw de Montfort north. Do not take risks. The prince wants a way in. We both know the castle, but I confess that neither of us took much notice of the town itself. If we are to take it then we need to know how the town is defended. We know the garrison of the castle and are familiar with its layout. How many men will you need?"

"Just one, my lord. I will take Jack of Lincoln."

I gave Jack of Lincoln instructions and sought out Miles Beauchamp. He gave us two old cloaks. I thought it prudent to go in disguise if we were riding in the heart of the land of the de Montforts. We had almost a hundred miles to travel so we left before dawn. Thanks to our chevauchee we had plenty of food. Our ale skins were full and we even had grain for our horses. Spring was almost upon us and green shoots were sprouting everywhere. However, this was England, and that still meant rain and driving winds. We rode in silence through the de Montfort land.

One effect of our raids had been to make the manors we attacked better defended. That left the wilder places empty and we used those. We were both men who were comfortable in such places. We avoided any towns. De Montfort's manor at Tutbury and his castle at Derby would be well garrisoned, as would Leicester.

We stopped our weary horses in an oak wood some forty miles north of Northampton. There was water for our horses and just enough new grass to feed them. We did not risk a fire. We had eaten hot food for many days, and a few days of bread, salted meat and cheese would do us no harm.

As we curled up in our blankets Jack said, "Since Peter died, I have thought of nights like this, when we slept in the greenwood. They were hard times, but I miss them."

"You would go back to being an outlaw?"

He laughed. "I am no fool, Captain. This life is better. No man hunts us. We have food in our bellies and clothes on our backs. It is just that there are things about this new life I do not like."

"The chevauchée?"

"Aye, you knew?"

"I did not like hurting the poor people. The nobles for whom we fight do not see them as people. You and I have been poor. We have eked out a living. Given a choice, I would not have done it."

"What we do, is it right?"

"We serve the future king of England. God put his father on the throne and we are duty-bound to fight for him. At heart Prince Edward is a good man. If there were not rebels we would not have raided. I console myself with that. They are to blame. If they did not rebel, then we would not need to raid."

He was silent for a while. "You are a clever man, Captain. For one so young you appear to have wisdom. Your words have comforted me. I still do not like what we did, but you cannot undo that which you have done."

"And know this, Jack of Lincoln, when next you draw your bow, it will be against warriors. War is coming. We will be doing the king's and God's will. We will be fighting rebels."

Northampton was protected on one side by the River Nene. We knew that much from speaking with Sir John, who described the town for us. He had been there with Prince Edward when Prince Edward had been an ally and friend of Peter de Montfort. The town was walled, and the castle was situated in the south-west corner, where the river turned. We arrived after dark and camped across the river, close to the north-west corner. We would take the next day to scout out the walls.

We were woken in the early hours by the sound of chanting. There was a church close by. Once awake, I decided to begin our task early. We left our bows and went to the river. It was still dark, and it was a risk, but we forded the river. At one point it came up to our chests, but it was not wide.

We scrambled up the bank. There was a ditch before the wall. I think it was there as a drainage feature, for whilst deep, it was not broad. When we had arrived we had noticed the wall, but once we were close up to it we realised that it was not as substantial as we had thought. The mortar between the stones needed replacing. I took a risk and picked one of the stones up. It was not attached. The wall at this priory was rotten. We could hear the watch of the castle walls, some two hundred and fifty paces south of us. There was little point in risking discovery there. The prince knew of the castle. He had stayed there. It was the town with which he was unfamiliar.

Instead, we headed north, back along the wall of the town, with the river next to us.

As we walked around the unguarded walls, we could hear the sound of the monks in the priory as they chanted their prayers. As we headed east along the wall we saw the sky begin to lighten. The town walls ran towards the south-east. The ditch, which was supposed to protect it, had fallen into disrepair. De Montfort thought this town was safe. As we approached the road from the north the sky became much lighter. I decided to cross the road away from the castle and the north gate. We made it unseen, although from the north I heard the sound of carts. It would be a market day, and traders were coming to sell. The gates would be open at dawn. We moved along the fields to the east of the walls. It was a risk, for any who manned the walls would see us. As dawn broke it became clear that they did not keep a watch on the town walls. Emboldened, we moved closer to them.

We spied a church ahead and saw that there were three gates in the walls. The church was outside the gates. Roads with a steady stream of people came from the east to enter the town. We looked out of place and so I headed for the church. As I expected, it was open. We went in and knelt. It would do no harm to pray, and we did so. An archer always needed God's help.

When we left the church I saw that the wall began to curve around. I decided to take a chance. I nodded towards the east gate. Jack and I joined the throng of people heading to the market. Our swords were hidden by our cloaks, but it mattered not. The two men of the town watch were too busy talking to each other to notice us.

Once inside, we followed the rest of the people to the marketplace and All Saints' Church. There we could disappear. The first thing I noticed was the castle, which dominated the town. It was on a high piece of ground, whether a natural feature or man-made I was not certain. There was a curtain wall which ran around it and another gate. The town might be taken but the castle would remain a problem. However, as I examined it, I saw that the towers were roofless and some of the stonework was crumbling. It was not maintained.

If we had attempted to leave the town it would have looked suspicious, and so we returned to the market. We spent a few coins. I bought a narrow-bladed dagger and scabbard. It would fit inside my boot. Then we went to an inn for ale and food. We chose a busy one to hide us and to allow us to listen to the conversations.

It proved a productive time. We used some of our coin to eat and drink well. We stayed for a couple of hours and the innkeeper proved to be a useful source of information. We were good customers and spending more than most. By the time we left, in the middle of the afternoon, we were best friends! We also had knowledge which had been worth the outlay of silver. The two de Montforts were in residence, and there was a garrison. It seemed that there were more than fifty knights in the town, castle and surrounding manors. The innkeeper told us that most preferred their manors to the crumbling castle. He happily furnished that information. He made money from guests and it helped to make him a rich man. However, the innkeeper had been less than impressed with the young Simon de Montfort. He saw him as reckless, whereas his father was well respected. He confirmed that no watch was kept on the walls at night. He had laughed when we questioned the laxity. "Why do we need to? Our castle is the strongest north of London, and every man in the town knows how to use a weapon. If any tried to capture it they would have the town to fight."

We left by the south gate. We crossed the bridge and I noted the number, position and arms of the guards. We carried on south to cross the river and then headed first west and then east to return to our camp and our horses. It was late afternoon when we reached them. As we had headed deep into the land, we had been aware of the brooding presence of the castle. The keep dominated that side of the town.

It was still light, we were well fed and our horses were rested. We mounted and headed west. We would make camp in the night and try to make Oxford in a day. We had done that which the prince had commanded.

Oxford was a massive armed camp when we arrived. King Henry himself was there, as well as Prince Edward's brother, Richard of Cornwall. I looked at Jack as we approached. "I have a feeling that as soon as we give our report, we will be moving. When we enter I will find Sir John. You had better go and warn the men."

"Aye. At least this will be a battle worth fighting. It will be men we face."

Although it was evening and the evening food was ready, I was ushered into the presence of not only Sir John but Prince Edward, Richard of Cornwall and the king himself. They were definitely eager for my news. I was not certain which of them to address. It must have shown on my face for Prince Edward smiled and said, "Captain Gerald, you are my archer. Tell me all and what you think." I saw his father give him a sharp, disapproving look. "My liege, I trust this humble archer. He may look young, indeed he is, but he has saved my life on more than one occasion, and he seems to have an understanding of war."

The king nodded. "Proceed."

I told them what I had discovered. At first I was nervous, but once I began I gained in confidence. When I had finished Prince Edward said, "And where would an archer attack?"

Again, his father and his brother looked surprised.

"The priory has a weakened wall. If you sent a few men over at night-time, they could remove some of the stones. Horsemen could ride across the river easily. It is not deep. The priory grounds are extensive."

King Henry spoke. "My son might be right. There is more to you than meets the eye. Tell me, archer, the south gate. Did it have a double gate?"

"No, your majesty."

"And you say the ditch is in a state of ill repair?"

"It is."

He looked at his sons. "Then we will attack the southern gate. A dawn attack might well catch them asleep. We can use the bridge over the Nene to bring all of our men to the attack."

"But my captain's idea is a good one."

"It is, and I commend your choice of archer. Nonetheless, an attack on the priory wall would necessitate fording the river, and there is no guarantee of success." He smiled and took out a golden mark. "You have done well. This is for your trouble, and I will watch you when we go to war."

I bowed and left. A short while later Sir John hurried out after me. "Well done, Gerald, that cannot have been easy. I think the prince likes your plan. Come to his quarters on the morrow, and bring Captain William with you."

At *that* meeting we formulated a plan to attack the priory. Our master was confident he could persuade his father to go along with his idea.

We left for Northampton on the third day of April. We rode behind the dragon standard, which I was told meant that no quarter would be given. Captain William did not think that meant much. "It is to terrify the rank and file. King Henry hopes that they will flee when we are near."

We camped on the Friday night so that we could be in a position to attack the town on the morning of Saturday, the fifth day of April.

We would not be attacking with the rest of the army. Prince Edward had persuaded his father to allow us to make a diversionary attack on the walls. His father had liked the idea of drawing defenders to the north-west of the town and allowing his men to use ladders to scale the southern defences. I knew that he would lose more men there than Prince Edward would. However, I had a great responsibility. I had told the prince that we could remove the stones and gain entry for our knights. I had to do as I had promised.

Prince Edward himself came to speak to Captain William and me. "When we fight tomorrow, do not slay the knights! They are worth coin to us. Demand that they surrender. Wound them if you must, but do not slay them. They are worthless if you do. Alive, they can be used to bargain."

After he had left us I said, "He puts men's lives at risk. What if they do not surrender? Do we let them slay us?"

"Did you not hear him? Wound them. Your archers are good enough to put an arrow where they will be incapacitated and not dead." He was right, and I nodded.

It was impossible to move such a large army through the land and remain hidden. We knew that Simon de Montfort would be summoning his men to London so that he could march north and meet us in the field. Attacking Northampton was a declaration of war. We camped separately from the rest of the army. We would be assaulting the wall with just five hundred men. Half would be the local levy, and the rest would be knights and professional soldiers. It would be Prince Edward's own men who would break down the wall and hold it until the knights could enter the priory and thence the town. A fifth of our band had fought together in the chevauchée. We knew each other. All enmity had been forgotten. We had all profited from the chevauchée. More than that, we had all fought alongside one another. We were fast becoming a band of brothers.

The next morning we headed for Northampton. In one way, King Henry's strategy was a good one. His attack would be on the main road from London. If relief was coming, they would have to get through our forces. We arrived in the middle of the afternoon. Camp was made. Those inside the town knew we were there but could do nothing about it. They were needed on the walls, and our attack had negated their numbers. Richard of Cornwall was sent to the east gates to prevent those being used. As soon as it was dark, we left.

Jack and I led. We had ridden this route in daylight and knew it. The trees and the undergrowth around the river disguised our movement, although I have no doubt that the sentries on the walls would have heard us. We halted in the place where Jack and I had left our horses on the scouting expedition. We did not speak. Prince Edward and Sir John, along with Captain William, joined us. I pointed to the wall. Prince Edward had asked us to demolish a section, forty horse-lengths wide. Captain William's men would aid us. Leaving our bows on the west bank, Jack and I led the two bands across the river. The ditch was slightly wider than I remembered. I hoped that the others would think to put the stones we removed into the ditch.

We worked silently. The monks were in their church, for we could hear them chanting. The smell of incense drifted over to us. I was working with my men, and they emulated me, laying the stones into the ditch so that the horses would be able to cross. It was slow and painstaking work. The archers were stronger, and I could see that we were demolishing the wall faster than the men at arms. The hint of dawn was in the sky when we heard the shout from the south gate. King Henry had launched his attack. It was early in the day, and he would lose men as a result. The idea had been that we would launch a surprise attack from within the town, rendering the defence of the south gate irrelevant. That was when I realised that Prince Edward was a better leader than his father. We worked on urgently. We removed our section, and I sent half of our men back to fetch the bows and tell the prince we were almost ready to attack.

I was just stringing my bow, the sun visible in the sky, when there was a shout. Men ran towards us.

Captain William shouted, "Stand to!"

I looked across the river. The prince was not yet ready. His father's premature attack had caught him out. It was men from the town who ran at us first. Our arrows found flesh, for they wore no mail. None came even close to the men at arms. Then I heard a shout and saw three riders approach. There was a warhorse ridden by a knight. The other two were a squire and a sergeant at arms. My men would leave the knight and squire alone. Six arrows struck the unfortunate sergeant at arms. The squire wisely reined in, but the knight dropped his reins and bravely charged towards us. I dropped my bow and drew my sword. I could not risk him falling from his horse and breaking his neck. His horse took the decision for him. My waving arm and sword made it swerve. It baulked at the partly demolished wall, close by Captain William's men. The knight soared over his horse's head, cleared the wall and landed in the ditch.

I ran directly to him. I hoped he was not dead, for we might be blamed. Already the prince and his men were fording the river. The knight's helmet had fallen from his head and he looked up at me. I shouted at him, "Surrender, my lord, or die!" He did not know that I would not kill him. Behind me was Jack of Lincoln, and with his split nose we looked like bandits rather than members of Prince Edward's retinue.

He held out his hand, "I yield, bowman!"

I pulled him out as Prince Edward arrived. The prince was grinning, "Well done, Captain, you have captured Simon de Montfort the Younger." He turned in his saddle, "Sir Aubrey, escort him to safety!" Then he stood in his stirrups, unsheathed his sword and shouted, "God and King Henry! On my warriors!" The horsemen clambered over the half-demolished wall. I sheathed my sword and picked up my bow. We followed the horsemen.

We had slain some of the townsfolk, but others were racing to try to send us back from whence we came. The horsemen were terrifying enough, but when our arrows began to fall amongst them they surrendered. They were forced to ride down the streets of the town, but we were able to go through the gates of the Black Friar's monastery, which was next to St Andrew's Priory. We saw the men on the castle walls. Amazingly, I saw that part of the wall had fallen and been hurriedly repaired with wood. The turrets had no wooden roof to protect them. We had the opportunity to end this battle quickly.

"Dick, son of Robin, find Captain William and bring him hence. We have a God-given chance to enter the castle without casualties."

"Aye, Captain!"

There was no ditch, and the curtain wall was undefended. Part of King Henry's plan had succeeded. The attention was on the south and the east. The north and west were deserted. We were fewer than thirty paces from the inner wall and keep when I saw the first soldiers run to the fighting platform on the wall walk. All three of them were hit by a shower of arrows.

"Start to pull down the wooden repairs! Quickly! The first in will have the first choice!"

My men set to. While half watched, the other half began to tear at the wood. Some of my men had hatchets which we used to cut kindling. They began to use them to make holes in the wood. Ralph Dickson was the first to reach us.

"A stroke of luck, Gerald!"

"Aye, let us not waste it."

The men at arms had axe-armed warriors amongst them and made short work of the wood. With an arrow nocked, I led my men through the breach. The gate to the keep was open. Captain William arrived and shouted, "Hold the keep, Captain Gerald, and I will secure the gate! We have them!"

I saw a man running from the main gate. He spied us and shouted a warning. My arrow struck him in mid-stride. I dropped my bow and drew my sword, "Archers, follow me." I ran to the door, which remained enticingly open. I could hear shouts from within as they saw Captain William and his men running to the defenders at the main gate and into the inner ward. I saw a hand gripping the edge of the door, and I swung my sword, slicing through the fingers. I hauled it open. A man at arms stood there. He was fully mailed, with helmet and shield. He raised his sword. I was a dead man. Two arrows flew from behind me and he fell dead.

"Robin, you and Matty hold the gate. Keep it open. The rest of you, with me."

The interior was in as bad a state of repair as the outside. Men at arms ran down the stairs towards us. At such close range my men could not miss. With the ground level cleared I hurried to the stairs. John of Nottingham had also discarded his bow, and we moved up the stairs with Jack of Lincoln and Dick, son of Robin, behind, with bows drawn. The others were ensuring that no defenders remained hidden to ambush us. The keep had an open wooden staircase. I had my dagger out, as well as my sword. As with all castles it was designed to favour the defender. As I turned the corner of the keep, a pair of men at arms suddenly leapt from the door. They had the space to swing their swords. Even as I lifted my dagger to block the first sword, two arrows flew to end their lives. The door ahead of us slammed shut.

Below me I heard the sound of feet running in, as Captain William led a handful of his men into the keep. "Come, you lazy lummoxes! The archers will have all the treasure."

The ill-repair of the castle was shown when John of Nottingham and I hit the door with our shoulders. Instead of remaining unmoved, there was a definite creak, and powder came from the hinges. The door had not been well made and the mortar was deteriorating. Captain William and four of his men appeared on the step below us.

"This needs men with mail." We moved down the wall to allow the four of them to charge the door. "On three. One, two, *three!*"

John and I had weakened it, and when they hit the door it collapsed inwards, taking them with it. We ran over their prostrate bodies and into the chamber. It was the main hall, and there was a table, chairs and wall hangings. More importantly, there were twenty men. I saw two knights with their squires. The rest were men at arms and fair game. My two archers had followed us, and they sent two arrows into the nearest men at arms. John and I moved closer together. Neither of us were as good with swords as the men at arms.

Four enemy men at arms ran at us. I was dimly aware of Captain William and his four men at arms getting to their feet. Two of the men trying to get at us were slain by my archers. The other two realised that their best chance of avoiding an arrow was to close with us. They rushed us. Like John and I, they were armed with sword and dagger. The difference was that they knew how to use them. I reacted. I blocked the sword strike with my dagger. Had I not been as strong as I was, then I would not have held it.

Captain William and his men at arms were carving their way into the enemy. My two archers had less chance of hitting anyone, for the room was crowded, but all that I was trying to do was stay alive. I swung my sword somewhat clumsily at the man I was fighting and he flicked it away with his dagger. I saw him twist the dagger and begin to bring it back to stab me. I had to resort to street fighting and brute strength. As the blade came up, I hooked my right leg behind his left and pushed with my shoulder. We tumbled to the ground. His sword arm dragged me down. As we landed he gave a soft sigh. I felt blood in my hand. As I stood I saw that my body weight had forced the dagger into his body. I rose and turned in time to see the other man at arms with his sword ready to skewer John of Nottingham. I brought my sword around with such force that it cut through his mail and into his body. He fell, dying.

"I owe you a life, Captain! I was a dead man for sure!"

"We are brothers in arms, John, we owe each other nothing."

The two knights and squires stood before the remaining ten men at arms. It was a stand-off. Captain William shouted, "Yield, Sir Peter!"

"To a man at arms? Never! We will die first!"

Captain William was hamstrung. We could not kill them. I said, "Jack of Lincoln. Choose a squire and pin his foot to the floor."

The squires heard me, but the speed of Jack was such that the arrow buried itself up to its fletch and pinned the foot of one of them to the floorboards before either of them could react.

"Sir Peter, there are worse things than death. My archers are so accurate that I could have named a toe. Prince Edward and the king will be here soon, and then you will surrender. Save the lives of your men at arms. Yield to Captain William!"

The whimpering squire ensured that they obeyed. They sheathed their swords. It would not do to hand them over to a commoner, but the men at arms handed over their swords. Two bows, with arrows aimed at them, ensured their compliance. Captain William escorted the two knights and the squires downstairs. Ralph Dickon bound the foot of the squire, who glowered murderously at us as he left.

Before the nobles came, we made sure that we took all that there was to take from the dead and the purses of the men at arms. They allowed us to do so. There was an understanding. We were all men of war. Had the roles been reversed, then we would have expected the same treatment. We would share with Captain William and his men later. After escorting the prisoners to the inner ward, we ransacked the upper floors. To the victor goes the spoils. I had heard the phrase, and it was now that I truly understood it. We had taken the risks and our chances, and we had been rewarded.

We used two chests to carry our booty down the stairs. The inner ward was filled with horses, knights, prisoners and, of course, the king and his son. John of Nottingham and my men slipped out through the hole in the wall we had made, carrying the chests. Our horses were still across the river by the priory.

Prince Edward was speaking with Sir John and Captain William. King Henry nodded to me and said, somewhat grudgingly, "It seems your archer has ideas, my son. I am surprised. I did not think that the common man had the wit for such thoughts. Perhaps, in the past, some lord laid with one of his ancestors. Still, if he comes up with such devices, perhaps you are well advised to keep him around you."

Sir John felt honour bound to defend me, "My liege, Captain Gerald captured Simon de Montfort and he and Captain William captured Peter de Montfort! Had they been knights, then they would both be rich men."

King Henry gave a reptilian smile and said, "But as they are commoners, then the crown will benefit from their capture. Sir John, have the keep searched. There must be valuables inside! Let us profit from its capture, eh?"

"Aye, my lord."

I gave a wry smile to Captain William. They would be disappointed. I might be Prince Edward's archer, but I knew enough about nobility to be my own man. Gone was the innocent who had followed a faithless knight. Now I followed a future king, but I would always watch out for myself.

EPILOGUE

The capture of Northampton was the first act in a civil war which would last for two years. King Henry and his army were full of hope. When we went north with Prince Edward and took first Leicester, followed by Nottingham and Grantham, we did not have to fight at any of them. The sight of our host made their castellans surrender. The defeat at Northampton had been like a dam breaking. We thought we had destroyed the de Montfort power. Taking Tutbury involved a short siege where we did not have to loose a single arrow. Prince Edward then showed that he had a harder side. He burned every de Ferrers and de Montfort manor that he could find. He was making a statement.

As we were finishing burning Tutbury, a messenger came from the king. John de Warenne was being besieged in Rochester Castle. Simon de Montfort had roused himself and come east with an army, to take the southern half of the kingdom. The civil war had begun in earnest, and we headed south. None of us knew what the next two years would bring, but I knew that I was now the captain of the archers, who served the next king of England. My fate was inextricably bound with his. I would rise and fall with him.

This was meant to be.

GLOSSARY

Candlemas – a Christian celebration, forty days after Christmas – February 2nd

Chevauchée – a raid by mounted horsemen

Coningeston – Coniston, Cumbria

Oswald's Cross – Oswestry

Lothnwistoft – Lowestoft, Suffolk

Matlac – Matlock, Derbyshire

muntator –light horseman (hobelar)

Rocheberie – Rugby, Warwickshire

sennight – a week (seven nights)

Thelwæl – Thelwall, Cheshire

Uluereston – Ulverston, Cumbria

Wrechcessham – Wrexham

HISTORICAL NOTES

The events based around Northampton and the chevauchée into Derby happened almost exactly as I wrote them. The capture of de Montfort was just as I described it. Truth is often stranger than fiction. Prince Edward's brief war in North Wales was, like the one I write about, less than successful, but I have changed the time scale and events to suit my story. I am a writer after all!

The next book in the series will begin with the campaign which led to the infamous battle of Lewes and end with the even more notorious battle of Evesham. They will be the backdrop for my story of Gerald the Archer. The kings and lords are incidental. It is the archers of England and Wales that I celebrate in this series of books.

Books used in the research:

The Normans – David Nicolle

The Knight in History – Francis Gies

The Norman Achievement – Richard F Cassady

Knights – Constance Brittain Bouchard

Feudal England: Historical Studies on the Eleventh and Twelfth Centuries – J. H. Round

Peveril Castle – English Heritage

Norman Knight AD 950–1204 – Christopher Gravett

English Medieval Knight 1200–1300 – Christopher Gravett

English Medieval Knight 1300–1400 – Christopher Gravett

The Scottish and Welsh Wars 1250–1400 – Christopher Rothero

Lewes and Evesham 1264–65 – Richard Brooks

ENDEAVOUR QUILL

Endeavour Quill is an imprint of Endeavour Media

If you enjoyed *Lord Edward's Archer* check out
Endeavour Media's eBooks here:
www.endeavourmedia.co.uk

For weekly updates on our free and discounted eBooks
sign up to our newsletter:
www.endeavourmedia.co.uk/sign-up

Follow us on Twitter:
@EndeavourQuill

And Instagram:
endeavour_media

ENDEAVOUR MEDIA